The woman wa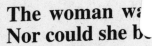
Nor could she b

Gavin pulled his gaze away. What was it about Clare that called to him? Strong, yes. But, like her bird, alert, expecting danger any minute. Her strength was a shield. He wondered what it hid.

She acted as if she'd never been tempted, let alone succumbed.

He'd like to see it happen.

He'd like to help.

The vision filled him. Clare. Naked. Tight braid undone. Hair tumbling across her shoulders. Eyes soft, lips yielding with want.

He downed the rest of his drink. If she knew what he was thinking it would confirm everything she believed of him.

And she'd be right.

Praise for
Blythe Gifford

HIS BORDER BRIDE

'Using falcons as metaphors, Blythe Gifford
has successfully soared with this Highland romance.'
—*Fresh Fiction*

IN THE MASTER'S BED

'…expertly crafted…fascinating historical details…
give this sexy historical a richness and depth…'
—*Booklist*

'…excellent…Blythe Gifford is the true Master…'
—*Cataromance*

INNOCENCE UNVEILED

'Blythe Gifford takes a refreshingly different setting
and adds a plot brimming with dangerous secrets
and deadly intrigue to create a richly detailed
and completely compelling medieval romance.'
—*Chicago Tribune*

THE HARLOT'S DAUGHTER

'Blythe Gifford finds the perfect balance between
history and romance in THE HARLOT'S DAUGHTER
as she expertly blends a fascinating setting and beautifully
nuanced characters into a captivating love story.'
—*Chicago Tribune*

'Gifford has chosen a time period that is filled with kings,
kingmakers and treachery. Although there is plenty of fodder for
turbulence, the author uses that to move her hero and heroine
together on a discovery of love. She proves that
love through the ages doesn't always run smoothly,
be it between nobles or commoners.'
—*RT Book Reviews*

THE KNAVE AND THE MAIDEN

'This debut novel by a new voice in medieval romance
was for me…pure poetry! The sweetness of the ending
will have you running for your tissues. Oh, yes,
this is a new star on the horizon and I certainly
hope to see much more from her!'
—*Historical Romance Writers*

HIS BORDER BRIDE

Blythe Gifford

First published in Great Britain 2011
by Mills & Boon, an imprint of Harlequin (UK) Limited,
Eton House, 18-24 Paradise Road, Richmond, Surrey TW9 1SR

© Wendy B. Gifford 2010

ISBN: 978 0 263 88776 1

Harlequin (UK) policy is to use papers that are natural, renewable and recyclable products and made from wood grown in sustainable forests. The logging and manufacturing process conform to the legal environmental regulations of the country of origin.

Printed and bound in Spain
by Blackprint CPI, Barcelona

After a career in public relations, advertising and marketing, **Blythe Gifford** returned to her first love: writing historical romance. Now her characters grapple with questions about love, work, and the meaning of life, and always find the right answers. She strives to deliver intensely emotional, compelling stories set in a vivid, authentic world. She was a finalist in the Romance Writers of America's Golden Heart™ Award competition for her debut novel, THE KNAVE AND THE MAIDEN. She feeds her muse with music, art, history, walks and good friends. You can reach her via her website: www.BlytheGifford.com

Previous novels by the same author:

THE KNAVE AND THE MAIDEN
THE HARLOT'S DAUGHTER
INNOCENCE UNVEILED
IN THE MASTER'S BED

AUTHOR NOTE

This book represents a 'border crossing' for me. It is my first to be set on the Scottish side of the line. As I wrote, one of my touchstones was an old Kris Kristofferson song called 'Border Lord'. The mournful lyrics tell of a man about to cross the line, both literally and figuratively. They seemed to sum up my hero perfectly—a man who cares little for rules, boundaries, and the opinions of others. What kind of woman would be a match for such a man? A woman who has lived her life prescribed by all of these. I hope you enjoy their story.

Dedication

To all our parents, and their secrets.

Acknowledgements

Thanks to Jody Allen
and the Writers of Scottish Romance group for helping
a newcomer to the northern side of the border and to
the staff at the Center for Birds of Prey, Charleston,
South Carolina, for helping me understand the falcons.
(All mistakes on both fronts are my own.)

Chapter One

<figure>Decorative flourish</figure>

Haddington, Scotland—February 1356

After ten years away, he had come home.

War had come with him.

Fog, cold and damp, darkened the fading light of a February day and crept around the corners of the church before them. The iron links of his chainmail chilled the back of his neck and the English knights by his side shivered on their mounts.

Winter was no time for a war.

Gavin Fitzjohn looked over at his uncle, King Edward, proud lion at the peak of his prowess. More than twenty years ago, this king led the English on a similar charge into Scotland.

That time, the King's brother had left behind a bastard son of a Scottish mother.

Today, that son, Gavin, rode beside his uncle, just as he had done for the last year in France. There, they had wreaked havoc on soldiers and villagers alike without a qualm until the smell of blood and smoke permeated his dreams. But he had done it because he was a knight in war.

Now, the King assumed Fitzjohn was fully his.

But this was not France. Now, Edward had brought the scorched earth home. In the fortnight since they had retaken Berwick, his army had slashed and burned what little the retreating Scots army had left standing.

Gavin's horse shifted, restless. Through the windows of the church, the choir where services were sung glowed like a beckoning lamp, light and lovely as any church he had seen across the Channel.

The villagers huddled before their spiritual home, uncertain of what was to come. Gavin watched a man at the crowd's edge, hands clasped, eyes closed, lips moving in prayer.

The man's eyes opened and met Gavin's.

Fear. Strong enough to taste.

His stomach rebelled. He was sick to death of killing.

A squire ran up to the King, carrying a torch. In the darkening twilight, the shifting flames cast unearthly light and shade across the mud-splattered surcoats and armour.

He looked at his uncle. No more, he thought, the words a wish.

But anger, not mercy, gripped Edward's face. The Scots had talked truce only to gain time to prepare for war. So, when Lord Douglas finally rejected the English offer of peace, Edward vowed to give them the war they wanted.

The King motioned the squire towards Gavin.

'Take the torch,' he said. The fire flickered between them like Satan's flames. He nodded towards the church. 'Burn it.'

The squire shoved the torch into Gavin's outstretched hand. He took it, as he had so many times before, but his grip was unsteady and the firebrand trembled. Or was that just a trick of the wavering light?

The villagers' wary glances shifted from him to the church. What would happen to them if they lost their link to God?

A baby's wail bounced off the church's stone walls.

He shoved the torch at the squire, trying to give back the flames.

'What are you waiting for?' Edward roared, releasing all the frustration of a failed campaign. Storms had sunk his ships. There would be no new supplies and nothing left to do but retreat. He meant to leave destruction behind him.

'Leave it. They never warred on us.'

'They laid waste to their own lands, so we'd have no cattle to eat nor ale to drink.'

Edward's knights grumbled their agreement. Hungry bellies made vicious warriors.

Gavin looked from the torch to the church. Stone walls were no protection. He knew that. He had lit fires large and small from Picardy to Artois. Heard the crackle of the roof catch fire, seen the timbers crash to the floor and ignite wooden altars, felt the heat sear his chest through his breastplate. Cinder burns pitted the gold lions and lilies on his surcoat.

But this was different and had been from the moment they crossed the border. He had breathed the familiar smell of the earth, felt the gentle slope of the hills rise below his stallion's hooves, looked up at the perpetual grey mist of the sky. And knew.

No matter how long he had been away, where, or with whom, this was home.

'What's the matter, Fitzjohn?' the King yelled. 'Is your Scottish whore's blood holding you back, boy?'

His mother was no whore. But the King had never forgiven Gavin's father for his sin, even after death. 'There's no reason for this,' he answered. 'These folk fight us no more.'

'Your father would have done it!'

His father had done worse.

But Gavin no longer could.

He dropped the torch and heard it sizzle as it hit the soggy ground. Then, he pulled off the red, gold and blue surcoat bearing his father's arms and held it over the sputtering flame until it was ablaze.

'My father might have done it. But I will not.'

He grabbed the reins and turned his horse away to ride into the darkness alone.

He was not the man his father had been.

Or so he prayed.

A few weeks later, in the Cheviot Hills

The falcon paced on her perch that morning, pecking at her jesses, on edge even after Clare slipped the hood over her head to cover her eyes. Strange. Typically, she feared nothing when she could see nothing.

'What's the matter, Wee One?' Clare crooned, as she closed the door and motioned the falconer away. She pretended the birds were part of her duties as mistress of

Carr's Tower, but the falconer was rewarded, and well, to tend to their constant needs. She simply preferred to do it herself, particularly with this one. 'Don't you want to take a morning flight?'

She stroked the striped feathers of the bird's breast, talking nonsense until Wee One recognised her voice and stilled her wings. Clare held out a titbit and the bird nipped it from her fingers.

'Ye're spoilin' the bird, Mistress Clare,' the old falconer said. His grey-tinged brows nearly met as he frowned. 'She'll nae hunt if she's nae hungry.'

'It's no more than a crumb.' A bribe was more the truth, something to fool herself into believing the bird cared about her instead of only the food she brought.

She checked to be sure the jesses on the falcon's talons had not come loose. 'I think it does her good to have a treat from time to time.'

Neil shook his head. 'Ye won't think so when ye lose her. If she ever discovers she can eat her fill without our help, she'll nae return to your fist again.'

He had grumbled the same thing to her for years. But except for this small infraction, Clare had studied all the rules and followed every one when she trained Wee One.

She pulled on a thick leather glove and held out her left hand. The bird hopped on to her wrist and Clare swept out of the mews and into the barmkin where young Angus awaited her.

The page, on the edge of squirehood, had been left behind when her father took most of the men to war, so he viewed himself as protector of the ladies left in the tower.

'Get my horse and the dog, Angus.'

He hesitated. 'Ye shouldna go out alone, Mistress Clare.'

She knew that, but she had picked the boy because he would not refuse her. 'Both the bird and I need exercise. And my father sent word. He'll be home soon. The Inglis are halfway to Carlisle by now.'

In truth, the Inglis might be as close as Melrose, but she was tired of hiding, tired of winter, tired of being caged like the birds. Besides, the wild hills surrounding their border castle offered as much protection as an army. The 'Great Waste', some called it. No one would come here unless he wanted to escape the civilised world.

Angus brought her hound and horse and held the falcon as she mounted. Then, sitting proudly on top of his pony, he rode beside her. As they left the shadow of the tower's wall, she took her first deep breath and looked up at the blue, cloudless sky. They had not seen the like for months.

'Clare! Wait!'

She turned to see Euphemia, daughter of the widow Murine, galloping after her. Clare stifled a sigh for the loss of her private moment with the falcon and freedom.

She held her horse to let the girl catch up. Far from looking ready to hunt, Euphemia, on the edge of womanhood, looked as if she were ready to fall into bed with the next man she stumbled across. Not because of her clothes—her dress was as temperate as Clare's—but even at sixteen, the slant of her smile and the flutter of her eyelashes put men in mind of night pleasures.

Just as her mother's did.

'I had to come,' the girl said, as she caught them. 'We may not see another day so warm 'til June.' A flush touched her cheek and her dark hair tumbled across her shoulders.

Clare's tight braid insured her hair would never fly loose, even after a day on horseback. 'You may join me, but stay close. She's not been out for days and I intend to be sure she has a good flight.'

She gazed at the sky, looking for potential prey. Instead, she heard the flapping wings of another falcon. Wee One, hooded, swivelled her head, as if searching for the sound.

'What's that?' Euphemia asked.

Clare peered at the bird—male, she thought, from his smaller size. He flew back and forth across their path, fierce, dark, yellow-rimmed eyes glaring as if he wanted them to stop.

'I don't know.' She frowned, suddenly afraid the strange bird might tempt Wee One to freedom. Thinking to escape him, she urged the horse into a gallop, not stopping until she was halfway up the ridge and the tercel was no longer in sight. Waiting for the others, she felt the south-west wind nudge her back.

Maybe summer would come early.

'Look!' Angus whispered as the hound pointed.

A few yards away, a fat partridge huddled under a bush. She would be easy to flush into flight, the perfect quarry for a falcon.

Clare glanced over her shoulder to be sure they had lost the tercel. Then she removed Wee One's hood, struggling to hold on to the leather jesses as the wind nearly jerked them out of her fingers. She raised her arm and Wee One took off, wings flapping, until she was just a speck overhead. There, she would wait, as she had been trained to do, until the humans sent her prey skywards.

Angus set the dog towards the bush, scaring the partridge into flight, where the bird expected to be away from danger, but the small dot in the sky dived for her prey, falling faster than a horse could gallop.

They stirred their horses and gave chase.

They were halfway down the valley by mid-afternoon. The bird had worked, tireless, through the day. She had several fine stoops, killing three fowl. Each time, Clare rewarded her with a taste of the flesh. Then, she whisked the prey into the sack for Angus to carry.

Food rewarded the falcon for a successful flight, but the bird was never allowed to eat without her master's help. Otherwise, she would learn that she did not need the help of humans after all.

The last partridge escaped. Clare called her falcon with a shrieking whistle and smiled as Wee One swooped on to her fist, obedient.

This bird would return to her. Always.

At the thought, the list of duties left undone rushed back, sweeping away the freedom of the day.

She turned her horse around, motioning to Angus and Euphemia to follow her. The morning's warmth had ebbed, and a chilly mist huddled in the valley and obscured the hills, reminding her of the dangers that lurked all around. The Inglis army might be far away, but the Inglis border was not.

That was her last thought before he rose out of the fog, a golden man on a black horse, like a spirit emerging from the mist.

A man without a banner.

A man without allegiance.

The hound barked, once, then growled, as if cowed.

The man's eyes grabbed hers. Blue they were, shading as a sky does in summer from pale to deepest azure. And behind the blue, something hot, like the sun.

Like fire.

Any words she might have said stuck in her throat.

Next to her, Euphemia gasped, then giggled. 'Where are you going, good sir?'

Clare glared at her. The girl was hopeless. They'd be lucky to get her married before she was with child.

'Anywhere that will have me,' he answered Euphemia, but his eyes touched Clare.

Her cheeks burned.

Beside her, young Angus drew his dagger, the only weapon he was allowed. 'I will defend the ladies.'

'I'm sure you will.' The stranger's smile, slow, insolent, was at odds with the intensity in his eyes. 'That's a handsome dirk and I'm sure you could wield it well against me, but I would ask that you not harm my horse.'

His tone was oddly gentle. Where was his own squire? 'Who's with you?'

'No one.'

'A dangerous practice.' Did he lie? An army could hide behind him in this mist. Her fault. She had ridden out alone and unarmed and put them all at risk. 'Don't you know Edward's army still rides?'

He frowned. 'Do they?'

His accent confused her. It held the burr of the land closer to the sea, but there was something else about it, difficult to place. Yet over the hill, in the next valley, each family's speech was different. He might be a Robson from the other side of the hill, scouting for one last raid before the spring, or loyal to one of the Teviotdale men who had thrown their lot in with Edward. 'You're not an Inglisman, are you?'

'I have blood as Scots as yours.'

'And how do you know how Scots my blood is?'

'By the way you asked the question.'

Did her speech sound so provincial to Alain? She winced. She wanted to impress the visiting French knight, not embarrass him. 'What's your name, Scotsman?'

'Gavin.' He paused. 'Gavin Fitzjohn.'

Some John's bastard, then. Even a bastard bore his father's arms, but this man carried no clue to his birth. No device on his shield, no surcoat. Just that unkempt armour that, without a squire's care, had darkened with rust spots.

No arms, no squire. Not of birth noble enough for true knighthood, then.

'Are you a renegade?' On her wrist, Wee One bated, wings flapping wildly. Clare touched her fingers to the bird's soft breast feathers, seeking to calm them both.

His slow smile never wavered. 'Just a tired and hungry man who needs a friendly bed.' His eyes travelled over her, as if he were wondering how friendly her bed might be.

'Well, you'll not find one with us.'

'I didn't ask. Yet.'

Did he think she'd offer to be his bedmate? She should not be talking to such a man at all. 'Well, if you do, I'll say you nae.'

'I don't ask before I know whether I'm speaking to a friend or an enemy.'

'And I don't answer before I know the same.' Her voice had a wobble she had not intended.

'Are you a woman with enemies?'

'Three kings claim this land. We have more enemies than friends.'

'Aye,' he said, nodding, a frown carving lines in his face. He flexed his hand as if it itched to reach for his sword. 'Who are yours?'

Her eyes clashed with his. She should have asked him first. Where was his loyalty? To the de Baliol pretender, recently dethroned? To David the Bruce, still held for ransom by the Inglis Edward? Perhaps he had lied about his blood and was Edward's man himself.

Next to her, the young girl sighed. 'This is Mistress Clare and I'm Euphemia and I have nae enemies.'

'Euphemia!' Was she batting her lashes? Yes, she was. 'Do you want us to be killed?'

'He wouldn't do that. A knight is sworn to protect ladies, aren't you?' She fluttered her eyelashes at him again, then turned to Clare. 'Don't treat him as an unfriend.'

'If I do, it's because I have a brain in my head.'

If she kicked the horse into a gallop, could she outrun the man? Not with Angus and Euphemia in tow and Wee One on her wrist.

She lowered her voice to a whisper. 'He looks like a dangerous ruffian, not a knight. He carries no markings and he's wearing dirty armour with rust spots!' The man, if he knew the maxims of chivalry, cared little for them.

Euphemia shrugged and turned to the man. 'You're not dangerous and dirty, are you?'

Something darkened his face before a smile waved it away. 'Well, that may depend on how you mean the words, but I'd say Mistress Clare has a gift for judging character.'

He said it with no sense of outrage. No knight would allow his honour to be so challenged. Certainly Alain, epitome of French chivalry, would never let such a slight pass.

'On whose lands do I ride, Mistress Euphemia?' he asked.

'Not Mistress. Just Euphemia,' Clare said, refusing to elaborate. Disgrace enough that her father had shamed her dead mother by taking up with the widow Murine. Worse that he'd treated another man's by-blow as his daughter. 'And you're on Carr lands.'

'Held of who?'

'Douglas,' she answered. There, that declared their loyalties, but if she hadn't told him, the girl would have.

She thought his shoulders relaxed, but she must have been mistaken. 'It's difficult *not* to be on Douglas lands in the Middle March, isn't it?' His slow nod revealed nothing of his thoughts. 'Are *you* loyal to the Bruce?'

'You ask that when the heart of a Bruce adorns Lord

Douglas's shield?' In her surprise, her tongue forgot its courtly inflection. 'Are ye daft?'

'Nae, but Carr men have been known to lapse in loyalty to an absent king.'

King David the Bruce had been England's captive for half her life, it seemed. In his absence, a Douglas and a Steward ruled Scotland in his name. 'Does that make you an enemy of Douglas and Carr, Gavin Fitzjohn?'

'Not as long as they are no enemy of mine.'

His eyes met hers and they took each other's measure in silence. On the Border, an allegiance could be as strong as the relentless wind. And as variable.

'See, Clare? He's no enemy and we should all go home. I, for one, am chilled to the skin and ready to sit by the fire.' Euphemia kicked her horse into a trot and the stranger fell in behind her.

Clare handed Wee One to Angus, then hurried to catch up, letting the squire and the hound follow.

She brought her horse beside Euphemia and the stranger dropped further back, complimenting young Angus on his mount.

'You're leading him straight home!'

Euphemia shrugged. 'Why are you so worried? There's one of him and three of us.'

'And he's the only one carrying a sword.'

A few men still manned the tower, but if he was scouting for raiders, they were leading him straight to what he wanted. Still, she would feel safer, she decided, home in the castle, where he would be outnumbered by her men-at-arms.

At the silence, the stranger moved closer. 'Angus tells

me your falcon killed three today that were twice her size. That's a bird with courage.'

'Well that you say so.' Euphemia smiled. 'Wee One is Clare's favourite.'

'Then it seems your sister is as good a judge of bird flesh as she is of men.'

She glanced at him without turning her head, still puzzling him out. He'd displayed none of the courtly respect a knight should, yet he controlled his destrier with a warrior's ease, confident of his strength.

He caught her studying him and she snapped her gaze away, gritting her teeth at his laugh. 'It's too late to flatter me, Fitzjohn.'

'Oh, Mistress Clare,' he began, his voice still edged with humour, 'no man who was any judge of character would try flattery on you.'

'But a true and noble knight would always speak sweetly to a lady,' she countered. Alain always did. 'That must mean you are not a true knight.'

'Or that you are not a true lady.'

She stiffened. What gave her away? 'I am certainly a truer lady than you are a noble knight.'

He cocked his head. 'Perhaps, Mistress Clare, it may be too early to come to that conclusion.'

She gulped against his gentle rebuke. A lady would never have made such a statement. In this wild land, it was hard to cling to the courtly graces she had learned as a child in France.

In sight of the tower, she was relieved of the need to answer, and waved to the guard standing on the wall to open the gate. 'Who's with you, mistress?'

The man beside her called out without waiting for

her answer. 'A hungry, tired man looking for a warm bed and a hot meal.'

The guard waited for her sign. She nodded. 'Open the gate.'

They rode into the barmkin and she handed the sack of game to the falconer, closing her ears to his complaints. She started to dismount, expecting young Angus to help her off her horse, but instead, she faced the stranger.

He appeared before she saw him move, fast as a falcon diving for its prey.

He reached to help her down. She hesitated. Somehow, his hand offered an invitation to touch more than fingers.

Without waiting for her to accept, he grabbed her waist, lifting her off the saddle. She had no choice but to slide down into his arms.

He held her too tightly. As she stretched her toes towards the ground, she felt her breasts press against his chest. Something like the stroke of a bird's feather rippled across her skin. She held her face away from him, but his lips, sharp and chiselled, hovered too close to hers.

Her feet hit the earth.

Standing, he was a full head taller than she. Though journey dust clung to him, he carried his own scent, complex and dangerous, like a fire of oak and pine, smouldering at the end of a long night.

His smile didn't waver. Nor did his eyes. Blue, startlingly so, and framed by strong brows, they held her gaze strongly as his arms held her body.

'I'm ready to dismount.' Euphemia's pout was audible.

And just like that, he was gone.

Clare sagged against her horse, realising she had held her breath the entire time he touched her. This was no perfect knight, but a dangerous man. Anyone who trusted him would find herself abandoned and alone.

Or worse.

She forced herself to walk away, ignoring the tug of his eyes on her back. The cook and the steward approached, stern looks on their faces. She hoped fresh fowl would soothe their anger at her for avoiding her day's duties.

'Mistress Clare.' The man's words were a command.

She turned at her name, hating herself for doing it and him for making her. 'If it is food you want, the evening meal will be served shortly.'

'What I want is to see the Carr in charge.'

Now she was the one who smiled, long and slow and she watched his face, savouring the moment. 'You've seen her.'

And when she turned to the steward, the smile lingered on her lips.

Gavin watched the woman turn her back on him, never losing her smile.

You've seen her.

And he had. With her fair hair pulled into an immovable braid, suspicious grey-green eyes and straight brows, hers was not a perfect face. But she had the air of a woman accustomed to being obeyed, and he could well believe she was the castle's mistress while her father or her husband was at war.

He had made no friend of her yet, he was certain, but

he must try to do so now. He strode over and interrupted her conversation. 'Then you're the one I want to see. I want to join your men.'

The quiver on her lips might have been irritation or fear. Should she discover who he was, it would certainly be fear. Eventually, there would be no way to hide it. She had not recognised his name, but even the smallest band of warriors seemed to know it now.

Yet he refused to cower behind a lie. Men would think what they would. He had learned not to care.

'No. You cannot.' Her tone brooked no opposition.

'Why not?' Most of the castle's men were, no doubt, harrying Edward all the way back to England. 'An extra man-at-arms should be welcome.'

'Oh, we'll have men enough, just as soon as they capture Edward and come home.'

He stamped on a pang of regret. He had known his decision would mean abandoning the man who had brought him to knighthood, but he had hoped not to care so much. 'Well, until they do, I've a sword to offer in your service.'

'Do you always march in, demand what you want, and expect to get it?'

What he wanted was an end to endless war. That, he did not expect. Or even hope for. 'I only expect that, as a knight, my duty is to fight.'

She studied his face until he feared she would see the English blood in it. 'So you truly *are* a knight?' The wonder in her voice implied that a knight was a special soul instead of a man trained, like her hawk, to kill on command.

'Aye,' he answered, the Scottish accent of his childhood remembered on his tongue. 'I'm as true a knight as you'll see.'

He watched her turn over his answer before she spoke again.

'My answer is still no. If you're hungry, fill your belly at the evening table. If you're weary, sleep in the hall tonight. But tomorrow, I want you out of the place.'

He bowed as she left him, grateful, at least, for one night under a roof.

Fuelled by anger and desperation, he'd spent the last few weeks hiding in these desolate hills, avoiding both the Scots and the English. Just to the south, near the peaks, lay the border that two kings had drawn more than one hundred years ago.

Now, he had chosen his side.

And lonely and bleak as it was, Mistress Clare, by all that was holy, was going to let him live on it.

Chapter Two

Euphemia ran after her as Clare entered the hall. 'No wonder you're still unmarried. A braw man appears and you do nothing but insult him.'

'Euphemia, you talk as if I should open my skirts to anything with a pillicock.' Of course, the girl's mother did, so she knew no better.

The girl shrugged. She knew who, and what, she was. Her mother might have been the baron's companion for ten years, but she would never be his wife. 'What's the harm?'

'He's someone's bastard son, attached to no lord. He may have been banished from his fellows. We'll be lucky if he doesn't murder us in our beds.' And if he did, the fault would be hers.

'Well, I'll be friendly, if you won't.'

'No, you won't. I don't want to see his bastard in your belly after he's gone. Now go and find out whether cook needs help with those fowl.'

The girl smiled and left, without answering yea or nae.

Clare gritted her teeth. She had tried to bring order to this place, but France and all she'd learned there was far away. The wildness of these untamed hills crept into everything and everyone. Even *she* had mornings, like this one, when nothing would soothe her but watching the falcon soar and taking pleasure in its kill.

She glanced up. Fitzjohn was still regarding her. He smiled, as if sensing her unruly urges.

She turned her back on him. Let the man fill his belly and be gone.

She tried to ignore him when he appeared in the Great Hall for the evening meal, sitting far below the salt. He seemed at ease there, among the men-at-arms, yet something set him apart, as well.

Euphemia leaned over to serve him soup, her breast pressing close to his shoulder. Clare clenched her fists.

He caught her looking at him and his eyes, in turn, travelled over her as if he saw not just under her clothes, but under her skin.

She looked away. He was not worthy of a lady's attention. She rested her gaze, instead, on the small tapestry banker, a gift from Alain.

Alain, Comte de Garencieres, had come to Scotland a year ago with soldiers and money to aid, or more precisely, to rekindle the Scots' war on England. He had brought with him the reminder of all she had left behind when she had returned two years ago after years of being fostered in France.

The banker, in threads of red, white and gold, depicted a man and woman, arms outstretched, about to reunite. On the woman's shoulder perched the falcon who had already returned to her.

It was too beautiful to sit on, though it was designed as a bench cover. Instead, she had draped it over a chest beside the great hearth where she could see it.

Alain's gift was a reminder of a better world, one where grace and chivalry reigned. And as soon as the fighting was over, they would be married. She would return to France as the *comte's* lady, far from this crude and brutal land of her birth.

She glanced at Fitzjohn through her eyelashes without raising her head. A boorish Scot, like the rest. Interested only in fighting, eating and women.

He had left her thoughts by the time the evening meal was finished and she started up the spiralling stairs to her bedchamber. But as she reached the third level, Fitzjohn loomed before her, just beyond her candle's glow.

The flame trembled. 'This is the family floor. What are you doing here?'

'Looking for a bed.'

She glanced towards her door, still closed. Had he dared look inside? 'I told you to sleep in the Hall with the rest.' She took the final step up to the floor, yet still he towered over her.

'You might at least offer me a blanket and pillow.'

'I've offered you a roof.' And it was more than she should have. 'Don't make me regret it.'

'A lady's hospitality normally includes something more comfortable.'

Comfortable carried the lilt of an insult, but the words raised her guilt. A lady *should* show more hospitality. Yet his behaviour didn't befit a knight, so she had trouble remembering to act as a lady.

'I have given you the same welcome that I would give any other fighting man. If that is unacceptable, then you won't be sorry to leave tomorrow. Now stand aside so I can reach my chamber.'

He didn't move, yet something crept over her skin, as if he had touched her. She started around him, but the space was narrow and she bumped against him, stumbled and lost her grip on the candlestick.

He caught her with one arm before she hit the floor and when she looked up, she saw the candle, straight and steady, in his other hand.

Knees bent, she tried to stand, but only fell against his chest. Embarrassed, she had to cling to his shoulders as he straightened, giving her back her stance, and then her candle.

She backed away, her forearm branded with his palm, her breasts still feeling the press of his chest, held just a moment too long, against hers.

'Dream well, Mistress Clare.'

She reached behind her and pushed her door open, afraid to look away for fear he'd follow. But he didn't move, and as she took the light with her his smile faded into the darkness.

She shut the door and leaned against it, shaking.

Tomorrow. Tomorrow he would be gone.

As she slammed the door against him, Gavin struggled to subdue his anger. Her disdain was sparked by such small trespasses, things that reflected none of the darkness he concealed. If she was so concerned about the shine of his armour, what would she think if he broke down her door and forced himself into the comfort of her bed?

He'd seen men do worse. He had ridden away from the English because their war had made it too easy to act on such dark visions. As easy as it had been for his father to seduce a Scots lady and leave her with a child forced to fight the heritage of his blended blood.

He was weary of war—the one on the field and the one in his soul.

He descended the stone stairs into the hall. A few men still gambled in the corner. The rest had curled up for the night. The fire had burned to embers and his small bedroll offered little cushion from the unforgiving floor. For weeks, he had braved cold and rain, staying clear of Lord Douglas's men as they chased Edward's troops. Grass and dirt had been his bed. He ached for a moment of comfort.

Stretching out close to the hearth, he saw the tapestry banker covering the chest beside it, keeping the wood warm when a man was cold.

He reached over, pulled it off and rolled up in it. The memory of her fingers caressing it when she thought no one was looking warmed him more than the wool.

Clare smiled as she entered the Hall the next morning and went over to pat the banker covering the chest. It had become a daily rite, reminding her of Alain's expectation that she be a lady, cleaving to the ways his mother had taught her.

Her smile faded as she came closer. Black and grey smudges marred the red-and-gold wool.

She knelt beside the tapestry, anger mixing with a sick feeling in her stomach. What would Alain think when he saw what had happened to his beautiful gift?

She looked around the Hall. None of her men would have dared touch it. It must have been the stranger.

Fury swamped the anguish. First, fury with herself for being so foolish as to let him into her home. Then, fury at him.

She folded the tapestry carefully, exposing a back as neatly finished as the front. He had done it deliberately, she was sure—tried to destroy something precious to her.

She carried the folded fabric as reverently as an altar cloth, the pounding in her ears growing with each step. A lady must never show anger. A lady must be ever temperate. Yet rage pounded against her temples. She struggled to subdue it, blaming him for raising her temper. The strength of it frightened her nearly as much as the other feelings he'd raised.

The ones that had kept her awake last night.

She found him in the stable, kneeling before his horse, testing the animal's fetlock. At least the man had the wisdom to look after the beast, a possession no doubt more valuable than he deserved.

She wondered whether he had killed the knight who owned it.

Angus sat in the straw at his feet, head bent over the chainmail, patiently polishing an individual iron link.

'Angus!' Her voice was sharp. 'Ask the falconer if he needs help in the mews.'

'That's nae work for a squire.'

It was the first time the boy had ever crossed her and she added it to Fitzjohn's list of sins. 'And if you do not do as you're told, you'll never *be* a squire.'

Fitzjohn motioned his head towards the door. The boy put down the brush and hurried out.

'Blame me, if you must,' he said. 'Not the boy.'

'I do.'

The morning sunlight streamed through the stable door and poured over him, picking up streaks of gold in his hair. He did not wear his smile this morning. Instead, the light carved sharp shadows around his nose and mouth. He looked as fierce as a golden eagle. Powerful, graceful, beautiful.

Deadly.

Such a bird could pluck Wee One out of the sky without ruffling his own feathers.

She lifted the cloth in an accusation. 'This was a beautiful tapestry.' She swallowed, trying to clear the fury fighting to escape her throat. 'It came all the way from France.'

She held it out, but he didn't take it.

His wry look returned, masking the danger. 'That's a long trip.'

'You ruined it. Deliberately.' Her voice shook and she hated the power he had to upset her.

'Now that's a harsh accusation. You sent me to sleep in the hall without so much as a blanket. I wrapped myself up in it and it fell into the ashes during the night.' He shrugged, his expression holding no remorse. 'That's what it's made for. To ward off the cold.'

'To ward off the chill when one is sitting on the bench.'

His smile widened, slowly. 'But your bottom wasn't on the bench last night, so I didn't think you'd mind.'

He was savouring her anger. His very smile seemed to say *I know what you are. You are not the lady you pretend to be.*

She dropped it in the straw at his feet, releasing a puff of dust. 'You dirtied it. Clean it before you leave.'

He looked down at the banker, then back at her, half-smile still in place. 'That's a lot of fuss to be making about a spot of dirt on a piece of cloth.'

'It's a tapestry, not just a piece of cloth.' She bit her cheek to stop the tears. 'From Arras. It was a gift.'

'Are you sure that's really what's disturbing you?'

'What else would I be distressed about?'

'Me.'

'You?' The word fell from her lips as quickly as if he had slapped her. How did he know? His very presence violated the natural order. Knights were supposed to be noble, honourable and kind to women. He was the opposite and worse, he delighted in it.

'That's right. I think I just roil you inside.'

He did. In places she had never felt before.

'Yes, Sir Gavin, if you are a "sir." You do.' She lifted her chin and lowered her shoulders, trying to regain a lady's calm. 'But do not smile with pleasure at the thought. You "roil" me because you deliberately flout the laws of chivalry.'

'Chivalry?' His mocking tone had a dark echo.

'Yes. You must have heard the word.'

Gratified, she saw his easy smile vanish. His blue

eyes turned hard and he stepped closer, forcing her to retreat. But she could not move far enough away. He still stole her breath.

'Oh, I've heard of it. But I've been fighting in a war, not a tournament to entertain the ladies. You may not believe this, Mistress Clare, but we don't see much chivalry in war, so forgive me if I've forgotten how to bow and scrape and bend my knee. In a real war, we don't wave a lance and a lady's scarf in hopes of winning a silk purse. In a real war, when someone loses, they die. And sometimes, the victor even enjoys the killing.'

She shuddered. Had *he* enjoyed killing?

A momentary vision of Wee One, catching her prey, flashed before her. But that was not the same. Not the same at all. 'Christian knights do not kill one another. The code of honour requires a fellow knight to be spared, else war would be nothing but brutal murder.'

'War *is* nothing but brutal murder.'

What kind of man was this? Whose war had he fought and what demons had he seen there?

'I do not know where you've been, but you're in a civilised household now, where everything is done *to then anes,* which means to its proper purpose, though I don't expect you know that. I suggest you learn.'

The smiling mask returned, wiping the darkness from his face. *'Mais oui, demoiselle.'*

His French stunned her.

It was smoother than hers.

And his half-smile had grown large enough that she noticed, for the first time, a dimple on his right cheek.

Gavin's smile faded as he wrestled with the tapestry, a small, poor thing compared to those he'd seen in

Edward's palaces. First, he shook it, hoping the ashes would fly free. Then, he tried brushing the smudges away, but that only dirtied the rest of the cloth and his fingers.

He knew nothing of how to put things right, only how to destroy them.

And somehow, Mistress Clare had known. Even without knowing his name, she treated him like the deserter he was. Like a man who had stood outside a church holding a torch.

And carried the blood of a father who would have burned it.

If it showed so clearly in his face, he was right not to lie about his name. People would judge him without caring that the truth wasn't as bad as they thought.

Nor as good as it should be.

And Mistress Clare, mired in her fantasies, was very, very good at judgements.

Blind to the crude tower and the rough life that surrounded her, she acted as if she wandered Windsor Palace.

Her illusions reminded him of King Edward. A few years ago, the King had gathered his friends at a round table and dubbed them Knights of the Garter: the garter of a woman the King had raped, if the rumours were true.

Mistress Clare wouldn't like that part of the story. It would violate all her illusions about chivalry, making her angry. Anger would bring colour to her cheeks and warmth to those stony, grey-green eyes. That, he would enjoy seeing. He had the feeling Mistress Clare didn't let her emotions show if she could help it.

A woman like that, well, it would be a pleasure to turn her inside out and force her to feel the passion she disdained. He would unravel her braid, so tight it smoothed her brow, and make her whimper with feelings the woman didn't know she had.

Or didn't want to know.

He looked back at the tapestry. It showed a man, arms outstretched, flying towards a woman and about to embrace her. One hand hovered behind her head. His face was near her breast. The other arm was reached around her hip.

He wondered whether Mistress Clare knew how sensual a piece it was.

He stopped his thoughts from going further. He had to keep his feelings in check. He'd heard from the men that her father was fighting with Lord Douglas and would soon be home. Gavin must humour her until Baron Carr returned. That man would know that a knight's value was in his sword, not his manners. Surely Carr would let him stay on, hidden, in this god-forsaken corner of the Border.

He looked at the tapestry again and sighed. To clean his body, he dunked it in water. Perhaps he should do the same with this.

He headed for the spring with a leery feeling neither one of them would like the outcome.

Fitzjohn, Clare noticed, missed the midday meal. She didn't observe it because she wanted to see him again, but only because she was eager to have her tapestry back. He needed only to hang it on a line, beat it from the back, then brush the front with a small broom. Simple task.

But as her fury faded, doubts crept in. Simple for her, but she had foolishly assumed he would know what to do. She should have never let it out of her sight without giving him thorough and precise instructions.

As the sun reached its zenith, she ignored the rest of her duties to search for him. Finally, outside near the mews, she caught a glimpse of red.

Draped across a rope was the wet, limp banker, no longer a beautiful depiction of courtly lovers, but a rumpled, sodden wad of cloth.

She closed her eyes against quick tears. How would she explain this to Alain?

Fitzjohn, apparently realising his mistake too late, was pulling on one end of the piece. Euphemia held the other as they tried to stretch it back into shape. The sight of Murine's girl helping him angered her as much as anything he had done.

'Euphemia! Get inside.'

'You're nae my mither.'

Did they all think to defy her once tainted by Fitzjohn? 'No, but I, not your mother, am mistress of this castle.' And yet she continued to make mistakes. Mistakes she would never have made if *her* mother had been alive to teach her. 'Now go!'

Euphemia did, throwing Fitzjohn a sunny smile as she left.

Clare stepped closer, torn between wanting to hit him and cry. Two things a lady must never do.

'Are you always so harsh?' he said.

'Not nearly so harsh as I'm going to be with you. You've ruined it!' The words tumbled out in a rush.

He shrugged, but said nothing. She had wanted an apology and expected an argument. Her father would have yelled back. But this man absorbed abuse and returned it with a half-smile, as some men would take a blow, roll over and leap to their feet again. He left her with nothing to do but get angrier or to give up.

She was not ready to give up.

'You've destroyed something valuable and precious. I expect payment.'

'Payment?' He raised his brows. 'I've seen warriors dead on the ground with no payment for their loss. I cannot mourn woven wool.' His words were mocking, bitter.

Dead on the ground.

She choked back her fear. *Not Da.* The phrase like a prayer. *Not Alain.*

Sometimes, the only thing a woman could do to hold back the dangers of the world was to maintain order in the small corner of it that was hers.

She looked back at the tapestry. 'I don't know what I was thinking, to expect a warrior to know how to treat such a treasure.'

This time, a trace of compassion touched his smile, as if he knew what was happening to her men, things she couldn't possibly imagine and didn't want to.

'It's not something that I was trained to do.'

For once, he made her smile, a rueful hiccup of laughter clearing the tears from her throat. She must take the first blame. Perhaps if she stretched it on the tapestry frame she might salvage it.

She stroked the damp cloth with her fingers and ventured a smile. A knight's lessons would never be so domestic. 'What are you trained to do?'

'Kill.'

She snatched back her hand. 'You have an ignoble view of war. A knight should be thinking of noble quests, of honour.'

'You talk as if King Arthur's knights still ride. Now we quest for land and ransom, not for the Holy Grail.'

She had been weak enough to share a momentary smile and in return, he'd thrown his brutal view of the world in her face. But there was something more in his eyes. An unaccustomed challenge. An unwelcome lure.

'If you do not seek the Holy Grail, have you at least had the honour to fulfil a lady's request?' It was one of the sacred tenants of chivalry, to honour a lady's wish.

The wind swirled around the edge of her skirt, blowing it towards his boot.

His smile, taunting, returned. 'Generally, what they've desired of me has not included holy objects.'

She grabbed her skirt back from the breeze. 'Neither does what I desire. I'd like you to clean the mews. Make it spotless.'

Here was a man who treated chivalry with disdain. Would he honour her request? Or, better, would he find the task so demeaning that he would, finally, ride away?

The harsh lines of his face eased, his smile suddenly genuine. 'I've spent more time with falcons than with fabric. I will certainly do my best to fulfil your wish, no matter how hard the work.'

'Good.'

The vision of him on hands and knees scrubbing gave her some satisfaction.

'And no matter how long it takes.' His smile took on a wicked edge. 'Even if it takes all night and all day tomorrow.'

She gritted her teeth, realising he had turned her demeaning request into his victory.

'One more night then. But no longer.'

She had judged him unworthy as a fighting man, but she must not underestimate his prowess in verbal battle again.

Chapter Three

The next morning, Neil accosted her, brows creased, complaining that she'd sent a stranger to meddle in his mews.

Clare sighed and went to face Fitzjohn, wary of the next trick he might try in order to extend his stay. As she opened the door to the mews, a shaft of light cleaved the dimness and found his bare back. He turned from his raking and she swallowed. His chest, broad, seemed strong enough to need no armour.

'Mistress Clare,' he said, shielding his eyes as he looked towards her, standing in the open doorway. 'I hope you will find that I scrubbed the falcons' mute to your satisfaction.'

She forced her eyes to meet his. 'The falconer has some complaints.'

'He's a good man. But wedded to old ways.'

He spoke as if he knew falconry.

All the birds were leashed, so she left the door open to allow the light in. The gravel crunched beneath her feet as she inspected his work. Of course, there had been little for him to do but rake the droppings from the stones. The falconer was scrupulous about daily cleaning.

'Is everything to your satisfaction, Mistress Clare?'

Closer now, she could see sweat dampening his hair and the hose clinging to his legs. She peered at the falcons' blocks, surprised to see he had even scrubbed away the whitish mute smears from the side of Wee One's perch. 'You've taken great care.'

He shrugged. 'You've more blocks than birds.'

It was a pitiful mews, by most standards, she knew. Most of the birds there now belonged to the visitors, only temporary residents. 'We had more, once. But birds and war are both costly. War has won.'

She pulled on her glove and held out her wrist. Wee One hopped on the fist, fluttering her feathers in delight. Clare rubbed her throat feathers gently, noting her crop was almost empty. She might be hungry enough to fly again tomorrow.

'That's the bird you were flying in the hills,' he said.

'I've had this one since she was just a brancher. She's my favourite of all I've flown. Of course, I've never had one of the really fine birds from the cliffs near the sea.'

'The best I've flown were northern birds, captured in the Low Countries.'

She assessed him anew. She had heard of such birds, but she'd never seen them and couldn't have afforded them if a falcon dealer had brought them. If he had hawked with birds like that, he must be of better birth than she'd believed. 'Those would be worthy of kings.'

He shrugged. 'Origin means little. I've seen gyrfalcons refuse to fly and sparrowhawks take on rabbits three times their size. Did you train her yourself?'

She nodded. 'I'm all she knows. She'll not leave me.'

'You cannot keep her on a creance and practise the art. Each flight is a risk. Each return a choice.'

She clutched the leather jesses tight between her gloved fingers. 'This one will always come back.'

Behind her, she heard the flapping of wings. As she turned, a bird swooped down, talons nearly tangling in her hair. Then, he soared towards the ceiling directly above Wee One's perch, performing an ecstasy of swoops and turns.

'Stop him!' Impossible. Accustomed to the entire sky, the bird hurtled dangerously close to the wall. A crash would mean a broken wing.

'I think,' Fitzjohn said, with awe in his voice she had never heard, 'that he's doing it for her.'

Wee One's head followed his flight. Clare peered up through the dim light. It was hard to be sure, but the stripes under his wings and the ermine look of the feathers under his throat reminded her of the tercel she had seen two days ago.

She cupped her palm against Wee One's breast, reassured that the bird had not tried to fly. 'Please. I want him gone.'

Fitzjohn waved his arms and yelled at the bird.

As he widened his flight, the strange bird seemed to realise he was trapped. He flew towards the light from the window high in the wall, but the slats, designed to keep the birds inside, were too small for him to escape.

'Open the door wider,' Fitzjohn said.

She did, then stepped away to give the bird a clear path to freedom. The tercel made a final swoop and roll, then, close enough to the door to see his escape, flew through it and disappeared.

She released a breath, still shaking. 'Thank you,' she said. 'I was afraid he would hurt himself. He must have been wild and mad.'

'He knew exactly what he was doing.'

Surprised, she turned to him, expecting a cynical expression. 'What?'

'Trying to get her attention.'

'Why?'

'For the usual reasons a male wants a female to notice him. He wants to mate.'

Heat touched her cheeks and she looked away. 'I doubt that.' His bare chest was within reach of her fingers. Close enough to touch. Close enough to kiss—

'Where do you think falcons come from?'

Perhaps he didn't know falcons as well as he implied. 'The falcon dealer has brought most of these, but I caught Wee One near Hen Hole just east of here.'

His laugh cascaded over her. 'Before that, I mean.'

She flushed. 'Well, from eggs, of course.' Could the tercel mean to mate with Wee One? 'But a mews is not a nursery.' She had never seen an egg laid in the mews. Was that even possible?

'They mate for life, you know.' His words were husky.

'Unless one of them dies.' And when her mother had died, her father had not hesitated to take another.

She turned away and tied Wee One safely back on her perch.

'If the mews is cleaned to your satisfaction, I await your pleasure,' he said, his voice caressing her back. 'I offer again to put my sword in your service.'

'My father will be home soon,' she said, abruptly, not looking at him. Like the wild tercel, Fitzjohn had flown into her mews by accident, and now seemed trapped and out of place. Did he long for freedom? Or did he need a safe haven? 'He'll be the one to decide your fate.' She felt she owed him that, though she did not know why.

'Thank you, Mistress Clare.'

She started out of the mews, then turned. 'I've an extra blanket, Fitzjohn. It will be yours tonight.'

He bowed, with a courtier's grace. 'I'm truly grateful, my lady.'

And for the first time since she'd met him, she truly felt like a lady.

The tercel returned a few days later.

She saw him in the weathering yard, where the birds had been taken outside for exercise, hoods off, but still tethered. This time, the male bird swooped down and joined Wee One on her perch. They bowed to each other, heads bobbing up and down like overactive courtiers.

She laughed and Fitzjohn, crossing the bailey, joined in.

'They look so funny,' she said.

'They are courting.'

'What?'

'Now she'll try to fly. Watch.'

Wee One rose, swooping with the strange bird in a sky dance, tugging against her leash as if wanting to escape.

Clare rushed over, clapping to scare the male away. Wee One tried to follow.

Clare pulled on the leather leash, drawing her falcon back until the bird was again within reach of her hand. This one, she must not lose.

She had already lost too much that she cared for.

'Mistress Clare!' The call came from the barmkin wall.

She looked up at the man. 'What is it?'

'Your father approaches.'

Home. Safe. Relief left her limp.

The roar of his voice reached her before she saw him. 'We've run the Inglis back across the border. Now where are my girls?'

Euphemia had already run to him, oblivious of the cold that had followed their few blessed days of spring.

And when Clare saw who was with her father, she ran, too.

Alain was home.

She slowed her steps before he saw her, remembering she must walk as a lady instead of running like a child or, worse, an over-eager lover. A lady worthy of her knight's devotion must set an example.

But she could not slow her heart. How brave he looked, the French *comte* on his horse! Straight, dark, strong. The epitome of knighthood.

And she felt a moment's gratitude that she had managed to stretch and shape the banker after Fitzjohn's abuse. Alain would barely notice the damage.

Her father swirled Euphemia as if she were ten instead of sixteen summers, their breath making clouds in the air. Then, he turned his eye to Clare.

'Da.' Her word was a breath of joy. He enfolded her in his arms and she snuggled against him like a child, safe, for the moment, back in his arms.

Then, she leaned away to look at him. New lines weighed the corners of his eyes. 'Ye broke nae rules, did ye?' She asked in the Scots way, as she did every time he returned. It was her prayer of thanks.

'None I'll tell ye about,' he answered, as he always did.

She shook her head. She refused to think of the dangers of war when he was away, telling herself the rules of chivalry would protect him. Even when he was safely beside her again, she could barely admit to herself he risked death every time he faced the enemy. 'I'm glad you're home.'

'Ye may not be so glad when I start pestering ye again. I've a new reason to want ye married, daughter.' He said it in his best Border burr, knowing it would irk her.

'I know the old ones well enough.' He wanted grandsons, that she knew. Well, the time had come to make plans with Alain.

'Ah, Demoiselle Clare.'

She turned to him, beaming, and extended her hand, as she had learned to do. He took her fingers and brushed his lips near them, his moustache tickling her knuckles.

'I wish I had known you would return today,' she said. 'I would have prepared a meal in your honour and worn my finest gown.'

He dropped her hand and she smoothed the wool of her shirt. It was cheap, local cloth, woven of wool not fine enough to send to the Low Countries.

'*Ridicule!* You are a lovely flower in this wasteland, as always.'

'Prepare what food we have.' Her father's voice boomed. 'I've a hunger a whole deer couldn't fill.' He had his arm around Euphemia again, as if she were a real daughter. 'Where's Murine?'

'Here!'

Her father's lover ran out of the tower and into his arms. Clare turned away, refusing to witness their embrace. This woman had moved into his bed after Clare's mother had died. Not lady enough to be a wife, she had been his companion ever since.

Murine had tried to mother his daughter, too, but when Clare was fostered in France, she had seen women who looked like her memory of her own mother, women who wore silk gowns and spoke with sweet scented breath. Murine would never be one of those. Gradually, she stopped trying.

Now, they stayed out of each other's way.

Clare moved closer to Alain and turned him towards the tower to shield him from their display. The *comte* knew the code. And held to it.

Unlike the stranger.

'Ah, *demoiselle,* what a breath of fresh air you are amidst the stench of Scotland.'

He offered her his arm and she saw dried blood on his sleeve. 'You're wounded!' Fear shook her again.

'It is but a scratch. But your touch makes it feel *comme neuf.*'

'Let me see.' She pushed up the sleeve, gently, and ran her fingers over the skin of his arm. An unwelcome memory of Fitzjohn's bare chest made her hand tremble.

Alain was right. The wound did not look serious. 'Come. I'll clean and bandage it for you.'

She revelled in the words. They sounded like something a wife might say.

He gently put her hand aside, holding her fingers no longer than propriety dictated. 'You are kind.'

Out of the corner of her eye, she saw Murine pull her father towards the tower. 'Food first,' she said, laughing, removing his hand from her breast.

Clare knew what would happen next. After the midday meal, she would not see them for hours.

Embarrassed, she turned back to Alain. 'I'm glad you are safe. Tell me of your battles.'

'Battles? Ah, I wish we had seen battles! Edward is a monster, but Douglas is a coward.'

'A coward?' No Scot would call Lord Douglas a coward. Not if he wanted to live.

'Instead of forcing a fight, Douglas kept us always away from the English. Then, by God's mercy, Edward's ships were destroyed.' He crossed himself with muttered thanks to the Blessed Virgin. 'He had no supplies. He had to retreat. But still Lord Douglas would not fight, only chased him, like a dog after the deer, instead of confronting him on an open field of battle. We could have delivered the *coup de grâce.*'

She murmured a supportive sound. Douglas would

take the field with the bravest, but when a Scot waged war, he thought only of the end, not of the proper way to reach it. 'So they are gone now, the Inglis?'

He nodded. 'And left the land laid waste, just as they did in France. Burning, looting, even during the holy day of Candlemas. And it was not just the rabble. The worst was the King's bastard nephew. He burned the monastery church in Haddington to the ground, full of innocents who had sought sanctuary.'

Stunned, she crossed herself. 'I did not think the Inglis so devoid of honour.' Murder. Sacrilege. No knight would commit such acts.

Alain offered his arm as they walked towards the keep. 'Alas, it is so. I was told the man who held the torch was the son of John of Eltham, who did the very same twenty years ago. And the Edward who rules today was so angry when he heard of it that he killed him. His own brother.' He shook his head. 'Such murderous blood, the English. This Edward must kill for pleasure alone if he would murder a man and then encourage his son to commit the same sacrilege.'

She glanced across the yard to find Fitzjohn's eyes on them. *We don't see much chivalry in war,* he had said. As if he had seen such acts.

As if he could have committed them.

She stepped closer to Alain. Her men were home and safe. Fitzjohn could answer to her father now.

After he had eaten his fill, her father spent the afternoon in Murine's cottage. Clare closed her eyes to what the two of them did there.

Late in the day, he emerged to sit with her by the fire

in the Hall, his third cup of brogat cradled in his palms, asking of all that had happened while he was gone.

He said little of the campaign. Edward had retreated, yes, but he had burned everything in his path. In the end, it seemed, both sides had lost.

'I saw a strange face on the barmkin,' he said, finally. 'Who is he?'

'A knight separated from his fellows.' Did she sound unconcerned? 'I gave him a meal and a roof and work to do. He wants to stay on, but I told him you would have to decide.'

Her father's eyes narrowed. 'We lost James in a skirmish last month. I could use a new man.'

'He's said little of himself. I'm not sure of the nobility of his line.'

'That's nae something to bother a Scot.'

She wondered why she was holding her breath. 'And he hasn't the *comte*'s sense of chivalry.'

Her father's lips twisted into something between a scowl and a laugh. 'Few do. I'll judge him meself, daughter. What's his name?'

'Fitzjohn.' She said the name as if unsure of it.

Her father sat bolt upright, nearly dropping his cup. 'What did you say?'

'Fitzjohn.' She wondered at his response. 'Gavin, I think.'

Her father rose from his chair, towering over her. 'What have ye done, girl?'

Why had she ignored her misgivings about this man? Her mother would never have made that mistake. 'Tell me. What have I done besides get a clean mews and a dirty banker?'

'Ye've brought the murdering fire-raiser who torched half of Lothian into our hall.' His bluster flagged, replaced by the same haunted look she'd seen in Fitz-john's eyes. 'We called it Burnt Candlemas. And he carried the torch.'

She cursed herself with words a lady should not know. If they woke with the roof in flames over their heads it would be her fault. 'Forgive me. I didn't know.'

He reached for his sword and started to buckle it on. 'I'll deal with him.'

'Wait.' She rose and touched his shoulder, moving him gently back in the chair. 'I was the one who let him in. I'll go.' Did she hope somehow he would deny what she'd suspected all along? 'Let me be sure he is the same man.'

'Not alone, daughter.'

'I won't be alone.' She patted the sheath holding her dagger. Since that day in the hills, it had never left her side, another reluctant concession to this lawless land. 'Not as long as I have this.'

'Ah, daughter. I wish ye were as determined to give me grandsons as ye are to do things your own way.'

She shook her head. Not her way, but the right way, something her father neither appreciated nor understood. 'Give me just a little time. Then, come and do with him what you will.'

She swung out of the hall and up the stairs, skirt swishing between her legs, uncertain whether anger, fear, or shame drove her. She found him on the tower's wall walk, staring towards the snow-covered mountains, stark against the sunset-yellow sky.

'Fitzjohn!' she called, her dagger at the ready.

He turned, slowly, his face shadowed by the light of the fading sun. 'That's what I'm called. Why the blade?'

'You're also called a fire-raiser.'

Pain and anger mixed in his gaze. Did she even see a pleading look there? No mind. This man had shown no mercy. Neither would she.

'I'm called many things.' The words came slowly, as if by speaking he had been forced to crack a stone.

'That's no answer.'

'What kind of answer would you like, Mistress Clare?'

'One that's true.'

'Ah, then you're bound to be disappointed in life. People will say what they will, true or false.'

Always, he turned aside a question instead of answering it. 'They say you burned a church full of innocent people.'

He turned his head, quick and sharp as a falcon spotting its prey. 'Is that the tale now?' The words carved deep lines around his lips, yet unhurried they came as if he truly did not care what was said of him.

'Is it true?'

'What do you think?'

His shadowed eyes had witnessed acts no man should know and no knight should commit. But had he done them, too?

She didn't believe it. Or didn't want to.

She dropped her weapon and shook her head.

'I thank you, then, for that.' His voice held an echo of soft gratitude. 'May I stay, then?'

'My Da is coming. The decision will be his.'

'I understand.'

She struggled to join her father's words and the *comte*'s story. 'Does that mean your father was the son of a king?'

He nodded.

'And brother to another?'

His sideways smile showed no pride, yet she felt her knees begin to dip, as if to make her curtsy before him.

'Why didn't you tell me?' Royal blood in his veins, even though Inglis, yet she had suggested he was no better than a peasant. He must think her a barbarian.

'Would you have let me in if I had?'

'No, but you lied. You told me you were Scots.'

'My mother was a MacGuffin. She gave me as much Scots blood as English. So tell me where that puts the Border in my body.' He grabbed her hand, the one holding the dagger, and stroked the blade across his waist. 'Here? Is the Scots half below the belt and the English above? Or is the heart Scottish and the baws English?'

She tugged against him, but his stronger hold was the invisible one. 'I don't know.'

'Or maybe it's this way.' Fingers locked around her wrist, he made her wave the dagger from the top of his head down the centre of his nose, then along his torso until she feared he might slash his chest open. 'Right? Left? Which side shall we throw across the hills into Northumberland? And which side would you deem worthy to keep?'

He twisted her wrist and the blade fell away. His move bent her elbow, pulling her so close that the rise and fall of his chest brushed hers.

Dark fire, hot and dangerous, coiled inside her, rising from a place she'd long forgotten, if she ever knew. She swallowed. 'Do you mean to burn us in our beds, Fitzjohn?'

At first, he let the wind answer. Then he retrieved his smile and relaxed his grip. 'Would you like to be burning in your bed, Mistress Clare?'

She stepped back, knowing she should fear him, but fearing herself instead. 'If I do, Fitzjohn, it won't be you I'll be asking for help.'

He raised his brows and cocked his head. His fingers still circled her wrist, but the grip became a caress. 'I don't think your Frenchman can strike that kind of flint.'

Over his shoulder, she saw her father draw his sword and touch Fitzjohn's back. 'Let go of my daughter, you bastard, before I run this sword through you.'

Chapter Four

Gavin let go of her wrist, resisting the feeling of loss. He wondered how much the man had seen.

And heard.

Well, death might be a welcome escape.

'Now raise your hands and turn around.'

Slowly, Gavin did, assessing the man up close for the first time. The baron was broad and gnarled and lean with years of work and war.

'Am I speaking to another Carr?'

'You're speaking to *the* Carr,' he snarled.

He was careful with his smile, but he looked over at her, gratified to see she was flushed. 'I thought Clare was a Carr.'

'Out of my loins.'

He caught the hint of pride. 'Well, Mistress Clare invited me in.'

'And tell me why I should let you stay.'

'Is your daughter's word not reason enough?'

'I gave you no promise. I said—'

'Quiet, daughter.' His sword never wavered. 'She let you in, but you didn't tell her the whole truth about yourself.' The man's sword touched his throat. Gavin swallowed, feeling the cold point against his skin. One quick thrust and he'd be a dead man.

'I told her I had Scots blood. If you know my story, you know that's true.'

'Would you swear you didn't kill those people?' Clare asked.

He hesitated. Men would think what they liked of him. He had learned long ago not to care and no longer wasted breath trying to change their minds. Now, this woman, like all the rest, seemed to believe the worst.

Only this time, it mattered.

'I would.' He started to lower his arms.

'Keep your hands up,' she said. 'Swear you won't harm us?'

Did she really think he'd set fire to the place? 'I swear.'

'And that you won't open our doors to the Inglis,' her father added.

'I swear it.'

'On a knight's honour?' she prodded, not trusting him even now.

'On my knight's honour.' Words that meant much to her and nothing to him.

Carr lowered his sword, though his suspicious stare didn't ease. Gavin let his hands drop, slowly. 'So I can stay?'

'I'm still thinking on it,' the man replied sharply. 'What do you want and why are you here?'

To find peace, he thought. Vain hope. There was no

truce for the war within. 'I'm just a poor knight between wars, seeking shelter and a lord to serve.'

'A few weeks ago you served the King of the Inglis. Why should I trust you to fight with the Scots?'

'Half my blood's as Scottish as yours.'

'And the other half is as Inglis as Edward's.'

Her voice came from beside him. 'And which is the stronger?'

He wished he knew. Sometimes, he felt as if blood was at war with blood, tainted by his father's sins. 'As long as I serve you, it's my Scots blood that will be speaking.'

'Be sure of it.' The baron stepped closer and Gavin caught a whiff of a warm hearth and a welcome pint. Things he hadn't seen for a long time.

'Aye. You have my word.'

'And why,' she asked, 'should we trust your word?'

Silent, he gave no answer. Trust could only be earned, not promised.

The baron squinted at him and motioned Clare to the stairs. 'Leave us, daughter.'

'But, Da—'

'You asked for time alone. Give me the same.'

He wondered, as she picked up her dagger and turned towards the stairs, what she'd wanted from those moments alone with him. And whether she'd got it.

Carr leaned against the stone wall, his eyes searching the dark hillside. 'Why are you here, Fitzjohn? The truth.'

'I was born here. And now I've come home.' Or at least, he'd come looking for home again. 'England wasn't…' He let the word drift, then shrugged. 'It wasn't that.'

An owl hooted and then was silent, giving its prey no more warning.

'If I let you stay, Fitzjohn, you must know that if anything suspicious, anything at all, happens while you're here, I won't ask any questions. I'll just kill you.'

That was progress, Gavin decided. 'Do I scare you that much?'

'You don't scare me at all.'

'No?' He scared the daughter, though she tried not to show it. 'I've a dangerous reputation.'

The old man gave a snort. 'Well, so have I. And I've had longer to earn mine.'

They both grinned then. And he felt a kinship with the man, something he'd never felt on either side of the border. He wondered what his life might have been like, if he'd had such a father.

'Well, if you're as clever as you are dangerous, you'll put me to work doing something more than sweeping the mews and hooting at owls.' He watched the man's face for clues and saw none. 'You could use a seasoned man.'

'You think so?' He looked as if he didn't care what Fitzjohn thought.

'Well, at least you could use one who understands that you don't meet an army in the field when you can defeat them in the woods.' The *comte* had spent the afternoon whining about Douglas's tactics, as if how the war was fought was more important than whether it was won or lost.

The old man's grin split his face. 'He's a pompous,

puffed-up idiot, the Frenchman. You said it sure.' He
studied Gavin's face. 'I'll think on what you said.'

'Dangerous men don't need to think long.'

'What's the hurry?'

He couldn't escape war here. But maybe he could
hide from it long enough to stitch up the worst of his
wounds. The ones people couldn't see. 'I've been away
ten years. It's time I reclaimed my Scots side.' When he
had left this land, he had lost a piece of himself. Now,
he hoped it was still here where he could find it.

'Can you live up to it?'

'Do I have to kill someone to prove it?'

The man stared at Gavin a long time without a
word.

'Not yet,' the old man said, finally. The determination
in his eyes matched his daughter's. Gavin hoped the old
man would come to a better conclusion than she had.
'But there's six red cattle on the other side of the hill
on Robson land that used to live in the pen leaning up
against our wall. If they were to come home, you and I
might have more to talk about. A lot more.'

And their shared smile was as strong as a hand-
shake.

As the men in the corner of the Hall rolled their dice,
Clare rearranged her patterns one more time, trying to
fit a new hood, jesses, and bewits for Wee One's bells
on her last piece of Flanders leather. When she heard
her father's step, she abandoned the effort. 'Did you
send him away?'

He looked at her, something like a smile tugging at
the wrinkled corners of his mouth. 'No.'

'Why not?' She fought her feeling of relief.

'I don't have to explain my decisions to you, me girl.' He shook his head when the gamblers waved him over. 'Pour me another brogat and come upstairs. There are things I need to tell you.'

He said it in his most stubborn tone, so she did as he said, and followed him to the next floor.

In his chamber, she perched on the small stool, leaving the chair for her father. He settled in with a comfortable sigh.

'What did you want to talk about, Da?' she asked the question, even though she knew what he would say.

'How old are you, daughter?'

'Can't you even remember that about me?'

'Are you tryin' to avoid the question?'

'You know I'm eighteen.' Seven more years and she would have lived longer than her mother.

'Your mother was sixteen when I married her. It's time you married, daughter.'

'I know, Da.' Did he think she did not? She longed for Alain, children and their home in France a dozen times a day.

'Without your mother…' He sighed and took a sip. 'I'm no good with these things. After you came back, I was content just to have you home.' He put his gnarled hand on hers.

She did not return his squeeze. When her mother had died, he had sent her away to be fostered in France with a family of Lord Douglas's choosing. While she was gone, he had taken Murine to his bed and Euphemia to his knee. After, it seemed, he had taken no more interest in her until she had been trained to run his house and bear his grandchildren. By then, both he and Scotland were strangers to her and Alain's family closer to her than her own.

Now, she searched the cold, barren room in vain for any sign that her mother had ever slept within these walls.

'Alain is back now,' she said. 'We'll be able to resolve our future.'

Only the war had kept him from asking for her. She was certain.

Her father tossed back the rest of his drink. 'Well, if it's the lily-livered Frenchman you want, I won't stop you.'

'Alain was the one who wanted to fight the English honourably, by the rules of chivalry, as war should be fought.'

'Daughter, we've chased Edward back over the Border, whether Alain likes the way we did it or not. The enemy is out of the country. But you need t'know something. I made an agreement with Lord Douglas.'

The set of his chin made her uneasy. 'What kind of agreement?'

'Something that will secure Carr's Tower for my grandchildren.'

'What's that?' She cared nothing for the tower and the lands. While as the only child, she might hold them after her father's death, she had assumed that once she left for France, Lord Douglas would award them to some distant cousin of the clan.

'Well, it began the night we almost captured Edward near Melrose.' He sat forwards, launching into a tale. 'We had the trap all set. We would have caught him, too, if William Douglas had listened to me. I told him not to wait for better weather, but he was listening to no man and—'

'Da! What have you done?'

'Well, we broke into the ale and I got William good and bungfued and reminded him of the promise he made to your mother as she lay dying on her bed.'

'What promise?' Her father was well on his way to being bungfued himself. 'You've never said a word of this before.'

'He promised that her wee daughter, only child of my poor darlin' wife, could keep Carr's Tower when she married and that I could choose the man.' He leaned back, a satisfied smile on his face. 'I've got William's word, and witnesses.'

She blinked, searching for her tongue. Difficult to imagine her French-born mother forcing such a promise. 'I'm sure Alain will be glad of that.' He would appreciate the income, at least, meagre as it might be. A steward could see to things. 'We'll certainly visit every few years.'

'No! Ye canna protect the border from France! If it's Alain ye want and who wants ye, you'll have to stay here, or I'll not approve the match.'

'But he has his own lands, his own responsibilities.'

'So do you. Your husband must be here to hold it. Himself.'

She closed her eyes in dread. Surely her mother, no lover of Scotland, had not foreseen this. 'I'm sure Mother never meant to tie me here.'

'Ye don't know everything, daughter. She trusted me to do what was best for you *and* for Carr's Tower.'

Clare bit back further protest. If Lord Douglas had made a promise to her mother and her stubborn father had his way, her wishes would have little sway. She must think of one thing at a time. First, Alain must speak for her. Then, she would raise the conditions with him, and find a solution.

But now, the one thing she craved from this marriage appeared to be the one thing she could not have. Instead of leaving this place behind, she'd be trapped here for ever. She tried to picture sitting with Alain in front of the tower's hearth instead of in the chateau's hall. Suddenly, her life with him looked strangely different.

And not nearly so appealing.

As word of his identity emerged, Gavin's easy camaraderie with his fellows evaporated.

Men who had shared a trencher with him only a day before shunned him. He sat alone at meals. Spent his days in silence.

A few nights later, Gavin approached two of them after dinner in the hall and held out his dice. 'A wager?'

Dark eyes, sullen, met his. *Inglis. Fire-raiser.* The man did not have to speak it. 'You've nothing I want to win.'

'If I lose, I'll take your duty while you take your ease.'

'And if you win?'

'You'll come with me on a trip across the top. There are cattle that need help to find their way home.'

The suspicion on their faces melted just enough for him to sit down and trace a circle for the dice.

He did not intend to lose.

Several nights later, Clare lay restless and warm in her bed. Alain had not yet spoken of their future. She tried to imagine it, what he might say. How he might ask.

How a lady might raise the question if he didn't.

Instead, Fitzjohn crowded her thoughts. The twist of his smile. The darkness behind his eyes. The fire he had raised in her body.

Would you like to be burning in your bed?

She flopped from one side to the other. It should be Alain that filled her dreams.

She threw back the covers and went to the narrow opening in the tower wall, letting the damp breeze cool her face. Drizzly darkness hid the moon. The hills, one softly nestled against the next, offered only shades of black, this one tinged with green, that with blue, the next shading to grey.

A sound, subtle as the shadings of black on the hills. Muffled.

A man on a horse.

Fear stopping her breath, she stared into the darkness. It was late in the season for a raid, but the Robsons never cared much for the calendar.

No. Not horses coming. Someone *leaving*.

She strained her eyes and saw the dark outline of a man, cloaked. He rode a small, black horse with blanketed feet, stepping as quietly as if the mount could see the loose stones and avoid them.

She recognised the man. His height, his shape, the way he sat.

Fitzjohn.

He had sworn on his knight's honour not to harm them, yet he crept away in darkness. To rendezvous with the Inglis? She turned away from the window. She must tell her father, raise the men, stop him.

The tread of a second horse drew her back. Another man.

Finally, a third.

Silent, she watched the darkness swallow them as they rode towards the hills. A smile tickled her lips.

Perhaps Fitzjohn was a Scottis man after all.

The baron flopped over in bed, snoring like the devil.

Murine sat up. 'Wake up, ye piece of horseflesh. I hear something.'

He snorted. Murine sighed. He could be a lout, but she loved him, for all the good it would ever do her.

She shook him. 'Ralph! Wake up and listen.'

He snorted awake then, and closed his mouth to let his ears work.

'It's a horse.' She didn't wait for him, but left her bed and went to the window of her small cottage. 'No. Three of them. Someone is leaving.'

He didn't bother to get up. 'Come back to bed, Murine. It's the boy.'

She turned. 'The boy? Fitzjohn? How can ye be sure?'

He turned on his side and patted the mattress for her to come back. 'Because I sent him. Thought he would take the bait. Three horses, ye say?' He nodded, smiling. 'He's done well already.'

She put her hands on her hips, bigger now than those years ago, when he had first taken her to his bed. 'Ye're a thieving rascal. Did ye send him after the Robson's cattle?'

He grinned, eyes still closed. 'Well, if I did, I wouldn't tell ye, would I? Now come back to this bed and keep me warm, woman.'

She laughed. And did.

Over the next week, Clare's father smiled like a man with a secret.

She refused to ask where Fitzjohn and the others had gone, for fear it would sound as though she cared. Alain commented they were well rid of the man, but her father said nothing.

Proof he knew more than he said.

Well, better, she thought, not to be distracted by Fitzjohn when Alain should be first in her thoughts. They needed time together, she thought, time alone. Perhaps hawking.

'Splendid!' he said, when she suggested it. 'You can fly my merlin.'

'I would rather take Wee One,' she said.

'Why do you persist in hunting with that bird?' he asked. 'She has even scratched you.'

She hid her hand in her skirt.

Alain, already on his way to the mews, did not wait for her answer.

She sighed and followed.

Conferring with the falconer, Alain selected birds

for the rest of his party. Neil, pleased to be restored to his rightful place, rode with them. The cadger carried the hooded birds, bouncing on the wooden frame hung from his shoulders. Two dogs and three of the *comte*'s knights joined them.

With a silent apology to Wee One, she held her tongue and mounted to ride. She and Alain had rarely been hawking together. She had forgotten that an outing with him shared little with her wild escapes.

This hunt seemed to be as much about the conversation as the chase. Alain and his men discussed the history of each bird with the falconer, then debated which should fly first, second and last. Alain's bird looked large enough to bring down a heron, yet he never attempted it. For all the discussion, his birds seemed to be ornaments, chosen for looks instead of for heart.

The sun climbed higher. The sacks remained empty.

Finally, one of the hawks ran a rabbit to ground. Alain's falcon gave good chase, but failed to catch a pigeon. The merlin, smaller even than Wee One, tail-chased two larks without success before snapping up a large insect.

'I don't know why she's so sluggish today,' Alain said. 'Perhaps she is not accustomed to you.'

Clare held her tongue. Any serious falconer knew that a merlin was only good for one season. Keeping the bird over the winter was a waste of food. But she did not want to criticise Alain in front of the others, and there was no way to exchange a word without being overheard. The two of them had no more time alone than if they were riding in a royal procession.

She finally blurted out a question as he helped her dismount at the end of the day. 'When do you return to France?'

She wanted to say 'when do *we* return?', but that seemed presumptuous.

'Lord Douglas plans a pilgrimage in grateful thanks for his victory. I shall travel with him.'

'To the Holy Land?' Her hands grew cold. He had mentioned nothing of this before. Such a trip would take at least a year.

'Not so far. Amiens.'

The French cathedral housed the head of St John the Baptist. It would be natural for Alain to travel with the group back to France. 'When?'

He shrugged. 'Arrangements must be made. By summer. Sooner, I pray. I can't wait to leave this cold, damp place.'

Arrangements must be made. Of course. He had sent messages home, she knew. He must be waiting for his parents' formal consent before he spoke for her.

They would give it, she was certain. Alain's mother had fostered her as a child and taught her all she needed to know to run their household. Douglas would approve, since he knew the family well.

That left only her father and Alain to persuade. The one to give his blessing, the other to make his home in Scotland.

She was not sure which would be the harder.

A few days later, when Clare heard the soft moo of cattle, she didn't look up from chopping radishes.

But as the noise became louder and more insistent,

she went to the window. And there, riding into the yard, was Fitzjohn, warm with the sweat of hard work in early spring.

Behind him, flanked by two of her father's men, plodded seven fine, red, long-haired cattle.

Something that felt like happiness erupted into a chuckle.

'Glad to see him, daughter?'

She swallowed the laugh. 'Of course not. But *you* must be. You sent him after those cattle, didn't you?'

He shrugged, but his smile showed. 'If a Scot wants to steal cattle, he needs no one's permission.'

She looked back at Fitzjohn. He had dismounted, and Angus ran up to grab the horse's reins. Some of the men hung back, still suspicious, but more clasped his hands or gave him a hearty swat on the back.

Well deserved. He had crossed mountains still covered with snow, ridden into the Inglis homestead, liberated half a herd of cattle, and returned unharmed.

Perhaps his Scots blood ran strong after all.

Gavin herded the cattle into the pen, ignoring the old man as he strolled over to watch. The task had been near impossible, and the thieving rascal knew it. Still, bone tired as he was, Gavin felt a heady sense of triumph no battlefield victory had ever given him.

And he hadn't had to kill anyone.

He spoke to the baron without preamble. 'Here's the six you wanted and an extra for good measure, though I'm beginning to think you snatched them from the Robsons first.'

The baron lifted his eyebrows and tried to look

shocked. 'Well, you may turn out to be a Scottis man yet, laddie.'

He laughed. He might have proven himself a passable cattle thief, but Clare's father, no doubt, was a master.

Gavin held out his hand. 'What's my reward?' In battle, a captured knight meant a substantial ransom. Cattle should be worth at least a Scottish shilling.

'Oh, I've something in mind.'

His hand, still empty. 'Promises?'

He had abandoned two kings for this, taking no more than what he carried on his back. Had he known what would face him, would he do it again?

Yes.

'Sit at the high table tonight. Share a trencher with my daughter. We'll talk later.'

He shook his head as the man walked away. No doubt he would get frostbite dipping his bread in a trencher shared with Mistress Clare.

But as he started for the stable, he saw her face at the kitchen's window, touched with a smile.

The Frenchman, striding out of the stable, glared in Gavin's direction, eyes narrowed in disdain, and walked deliberately wide of him.

'Have you no courteous greeting for a fellow knight?'

His question forced the *comte* to pause, but he pursed his lips as if holding back words.

Gavin held on to a slow smile. 'You're working very hard not to say anything.'

'To speak to you soils my tongue.'

'Oh? Why is that?'

'Lichieres pautonnier.' The insult was a slap in

the face. 'You are a disgrace to the knighthood you profess.'

'The baron doesn't agree with you. He's asked me to sit at the high table tonight.'

'He's as bad as you are.' Behind him, a cow bellowed. The *comte*'s glance, disgusted, took in the animal, the tower, the hills and both sides of the border. 'Inglis, Scots, you are all barbarians.'

He'd been called worse. 'France is not the sole keeper of the code of chivalry.'

'I cannot wait to be rid of this island,' he muttered, as if to himself and not Gavin. 'Nothing worthy dwells here.'

'Nothing?' Over the man's shoulder, he saw Clare come out of the tower, the trace of a smile clinging to her lips. 'I thought you found Mistress Clare more than worthy.'

She paused, looking at them both, and he watched the sun turn her hair to liquid light.

Alain's gaze followed Gavin's. Her smile broadened to touch them both before she turned away towards the garden. 'My mother trained her well.' He sighed. 'She deserves better than this.'

Yet in the man's eyes, Gavin saw neither desire nor commitment, but only a touch of regret. 'Well, maybe I'll give it to her.'

'You?' The question was like a call to combat. '*Licheor plain d'anvie*. Do not dare defile her.' The man spat in the dirt at his feet.

'Then she's to be yours?'

He tried not to think about how much the man's answer meant to him.

'*La mienne?*' Alain's eyebrows lifted in surprise.

'*Non?*' This time, it was easy to smile, for Alain was a man who intended no claim on Clare, much as she believed otherwise.

'I meant only that she deserves better than a man so debased he is hunted even by the *Anglais*.' He turned his back and moved towards the tower.

Hunted by the English? His moment of triumph soured.

Edward must have named him a traitor. He should have expected no less. If a man could kill his brother, he would not hesitate to condemn a nephew.

But a faint wish lingered that, hunted though he was, he might be the kind of man worthy enough to deserve Clare.

Chapter Five

Gavin joined the family table that evening, moving up from the end where the men-at-arms gathered. He sat on one side of the baron, while, from the other, the Frenchman glared in his direction, eyes brimming with disdain, doing everything he could to avoid speaking to him directly.

He'd met the man's kind before. One of those who cared more for appearance than truth. Yet Mistress Clare's gaze rested on him, wide-eyed, as if appearance were all.

The moo of the cattle penetrated the walls. 'Glad to be back home,' the baron said, smiling.

'Until your *maudit* neighbours steal them again,' the *comte* said.

The old man turned on him. 'You don't like us much, do you?' A smile twitched on the old man's lips. Gavin didn't think the baron liked the Frenchman much, either.

'Da, please. Alain is a guest in our house.'

Gavin could hold his tongue no longer. 'Guest? That's not what I call someone who comes to make war on another country.'

Forced to acknowledge him, the *comte* stared with loathing. 'France came to Scotland's defence. It was you who invaded Scotland and burned her sacred churches. Everyone, they know who you are and what you did.'

The baron and Clare turned to watch him, waiting for his denial. He made none. Let the man think what he liked. Nothing Gavin said would change his mind. 'What everyone knows isn't always the truth.'

'That's not what I'd call an answer.' The baron looked as if he might reconsider his generosity.

'He didn't ask a question. He made an accusation.'

'You see?' the Frenchman said. 'He does not even bother to deny it. But the Scots are no more civilised. They torched homes and fields just to deny them to the Inglis.'

The baron's smile turned to a growl. 'You may not like the way a Scot wages war, but we've kept the Inglis at bay.'

'What you wage is not war. You either commit brutal destruction or you run like one with a tail. I came to fight in proper combat, not to skulk in the woods.'

This, then, was why Clare thought war was a pretty pageant, a tournament writ large instead of a life-and-death struggle. Strange. Her father knew better.

The baron chuckled. 'The Frenchman here's been spoiling for a big battle for months. Seems as if that's the only kind he's willing to fight. But the Bruce advised us to take away anything that might comfort the enemy, and we've found that a better tactic than standing in a line waiting for Inglis arrows to fall on us.'

'Da! Alain is a valiant and brave warrior!'

'He doesn't need you to defend his honour,' her father said.

Gavin bit back a smile and took a bite of his oatcake. He liked to see Mistress Clare with a flash in her eyes and a flush on her cheek.

'Monsieur le Fitzjohn is the one without honour,' the *comte* continued. 'He only attacks helpless people in the dark.'

'And I've seen enough of how Frenchmen fight,' he said, keeping a grip on his tongue and his temper, 'You offer to make an appointment, then can never agree on the date.'

De Garencieres's cheeks turned dark red and he exploded into French insults.

Clare put a hand on his arm in a vain attempt to soothe him, shooting an angry glance at Gavin.

The baron rose and pulled his knife. 'A Scot is worth two Frenchmen!'

The *comte* stood to meet him, brandishing his own weapon. 'One Frenchman is better than five Englishmen!'

Clare looked at Gavin, pleading for help. 'Fitzjohn?'

All eyes swung to him. Half-Scots. Half-English.

He kept his eyes steady. In Scotland, his father's name had been despised. At the English court, they called him savage. Which side was stronger? His mother's or his father's? Most days, he hated both. What would it be like, he thought, looking at them, to know so clearly who you were?

'Well,' he said, slowly, deliberately pasting the smile back on his lips, 'it appears that would make me worth at least three Frenchmen.'

The *comte* did not return his smile. 'You are no man at all. You are a beast who held the torch to burn the very—'

'No.' He rose then, and let his hand rest on his dagger. Think what you like, he had always said, for his father's acts clung to him, no matter what he did. But he would not have Clare believe he'd lied. 'I did not.'

The *comte* raised his brows in surprise. 'That is not as I was told.'

'You cannot believe everything you hear.' All the years, all the insults from both sides of the border. He wanted to be quit of them. But even here, they followed. 'Scottis. English. French. A man is what he proves himself to be.'

In the awkward silence that followed, Clare touched each man on the shoulder, gently forcing them to sheath their weapons and sit.

The baron smiled. 'You've proven to be at home in the hills, Fitzjohn. Let's see what else you can do. Take on the arms room. Repair the damage we did in the fighting.'

'Da! You know nothing about this man.'

'Neither did you when you brought him in. Now each of you claims to know a great deal about him.' He looked at Gavin. 'Why don't we let him show us who he is?'

He felt a moment's peace. Refuge, even for a while, was everything. He nodded. 'Thank you.'

Carr rose. 'Well, I think this calls for breaking out the brogat.'

The *comte,* scowling, held his silence as Clare filled their cups.

Gavin took a sip and let the drink's honey flavour soothe his throat. Mistress Clare's brew was both smooth and dangerous.

The baron lifted his cup. 'Here's at least one thing about Scotland even the Frenchman likes, eh?'

'I like several things about Scotland,' he said, his eyes lingering on Clare.

Gavin's fingers tightened on his cup. He took another sip. The woman was nothing to him. Nor could she be.

He pulled his gaze away. What was it about Clare that called to him? Strong, yes, but, like her bird, alert, expecting danger any minute. Her strength was a shield. He wondered what it hid.

She acted as if she'd never been tempted, let alone succumbed.

He'd like to see it happen.

He'd like to help.

The vision filled him. Clare. Naked. Tight braid undone. Hair tumbling across her shoulders. Eyes soft, lips yielding with want.

He downed the rest of his drink. If she knew what he was thinking, it would confirm every laidly thing she believed of him.

And she'd be right.

Chapter Six

Pouring another round, Clare felt pinned between Fitzjohn's gaze and Alain's. Her father delighted in pitting the two men against each other, even favouring the bastard over the *comte*.

Euphemia came up from the kitchen floor below to help clear. As she went to the end of the table, one of the men swatted her behind, hooting his appreciation.

Clare frowned. 'They should not treat her thus.' Her own cruel treatment of the girl pricked her conscience. 'You must stop them, Da.'

'Can't stop a young man from looking. I was young once. Patted your mither just the same way.'

She frowned. Her mother had been gracious, cultured. She would never have allowed such treatment. 'Mother wasn't even here. She was in France.'

'So was I. Went to make sure the King signed the treaty with us.' He grinned at the shock on her face. 'Didn't know that, did you, daughter?'

Alain was wearing his pained smile again. She nearly moaned.

Fitzjohn, curse him, shared a look with her father. 'Is that how you won her?'

She jumped in before her father could disgrace them further. 'Of course not. My mother would never have responded to something so vulgar. He is teasing.' She prayed that was true.

'That's all you know, lass.' Her father laughed. 'Your mother came out to play under the moon once or twice.'

She gripped the jug until her knuckles whitened. Clare's image of her mother was a child's picture of perfection. Was that memory or imagination?

Her father's easy smile raised doubts. She could easily imagine *him*—standing outside the castle, hooting and hollering.

Yet if her mother had been the kind of woman who would respond to such lewdness, what did that say about Clare?

She'd had those visions and tried to hide them. From Alain. From herself. Thoughts of a man looking, touching, kissing, more…

No. Her mother had not been that kind of woman. And neither was she. Alain would never marry a woman like that.

'Would you like someone to howl at you under the moon, Clare?' Fitzjohn's smile said he had read her doubts and wanted to encourage them.

'Demoiselle Clare is much too fine for that,' Alain said.

'Are you suggesting my wife wasn't?'

She put a hand on Alain's shoulder before he drew his blade again. 'We need no more fights tonight.' She cleared her throat, wanting to scream at all of them to stop speaking of her mother so. 'I think that Alain's experience is that no true lady, including my mother, would respond to such a display.'

Gavin's smile refused to budge. 'Is that what you meant, Alain?' As if he enjoyed seeing them devour each other with words.

Her father elbowed Fitzjohn with glee. 'Listen, lass. Your mother and I enjoyed our marriage bed. Where do you think you came from? A hen's nest?'

Alain's face had turned to stone. From the other side of the hall, a whistle greeted Euphemia again.

Anger rose in her throat. 'Stop it!' Clare slammed the jug down on the table. 'Stop it, both of you!' Brawls. Bawdy insults. When would she be free of this dreadful place? 'No wonder Alain thinks we are savages.'

The men at the end of the table turned from teasing Euphemia to stare.

Horrified at her own outburst, she ran from the Hall and down the stairs, nearly tripping on her skirt.

Outside, she gulped in the night air and shivered. The whistles and hoots subsided, or were muffled by the tower wall. Alain's footsteps, slower, echoed on the stairs and came up behind her.

Ashamed, she looked at the ground, blinking tears away. 'I don't know why Da doesn't stop them. He thinks it's funny, which just eggs them on.'

'But that girl, she is not of your family. She is nothing to do with you.'

'Thank you,' she said, relieved he believed so. But

while they shared no blood, Euphemia was the daughter of her father's mistress. Through him, they had a bond, one Clare did her best to ignore.

Ready to face him, she turned. 'Sometimes my father, well, I wonder…' How could she have been born of that man?

His eyes were gentle. Concerned. Polite. 'You're nothing like him.'

I'm glad was her first thought. Then guilt pricked her. He was her father. She could not deny him. 'He hasn't had the life you have. Things are different here.'

'But you're not a woman who could be howled at and dragged into the bushes.'

'Does that mean I'll never be kissed?' The question slipped out and she averted her eyes, mortified that she had asked it. But tonight, she wanted to be kissed. Hard.

'Mais non.' He touched her chin and turned her head towards his.

Now. Now, though she'd been too forward, he would finally speak. Finally take her in his arms.

His hand cupped her cheek and she leaned towards him, close enough that her breasts brushed his chest.

His hand dropped to his side. 'Everything will happen in the right time, *chérie*. Now come in out of the cold.'

She bit the inside of her cheek to stop the tears. He must not see her cry. 'You go. I'll be in shortly.'

When will the time be right, Alain?

No lady would say such words. She scolded herself with a silent recitation from *Miroir des preudes femmes*. Alain's mother had insisted she learn it by heart. A virtuous woman must wait until her lord speaks first. She must strive to perfect humility. She must never quarrel. She must never be angry.

These lessons would protect her virtue and her reputation. They would keep her safe.

They would keep her from losing anyone ever again.

She crossed the courtyard towards the darkened mews, wishing she could afford to keep lights burning there as she knew the kings did. Yet she paused, fingers on the door.

It was too late to visit. She would only disturb the sleeping birds.

'You've been left alone early. Where's the Frenchman?'

Her heart skipped at Fitzjohn's voice.

A soft glow spilled from behind the shutters of the servants' quarters at the top of the tower, throwing a faint light on his face.

'Alain went in.' He need not have asked. They must have passed on the stairs. She started back to the tower. 'I was just going to bed.'

He fell into step beside her, clucking his disapproval. 'And by yourself.'

'I don't like what you're suggesting.'

'That a woman might want to spend her nights with her man? That's no insult.'

'In your mouth, it sounds that way.' Yet he seemed to know she had waited for a kiss that never came. 'I am a woman of virtue.' So she prayed, hating Fitzjohn for making her feel as though she were something different.

'I'm not sure you've had enough experience to know what kind of woman you are, Mistress Clare. I'd be happy to help you find out.'

'I would rather be dead.' She regretted the words as soon as she spoke. A folly to speak lightly of death. Both of them had seen too much of it.

There was a long silence before he answered, 'Well, you're very much alive tonight and you could live any one of a number of ways if you choose.'

'You offend me.'

'Is it offensive to know what I think and say it?'

'It is offensive to imply that I would be so reckless as to listen to your lewd suggestions.'

There was that smile again. The one that said *I know what you refuse to admit.* 'And you're never reckless.'

'I cannot afford to be reckless. Not with my birds, my brew, or my reputation.'

He flinched and she realised she had returned his insult. He could be careless with his reputation, for he had none to lose.

'You ought to try it sometime. Try mounting that big horse of yours and ride across the hills, so fast the wind snatches the breath out of your chest.' He moved closer, snatching away her breath as she stood. 'And when you can breathe again, howl at the moon.'

How did he know she had ridden just that way? How could he sense that she craved…something? Something that would put everything she wanted at risk?

She struggled to speak through a ragged breath. 'Why would I do such a thing? It would only frighten the horse, panic the bird and curdle the brew.'

'Then try more quiet pleasures.' He grabbed her hand,

his palm warm and tempting on hers, then he bent close, whispering in her ear, 'Let's go search for a needle in the tall grass.'

He was so close she was afraid he could hear her heart whisper *do it, just to see how it feels.*

She pulled back and crossed her arms over her chest. 'You mistake me for Euphemia. That is not in my nature.' But she was afraid, now, that she lied.

'How do you know unless you try?'

'I know myself.' Or she knew who she must be. 'And I know men like you. You may fool my father, Fitzjohn, but you don't fool me.'

'I don't fool your father a bit. I think he knows exactly what I am.'

'You and he are two of a kind. Rude rascals, both of you.'

'Unlike your French friend?'

She stiffened. It was true. Alain did not belong here. Well, neither did she. 'I won't allow you to disparage him, too.'

'I didn't. I said he was nothing like me. Besides, a knight can defend his own honour.'

'But he's not here to defend himself.' She lifted her chin. 'Or me.'

'There's nothing to defend. For either of you. I respect you. I even respect him. He's got wonderful manners and can make pretty speeches that King Jean le Bon would applaud. I might even envy that chateau that's been in his family for five generations.' His tone was teasing, as if manners, honour and family were trifles. 'But if you are saving yourself for him, you'll be waiting a long, long time.'

The accusation jolted her. Did he know something she'd only feared?

No. No. He would ask for her. He must. 'You've no right to speak so. Our future is between Alain and me.'

Gavin took her arm and swung her towards his chest. 'If it had been me, I wouldn't have left 'til dawn.'

The coarse words grabbed her more tightly than his hand. 'If it had been you, you would have spent a long, cold night alone.

He lowered his head, lips too close. 'Would I?'

Just an inch more and she would have the kiss she had wanted. Rich, hard and deep.

Everything stopped. Breath. Heart. Thoughts.

His lips, firm and warm, met hers.

A rush of feeling, strong as the wind, scooped her away from earth.

Struggling to cling to the ground, she braced against the onslaught, telling herself she fought against him.

She did not.

She fought against herself.

Arms, legs, lips—she stiffened them all, fearing that if she didn't, all the lust locked inside would roar forth and she would be exposed as no better than the lowest limmer he'd ever bedded.

A rough laugh broke the spell and they stepped apart.

Arms around each other, her father and Murine teased each other as they came out of the tower. Clare tried to hide in the shadows, but they didn't look around as they walked to Murine's cottage.

Again tonight her father would sleep in her bed instead of his own.

'Yes,' Clare said, drawing a shaky breath. 'You will sleep alone. And so will I.'

'Don't wait too long.' He, too, was struggling to breathe and his smile had disappeared. 'Life is short.'

She knew that better than most. Had her mother ever howled at the moon or ridden faster than a falcon before she died? Was there a side of her mother that a child could not understand?

That only a husband could know?

'Yes. Too short to waste an evening with you. Goodnight.'

His smile returned, quickly as if a gust of wind had blown the darkness away. 'Don't be afraid of your dreams, Mistress Clare.'

She ran into the tower, gripped by a desire to live. To ride, wild and dangerous in the dark. To fly like the falcons.

To lie with a man.

No recollected lessons could crush those urges, urges that had stayed safely dormant until now.

Too late to discover that Fitzjohn's irreverent views could taint her, as they had Angus and Euphemia. Yet tonight, she felt as if she had been hoarding her life like a squirrel who refused to eat an acorn all summer because he feared that winter would come.

What happened when the squirrels died before winter? All those lost acorns they had buried just rotted in the ground.

A man's booted step gained on her as she climbed the twisting stairs. She turned, wanting, fearing, to see Fitzjohn again.

Instead, her father climbed behind her.

'I thought you'd gone to the cottage,' she said.

'Needed to talk with me girl. Was that Fitzjohn with you?'

He would notice, of course. 'We simply said good-night.'

'Where's the Frenchman?'

She glanced up towards the family floor, where Alain had a room. 'Getting a good night's sleep, I presume.'

'Alone?'

Of course, she thought at first. Then had to speak the truth. 'I'm sure I wouldn't know.'

'Well why not, girl? Has he had you yet?'

'Da!'

'No, of course not. I should have known. Well, I let you two alone long enough. The time has come. The man must speak, one way or another.'

Her hand touching the stone wall for balance, she looked behind her as she mounted the winding stairs, afraid her father would stumble. 'Is that the only thing you can think of to talk to me about?'

She lowered her voice as they climbed past the dark-ened kitchen and on to the next floor, where the men-at-arms lay sleeping in the Hall. 'Do you never want to know anything about me, what I want, who I am? I'm quite a good falconer. Even Neil says so. You drink my brew and sleep under blankets I've woven and never ask a question about how all this came to be. Did you treat my mother the same way?'

His face sagged, sorrowful, as they reached the third level and she regretted her angry tongue.

'I'm not here to talk about her,' he said, stepping

on to the floor. 'I'm here to talk about you. And my grandchildren.'

She looked at the door to the *comte*'s chamber, thankful to hear a snore. 'That's all we ever talk about.'

'And that's all I *will* talk about until you do something about it!' He braced himself against the stone wall as if the climb, or the anger, had tired him.

'Are you all right, Da? Here, lean on me.'

He pulled away when she reached for his arm. 'Just tired,' he snapped. They had reached the door to his room and he stood straight again, but he let her lead him to his chair. 'Some day, I won't be here, you know.'

He said it, she knew, to raise her guilt, yet he played to her worst fear. 'That can't be. You're too stubborn.' He had fought in wars all her life, yet like a child, she had thought that since God had taken her mother, He would not leave her fatherless, too.

'I want to see you married, both you girls, before I depart this life. Now Euphemia, she'll marry the first man who asks her and ride off to who knows where and have a gaggle of children and grow fat.'

Clare frowned. 'I do not care what Euphemia does and I don't know why you do either.'

She knew his teasing smile and his cantankerous temper, but this expression was new. Sombre.

'Ah, daughter. Some day you'll learn to forgive yourself as well as others.'

Startled, she studied his face. Did he know, then, all the blame she had heaped on his head for her lonely years? For Murine?

Did he know how she scolded herself for every misstep on the path Alain's mother had taught her? For tonight, most of all?

Her expression must have been answer enough. His face softened. 'I want to see you settled. You and the lands you'll carry.'

'I know you do, Da.'

'You may know it, but you've done nothing about it! I'll speak to the man if I must.'

'No!' She flinched, thinking of the embarrassment. 'He will speak in his own time.'

'That time must be soon. You've until summer, girl, to get that Frenchman to commit to you and to Scotland. I need an heir and without a son, if I don't populate the premises soon, the Inglis will sweep it back. Douglas won't see that happen and neither will I, do you hear? Dead or alive, this land will belong to men with my blood in their veins!'

He paused, out of breath. This campaign, she realised, had been difficult.

'I understand, Da,' she said softly, knowing her heart had not yet accepted all that he meant.

'By Beltane. It will be decided. One way or the other.'

'Alain will speak soon. I'm sure of it.'

Yet she was sure of nothing. Even if Alain did speak, he would never commit to a life on the Scottish border. And neither would she.

Murine appeared at the door, soundless, as if knowing the conversation was over. Clare rose and passed her, without speaking, as the woman helped the baron towards his bed.

She chided herself as the door closed behind her.

Of course it was time she married, but it must be done properly, not with her father's blunt tongue.

Yet the time for patient waiting was over. Beltane Eve and summer's beginning was only weeks away.

Perhaps she could put Fitzjohn's rude intentions to good purpose. Alain had no more love for the man than she did. Perhaps a little rivalry would persuade the *comte* to declare himself.

But she must carry out her plan with care. Stirring Fitzjohn's interest could be dangerous. To herself above all.

Chapter Seven

The next morning, Fitzjohn watched, astonished and wary, as Mistress Clare approached him in the Hall with a sway in her step and a smile on her lips.

A forced smile, but a smile, none the less.

'Good morrow, Fitzjohn,' she said.

'Mistress Clare.'

Silent, she nodded, the smile firmly fixed, looking, to his eyes, nothing like the self-controlled, sharp-tongued woman he'd come to know. He'd spent a sleepless night reliving the kiss. She was a woman of passion, that was clear, but it was passion denied, and he'd concluded that the Tweed would be frozen mid-summer before she would ever speak a friendly word to him again.

'What is it you need from me?' he asked, finally. Nothing else would have brought her to him. More was the pity.

'Need? Oh, nothing.' She looked down at her shoes, then gazed up at him with a flutter of her lashes. 'Are you well?'

'Well?' He recognised the seductive glance. He'd seen Euphemia use it, but on her, it came naturally as her breath. Clare looked as if she had practised without yet attaining perfection.

Then he saw her furtive glance over to the hearth where the Frenchman stood and recognised unwelcome disappointment. 'He's not watching, mistress. If you want to raise his interest, it will take more than a sideways glance at me.'

Her soft, welcoming expression disappeared. 'What do you mean, I'm not...?'

Her protest trailed off as she realised she had turned her head to see whether Alain was watching.

'If you want to make him jealous, you'll need to give him something to be jealous about.'

In fact, based on what he had seen of the man, jealousy would only raise his interest in besting his rival, not in Clare herself. Still, her plan would give him an excuse to linger in her company.

She stepped out of reach, though her scent, like sweet white flowers and tart red berries, still enveloped him. 'You are imagining that.' But her eyes no longer met his.

'No. I'm not.' Though he wished he were. 'I'd be glad to help you, Mistress Clare.' He moved closer and looked over her shoulder. 'Your Frenchman is watching now. I haven't touched you, but I can.' He put his hand on her waist, feeling that dark recklessness rise in him. 'I think we have his attention now.'

'Stop,' she said, but her breath was short.

Yet when he touched her back to guide her out of the *comte*'s sight, she came with him. He led her up the winding stairs to the watch tower, above and out of sight of the sentries.

Outside, he breathed in the cool air, full of the smell of fertile earth and new grass, waiting to be born. Through the narrow openings in the turret wall, the hills spread out before him like his own private country.

He looked back at Clare, but she neither saw him, nor the hills. Instead, she looked over her shoulder and down the empty stairs.

He touched her cheek, wanting her gaze again. 'Do you think he'll come?' His voice, harsher than he intended, as if he were the jealous one.

'Yes. It is his chivalric duty to protect me.'

Anger came first, then fear for her if she thought the rest of the world would follow her pretty rules.

'Well, yes, he may, but if you expect every man to do the same, you'll be eaten alive, Mistress Clare. This world belongs to warriors and they don't care who they hurt as long as they get their way. That's the only lesson that matters on these Borders.'

He had her eyes, then. And they flashed like green fire. 'That's why I want to leave. These hills are full of men who've never had a scruple they couldn't squash. And you're like all the rest. Or worse.'

'That's a harsh statement, *demoiselle*.' Yet, he feared, true.

She blinked to hear the French he'd spoken at court. He smiled, knowing his accent could match Alain's.

'Perhaps,' she said, finally, 'but if you weren't, you would defend yourself with the truth.'

The truth. He had seen too many battles fought

between men clinging to mutually exclusive truth. He was no longer sure what the word meant.

He brushed his lips with a smile again. 'Well, if I were to sort out the false from the true for you, it would take hours.' Blood fired, he leaned closer, so close that if she parted her lips, she would feel his words on her tongue. 'And there are much better ways to spend time alone with a beautiful lady.'

She swayed towards him. Just a little closer and he would kiss her again. They could start where they ended last night, but this time, she would truly surrender.

Her lips touched his, feather soft. Something more than lust answered this time. He cradled her gently, breasts warm against him. Soft and slow, he explored her sweet mouth with his tongue, wooing.

He felt her yield.

Then, she pushed him away. 'No!' Both of them staggered at the separation. 'I don't need you. I don't want you.'

He willed his pounding heart to slow. For just a moment, he had glimpsed what it might be like, to share so deeply that he could be fully known.

And be loved anyway.

Difficult for most, impossible for him, particularly with this woman.

'*Pardon, demoiselle.*' His accent mocked her. Or did he mock himself? 'I thought you needed me to make *le comte jaloux.*'

'He is not here. He cannot be jealous of what he can't see.'

The smile returned. '*Au contraire.* What is not seen must be imagined. Many people will describe events in detail that they never witnessed.' He leaned against the hard stone walls, crossing his arms to keep from reaching for her. 'I will say a word, two perhaps, and then it won't matter that he wasn't here to see us. He'll believe whatever I say.'

'You're a cruel man, Fitzjohn.'

'Because I have tried, like the perfect knight, to fulfil a lady's request? How jealous do you want him to be?' He leaned towards her again, unable to keep his distance. 'I can describe your eyes.' He peered at her, as if assessing what to say. 'Green, yes, but with a touch of grey, hard as a stone, unless, of course, they are gazing into mine.'

Her glance clashed with his. 'He has seen my eyes.'

And no doubt her eyes were soft as spring grass when they gazed on the *comte*. 'Your hair, then. I shall speak poetic lines to tell him how it looked, flowing across your shoulders like unbound silk.'

'He will not believe you. My hair is never down.'

'Then I will tell him of your skin.' His voice had deepened as he spoke of all he wanted and could not have. Imaginings unbound by what he could see. He drew her against him again. 'How fair and soft it felt beneath my fingers as I stroked the curve of your breast—'

'You mustn't!' She leaned away, but he did not let her free. 'If you imply that I, that we…'

He heard the *comte*'s steps, angry, mounting the stairs.

She heard them, too. 'Please. Don't.' Eyes wide, locked on his. 'He'll decide I'm not fit to be his wife at all.'

And for just a moment, he was tempted to tell the

Frenchman of her eyes and hair and skin and more. A man whose desire was so shallow did not deserve her at all.

'Well, we can't have that, now, can we?'

They were no longer alone. 'Let her go.'

He raised his head, dizzy from looking so deeply into her eyes. 'Ah, Comte de Garencieres. We were just speaking of you.'

Clare stepped out of his reach and into the other man's. Gavin dropped his empty, jealous hands.

'No, we weren't.'

'Oh?' He looked back at her, not caring who was watching. It had not been hard to play the swain when she asked. It had been difficult to stop. 'What were we discussing? Ah, yes. Your eyes.'

The Frenchman stepped in front of her. 'If I did not know already who you were, I would still know you're an ignoble traitor to one side or the other, or perhaps both. The lady doesn't want your company.'

Clare, behind the *comte,* refused to look at Gavin.

'You have his attention now, Mistress Clare,' he said. 'Do with it what you will.'

And he turned away, refusing to look back for fear he'd see the man touching her.

And care.

There had always been women. As he'd grown to manhood in David's court in captivity and then was drawn into King Edward's bright circle, there had always been a woman eager to help him ease his sorrows. He did not know whether his looks or his pedigree or his air of danger drew them and didn't care. He never tried to be anything other than what he was: a landless bastard with bad blood, despite its royal tinge. They expected no more.

But this woman did. Expected it. Wanted it.

Deserved it. Deserved all the things he couldn't offer.

He hardened his heart against her temptation. After disdaining the very sight of him, she was callous enough to tease, to use him to get to a man who was too blind to see what he could have.

Well, if she wanted to make the man jealous, he could oblige her. Perhaps it was time Mistress Clare learned what passion could be. But that, he knew now, would be dangerous, for him as well as for her.

Better he keep his distance.

Alain, Clare discovered, was a man who could be motivated by jealousy.

It was gratifying to find him attentive again. He even acquiesced to her desire to take Wee One for a day's hunt. Neil the falconer grumbled at hawking so late in the season. It was nearly time for the birds to be confined to the mews to shed their feathers in the yearly moult.

Organising a hunt for the entire household was as complex as riding into battle. Each must ride according to stature and status. She paid close attention. One day, she would ride out of the chateau at the head of even grander parties, not sneak out with her own bird like a scullion.

Her father would understand that some day. He must.

As the horses milled around the yard, Fitzjohn pulled

up beside her. 'I see the *comte* enjoys besting a rival. I have not seen you out of his sight for days.'

She was ashamed to admit it. Somehow, it was demeaning to think he was responding not to her, but to Fitzjohn, as if she were no more than a bone that two dogs might growl over.

'Perhaps it is only that you are unfamiliar with the way a proper knight attends his lady.'

He shook his head. 'I am only pleased that I have finally found a way to be of service to you, Mistress Clare.'

A most unladylike laugh escaped her lips. 'You don't even like me.'

A strange mix of pain and laughter crossed his face. 'Oh, Mistress Clare, I like you well enough. I just think you're flying the wrong falcon. You need someone who loves the hunt the way that you do.'

She twisted a strand of hair that had come loose and tried to poke it back in place. 'Ladies can hunt. It's allowed.'

'What if some day Alain decides it's not allowed?'

'He wouldn't do that!'

But he could, her mind whispered back.

Alain called to her then, and she turned the horse away, finally breathing freely once they rode out of the gate. The spring air made her feel like a child again. How could she have forgotten? She had loved these hills, before her mother died, tainting all her childish joys.

The hawks flew first, chasing their prey on the ground. She understood it, but it never really seemed right, seeing the bird fly so close to the earth that her wings nearly brushed the grass. A falcon took her prey in the air, flying so high, sometimes, that she was barely a speck in the blue. So high, that surely God must be within reach.

Alain rode beside her, but her eyes strayed to Fitzjohn. He sat on his horse like a warrior, out of place in such a domestic pursuit as a hawking party. The war he hated so seemed to ride with him, something he could not escape.

The hawk took off after a rabbit and the riders thundered behind. Bored with the ground fliers, she rode over to the cadger and pulled on her glove. 'I'm taking Wee One,' she said, picking up the hooded bird before he could protest. 'I won't be long.'

Wee One ruffled her feathers and settled, as if glad to be back on the fist. Then, Clare kicked the horse towards the hilltop, wind in her ears, nearly laughing with relief when the hunting party dropped out of sight.

Ride across the hills, he had dared her. *So fast the wind snatches the breath out of your chest.*

She left grass and trees behind, riding high enough that snow covered the soft ground beneath the horse's hooves. Reluctantly, she slowed. Bogs and sink holes littered the hills. She mustn't put her mount at risk.

Only when she slowed and the wind's whine dimmed did she hear the hoofbeats.

She looked over her shoulder.

Fitzjohn was gaining on her, his black stallion pounding the turf. He caught up quickly, grabbing her reins as his horse danced alongside hers. 'Are you safe?'

Only then did she realise he thought the horse had

bolted. She ought to let him think so. No lady would have ridden off as she had, wild and alone.

Instead, a smile, born of speed and wind, burst across her face. 'You were the one who told me to ride howling into the mountains.'

And for a moment, alone with him near the top of the hill, wind whipping her hair into her face, she relished his answering smile.

'Well,' he said, finally, 'Robson land is just over that next ridge. Perhaps you ought to stay on this side of the line.'

She sighed. She wanted to keep riding as if she could fly, but that temptation, and his, she must resist.

She summoned a warning into her glance and pulled her horse back a step. 'I would ask the same of you. Alain needs no more excuses for jealousy.'

A rueful edge touched his smile. 'Shall we hunt, then?'

Clare nodded. Wee One, hooded in blissful ignorance, had waited patiently, but the bird was hungry and she ought to return with a catch to justify her absence.

'Then we'd better ride down,' he said. 'The falcon and her prey care nothing for these lines.'

They turned the horses around and rode, side by side, wordless, until they reached brush and grass again. Then, he signalled, silently, that he would look for game to flush into the air for her. Sliding off the horse, who stood as commanded, he crept towards the undergrowth.

She took off Wee One's hood and lifted her glove. Released from blindness, the bird knew what she must do. She flew straight up, the jingle of her bells immediately whipped away by the wind. Then, she circled, a small speck in the sky, waiting in perfect faith that her human partners would provide her prey.

Fitzjohn crept close to the bushes where a grouse rustled. When he clapped, the bird burst from its hiding place, flapping into flight, expecting to be safe as soon as it flew beyond the reach of man.

The bird's wings were louder than the falcon's, but the flight so quick, Clare could barely follow her.

Above, Wee One plummeted from the sky towards her prey.

And missed.

The grouse escaped, flying wildly towards the valley. The falcon followed.

Fitzjohn remounted and Clare gathered her reins, ready to give chase. Then something whisked beside her ear, as if following, too.

It looked like the tercel.

Clare gave the shrieking whistle that always called Wee One home. Futile. Frantic.

The bird had disappeared. Along with the tercel that had been courting her.

'You've a powerful whistle,' Fitzjohn said, 'but she may be too far away to hear.'

She knew as much. And if Wee One caught the grouse and discovered she could feast without a human hand, it would be easy for the male to coax her into abandoning the mews for the wild.

She could hear the falconer clucking his warning. Neil would scold her for losing the bird, but not nearly as sternly as she scolded herself. She had broken the rules and brought on disaster.

Gavin waved his arm towards the hills. 'We'll ride across, then back.' His patient voice, bare of the darkness of sarcasm, surprised her. 'That way, we'll not miss anything.'

She hesitated, then nodded and followed his lead.

They rode back and forth across the hills as the sun rose and her heart sank. Could Wee One find her way home alone?

Would she want to?

Periodically, they stopped and she whistled again until her lips shook with weariness, barely able to form a sound the bird couldn't possibly hear.

Finally, she saw a speck in the sky, circling slowly. They stopped the horses and she whistled again. The bird flew towards them, close enough that Clare could see her.

Wee One. Obediently returning.

Clare's heart only quieted when the bird was on her fist and hooded, jesses clenched tightly between Clare's gloved fingers.

They found a cluster of oak trees and dismounted to sit, spreading a blanket to cushion the damp, soggy ground. Exhausted, Clare attached Wee One to her creance, not willing to lose her again. The bird flapped her wings, slow to settle.

'She must not have caught the grouse,' Gavin said. 'She would be long gone if she weren't hungry.'

Clare knew that. She knew that the bird only stayed with her in order to eat, but she wanted to believe Wee One came back for something more.

'The falconer has warned me a hundred times not to go out on my own. I might have lost her.'

'You may lose her still.'

She fought the chill his words raised. 'Not if I stay with the group and do as the falconer says.'

'You think that will protect you?'

'Yes.' The word popped out, though it sounded silly as she said it. But if she did things right, if she followed the rules, she would be safe.

No one would die.

He took her hands in his. The feeling was warm. Safe.

Until he spoke.

'Clare,' he said, his eyes honest in a way she had never seen them, 'it doesn't matter what you do or don't do. It won't guarantee that you'll never lose her.'

She ripped her hands away. 'How do you know?'

'Do you think I've lost nothing in my life?'

'What have you ever lost?' Thoughtless words. Regretted as soon as she said them.

Stunned pain lingered in his eyes. 'My father. My childhood. My country.'

Unwelcome sympathy welled into her eyes. She did not want to understand this man. She wanted to hate him. 'Lost your country? You *left* your country.'

'I was *sent* from my country.'

'But then you deserted the King, broke your knightly vow of fealty.'

'So you think I deserve my fate?'

'Yes!' If God did not punish the wicked and preserve the good, how could anyone be safe?

The set of his lips, grim, firm. Perhaps to prevent them from trembling. 'What heinous act of a child of three deserves to be answered with his father's death?'

Clare swallowed, speechless. She had puzzled over a similar question for ten years. What rule had she broken to cause her mother's death?

At least she had known her dear, perfect, beautiful mother. His father must have died before he could even become a memory.

But his father had been a monster. 'Your father's wickedness caused him to die, not yours.'

Strangely, his mask of amusement returned. 'And was he more wicked than his grandfather, the first Edward, who laid Scotland to waste, executed William Wallace and still lived for more than sixty summers?'

She opened her mouth, then shut it. She had no answer. Some very wicked people lived to a ripe old age. And some very good ones died young. God's way, unfathomable.

'I'm sorry,' she said, finally.

His expression turned wary. 'For my loss, yours, or for breaking some rule with your rudeness?'

'That you grew up without him.' Her childhood had died with her mother. His, too, had been snatched away.

He shrugged, breaking his gaze to look up at the clouds, threatening a bare sky. 'It was a long time ago.'

'Tell me about your mother.' She had asked the question many times, borrowing other people's mothers, to fill the void where her own should be. 'It must have been hard.'

A smile whispered on his lips. 'Her family, my uncles, would have been happy to see me dead. They even refused to train me for battle. But she protected me, as if we were a kingdom of two.'

'But she sent you to the enemy.' How could a mother do that?

'We were defeated.' His eyes, earnest, begged her to understand. 'King David captured.'

'But you could only have been twelve!' Not so young, she remembered. She had been even younger when she left for France. It was the way of nobles, to train their children.

'Old, to be a page to the King.' He smiled. 'She thought if I went with David I might learn something of my father's people.' He shook his head. 'My uncles agreed. They hoped I wouldn't come back. And I never will, to them.'

She tried to envision him as a boy, standing before a king, an uncle he'd never met. 'What did King Edward say when he found out who you were?'

He turned his gaze south, lost in memory. '"So you're the one."'

'But he accepted you.'

'He squired me to one of his own men, trying to make up for lost time and training. He thought I was glad to be back with "my" people.'

'And you weren't?'

'Have I not spoken plain? I am Scots *and* English. You keep trying to push me to one side or the other of that line.' He waved his arm towards the summit where the last of the snow still covered the invisible border.

'You were the one who crossed it. You were the one who chose.'

His shoulders dropped and he nodded, ruefully, his

gaze still on the hills. 'I canna live on the line itself, now, can I?'

He didn't look to her for an answer that was not there. She studied him in silence. The pain behind his eyes was older than the war, the harsh lines of his face sculpted long before these battles. The Fitzjohn who sat beside her was not the man she had thought.

'Are you sorry, then, that you didn't stay in England?'

He turned to look at her, though he didn't speak at first. It was as if he was searching for the answer in her face.

'No,' he said, finally. 'I could do nothing about my birth, nothing about my childhood. But the last, the coming home, that was my own doing. My choice, for good or ill.'

Wind filled the silence as they looked out on the hills together, white-capped peaks fading to shades of brown waiting for the spring.

Wee One bated, wings speaking her desire to fly again.

'How long have you had her?' he asked, as if glad to leave the past behind.

'Three years.' Too long, she knew. Catch the bird, train her, hunt for a season, then let her go. That was how it should be done. 'You know much of hawking.'

'The King brought hawks with the army when we went to France. That way, when we paused in our killing, we could watch the birds kill instead.'

She winced. 'When you say "the King," Fitzjohn, which man do you mean?'

He opened his mouth, but a name did not come.

Relieved, she felt her anger rise, rebuilding the wall

between them. This man had acted the knight today and she had shared too much. She needed him to stay the villain, because if darkness could mix with light in his soul, it might do the same in hers. 'Are you speaking of England's Edward or Scotland's David?'

'Both are lovers of the hunt.'

'But you, Fitzjohn, did not mean David, did you? David would never lead an army against the French, our allies.'

'No. I meant Edward.'

She heard no shame in his voice. 'If that is who you mean when you say "King," then I do not believe, Fitzjohn, that you are yet a Scottis man.'

Chapter Eight

The evening after the hunt, her father, unusually silent, called her to his chamber.

'You and Fitzjohn were alone for some time today. Have you a wandering eye?'

'No! I merely gave chase to the falcon and Fitzjohn thought I needed help, then Wee One flew out of sight and we had to find her.' When they returned, she had seen more than one questioning glance. And Alain's jealousy had turned from flattering attention to sullen fury.

Her father raised his eyebrows, as if waiting for her to say more.

She didn't. The jumble of temptation, fear and distrust the man raised in her wouldn't fit into words, particularly now, when it was glossed with empathy as dangerous as his kiss.

'And Alain hasn't spoken,' he said.

It was no longer a question, but she shook her head. 'He is not a man to be forced.' She had been reminded of that today to her sorrow.

'I'm not sure he's a man at all, but if he's the one you want, I'll dance at your wedding. But if he's not willing, it will be the other one.'

'What other one?'

'That red-blooded breeding bull Fitzjohn!'

'You can't mean that!' Had her father gone daft? Or had her misguided attempt to raise Alain's jealousy put the wrong idea in his head?

'Can't I? He's full of energy and brawny blood.'

'But he's half-Inglis!'

'So are most of the families on these Borders. Keeps the stock strong. Now I've no love for the Inglis. Been a Bruce man all my life, and my father before me and his.' He paused for a breath. 'But we've fought over this land longer than anyone remembers. Some day, it must end. I don't know how, nor whether I'll live to see it. But until that time, you'll need a strong man, with quick wits, to keep you safe. One who can sniff out the wind and ride the currents, like those birds you're so fond of. This man is one of those.'

'You would disgrace me to protect the land?' Her voice shook so that she could scarcely say the words.

'It's you I'm trying to protect!'

'Without caring who I am or how I feel?'

'Oh, you'll feel all right once it's done.'

'Never. Not with him. Not with a man who burned those people!' He had sworn it was not true, but she no longer wanted to believe him. Safer that he stay a monster.

'Whether he did or he didn't, do you think we didn't do the same or worse on the other side of the border?

War is hell, daughter, and only men so alike can hate each other so much.'

Clare shuddered. He sounded too much like Gavin. 'But *we* are in the right, Da, not men like him.'

A sigh shook his chest. 'Ah, daughter. God's not made the world so simple for most of us. Things we thought we'd never do, we will. To survive.' He patted her arm with a clumsy palm. 'To protect the ones we love.'

She shook off his hand. '*I* won't.' She sent up a prayer for her blasphemous father, left without Godly guidance when the plague took the Tower's priest. 'You gave me until Beltane.' The day was rushing towards her. 'Keep your word. Alain will speak by then.'

He must, or the life that loomed before her would be more terrible than she had ever feared.

Gavin went to the armoury that evening, escaping to the world he knew. War. Weapons. Killing. Keep them sharp, the baron had said. Keep them ready. Peace was only temporary, especially for a man like him. It would last no longer than Lord Douglas's patience or King Edward's temper.

Or Clare's tolerance.

But for now, the weapons rested quietly. He picked up a sword and ran his fingers along the blade, feeling for pits too small to see by the dim light of the torch.

Blood rusted a sword faster than water.

Light steps climbing the stairs, pausing at the door.

Clare.

Her eyes met his. Did she smile? A trick of her wavering candle. Nothing more.

The few hours of honesty they had shared in the hills had ended abruptly. Today, he had never touched her, yet still she had shut the door, locked him out, thrust him back into the role he knew so well.

Bad son of a worse father.

There, she could safely berate him and secretly be tempted by him, wondering what such badness would taste like and whether she would enjoy it.

That was a question he would be pleased to answer.

'What brings you out so late, Mistress Clare?'

'Visiting the mews.'

'Did you wake the birds?' The words, foolish, only a way to keep her near.

She had the grace to smile, but she didn't come closer. 'The tercel came back. I chased him out.'

He slid the sword back into its scabbard. 'He won't stay away.'

Neither could he.

He had ridden beside her all day, alone, and acted as nobly as she could have asked. But now, her sweet-sharp scent coaxed him across the room. Faster than she could step away, he grabbed her arm and blew out the candle.

In the fading torchlight, it was harder to see the aversion in her eyes.

'Now,' he whispered. 'It's dark. Your Frenchman's gone to bed. There's no one to see. I'm going to kiss you.' He slipped his arms around her waist, cupped her skirt and pressed her to him. 'And then you'll see how small and frail those little lines are when you step across them.'

He took her lips and the line was swept away.

* * *

Something low in her belly responded, and then all she'd tried to hide rose up to meet him.

She clung to his shoulders, telling herself it was only because she was too unbalanced to stand alone, but it was because she was hungry for something his kiss unleashed. Something that enabled her to soar, no longer bound to earth. Lines, borders, rules grew smaller and smaller and then she couldn't see them at all.

She bumped against the wall and fell to earth with a thud.

And slapped him.

Fumbling with a lock of fallen hair, she pushed him away with her other hand. He didn't resist.

'Well, you proved it.' Breathless, heart pounding, slack-jawed. She must look ripe for plucking. 'Your pretence of knighthood could last for no more than an afternoon.'

He rubbed his cheek, but his sideways smile didn't budge. 'Oh, I know what's bothering you. You hear those calls for Euphemia and you see your da and his woman laughing and all the time, you're waiting and waiting for that Frenchman.'

'I am behaving as a virtuous woman should.' Yet when he touched her, she forgot everything a virtuous woman should know and wanted only to mate like a beast.

Worse, he knew it.

He shook his head. 'The years are passing, Mistress Clare. Time's flying faster than a falcon.'

He didn't take a step, but she wanted him to. No man had ever looked at her like that, as if she were a woman he wanted as desperately as life itself. If she did not stop him, she wouldn't be able to stop herself.

She drew in a breath and uttered the foulest slur she could think of. 'Fire-starter.'

That shook the smile.

'Well, I can see my knightly airs and graces haven't fooled you at all. You asked me on my knight's honour whether I did those things and I told you no. But that wasn't enough, was it?'

She shook her head. *I don't want to believe you.* 'You made a vow to serve Edward and broke it. Why should I believe anything you say to me?'

He nodded, as if it was what he had expected. 'That's why I never worry much about my reputation. People will believe what they like. It's much easier than discovering the truth.'

He leaned closer, but not with the teasing seduction he had shown before. 'Believe what you will, Mistress Clare. Believe that I'm a menace to the countryside. Believe that any Scots man, woman or child who looks askance at me can expect to go up in flames.'

She crossed her hands across her chest, as if that might hold him at bay. His face, carved in anger, was the face of a man who could have done those things. And could do them again.

'Oh, yes. Back away, Mistress Claire. Because we're sleeping under the same roof. That ought to keep you awake at night.'

He stopped, as if catching himself. The anger in his eyes ebbed and the seductive smile returned. He reached for her, stroked her ear, and let his fingers trail the edge

of her throat until a moan started again. 'Or is it something else about me that keeps you awake?'

She pushed his hand away. 'Nothing about you keeps
me awake, Fitzjohn, except praying that you will leave
us soon.'

But as she fled up the stairs, she knew that wasn't
true. He was keeping her awake night after night. And
with that kiss, she was just beginning to realise why.

He slammed his palm against the unyielding wooden
table when she left.

Something beneath her cold exterior called to him
in a way no other woman ever had. And this was the
wrong time to be tempted. And the wrong woman to be
tempted by.

'I gave you my hospitality, but don't go breaking the
furnishings.'

He turned, startled, to see the old man leaning against
the door.

'What are you doing here?'

'Enjoying a spring evening.'

'You asked me to get the armoury in order. I'm doing
it. I don't need your supervision.'

'You had some words with my daughter.'

He wondered how many of those words the man had
heard. 'A few.'

'She doesn't fancy you.' It wasn't a question.

'Well, the feeling's mutual.'

'Really?' A smile carved deep into his face. 'Well,
you fooled me, then.'

He hoped it was too dark for the man to see the heat on
his cheeks. 'We don't mix well. We're very different.'

'That's not what I see. I see you as a contender.'

Gavin snorted. 'For what?'

'I took you in and I let you stay, even after I knew who you were. Do I look like I'm daft?'

A genuine laugh broke free. The baron was as sharp as they came. 'No, sir.'

'Do I strike you as a soft-hearted idiot?'

He was tempted to say yes, just to bait the man. 'No, sir, you do not.'

The baron strolled into the room and settled on to a bench, with his back against the table. 'Yet I opened my door and brought you into my house when most folks would have slain you on sight. Now why do you think that is, Fitzjohn?'

'Why don't you tell me?'

'I have something I'd like you to do.'

He should have expected a hidden motive. No one would accept him for himself alone. 'More cattle to steal?'

The man laughed. 'Not this time.'

'Then why don't you tell me what it is and I'll tell you whether I'd like to do it.'

'Get married! Have sons!'

A chill like chainmail in the rain prickled the back of his neck. He watched the old man smile and, suddenly, a vision flashed before him.

His chin dropped in shock. 'Well, I'll be damned.'

'Probably. But first, you'll make a bride of my Clare!'

No words escaped, but shock settled on his face.

The man chuckled again. 'Surprised, are you?'

Married to a woman who hated his guts. Was the man mad?

'Well? What do you think?' The baron leaned forwards, smile gone, expression earnest, as if he really cared whether Gavin gave a fig about his scheme.

He didn't want to disappoint the old man, but it was impossible. Clare would have nothing to do with it.

And he?

Well, he could offer a woman little and expect less. When he had left Edward, he had walked away from everything except what his sword arm would earn him.

'You've devised a very interesting plan.'

'Plan?' he exploded. 'I'm talking about carrying on the Carr name. Having grandchildren so my blood doesn't die out and my land be lost to the next pick-thank who curries Lord Douglas's chestnut horse!'

The man was serious as death. 'And to do that, you're willing to mix your blood with the torch holder of Burnt Candlemas?'

Clare didn't believe the truth. Did her father?

The man squinted at him. 'Move up to the family floor. See how you like fresh straw. Study that woman. And then we'll decide.'

Gavin's pulse beat faster, and it was Clare, not clean sheets, that caused it. 'And Clare agrees to this?'

The man looked away. 'She will. She will.'

'She certainly doesn't now.' His kiss had frightened, not tempted, her. 'So what do I get out of this besides a bride who can't stand to be in the same room with me?'

'The tower. The land. What money I have when I die.'

But none of that stirred his longing. It was the promise of a home. A side truly his. A haven, not temporary, but always there.

Something he had never been able to imagine.

He flattened the flutter of hope, afraid to let it grow too large. 'You're promising things that aren't yours to give. I've never heard of a Scots who could just hand over his property.'

There was a sly grin. 'Well, when my son died after the Battle of Neville's Cross, Lord Douglas, in a moment of sentiment he's never shown since, told me that if Clare took a mate before David the Bruce came home from captivity, he would approve any man I chose to hold Carr's Tower.'

Clare had never mentioned a brother. 'David's been in England ten years.'

'I don't think Lord Douglas expected him to be away so long.'

'Why me?'

He smiled. 'Because I like you. And I think you'll be good for her. And for the land.'

Tempted. He was so tempted and so afraid to believe. 'I'll think on it.' The man could change his mind.

'Dangerous men don't need to think long.'

The very words he'd thrown at the baron all those nights ago.

Now the man was pushing him just as hard. 'Now. Tonight. Decide.'

To have a home in the land of his birth—that was worth any hellion bride he'd have to face. 'She could still choose the *comte*.' He did not think the man would ask for her. But what if he were wrong?

Carr snorted. 'Do you think that if you really wooed her, she would choose that lily-livered Frenchman?'

'No, sir!' He could offer her things the other man never could…if only she could recognise them.

'Now I know I've picked the right man.' Carr stuck out his hand, their eyes met, and they shook. 'Now listen to me. You must treat her right. Once you're joined, if you ever take another, I'll kill you meself.'

And odd warning. He wondered when Murine had first come to the man's bed.

And whether he was condemning himself to a life of celibacy.

'She may seem delicate,' the baron said, 'but she's made of better steel with stronger seams than most men.' The man cleared a catch in his throat. 'Like her mother before her.'

And, Gavin thought, she was as close to quality as he or the old rascal would ever get. 'Who says marriages are made in heaven?'

This one, if it happened, might take him straight to hell.

Chapter Nine

The next evening, he moved into a room high in the tower with a view towards the south.

Angus carried his bag, though it wasn't necessary. He owned no more than one man could hold.

'Where do the rest sleep?'

'Mistress Clare, on the other side. The *comte*—' he pointed, wrinkling his nose '—over there.'

'And the baron?'

He nodded towards the closed door on the west side. 'At the end, but he doesn't sleep there much, I've been told.'

Gavin nodded. Everyone knew he spent as many nights in Murine's cottage as in his own bed.

'Thank you, Angus. That will be all.'

Gavin crossed to the window and gazed towards England.

It had to be there, somewhere. One of those hills, overlapping like waves, was Scotland and the next, covered with the same melting snow, was England.

But how would a man know when he crossed that line? No fence, no wall marked the boundary.

Dusk fell and the line he looked for was no longer visible, if it had ever been.

He turned abruptly from the window. If he was going to woo her, he'd better start.

Clare's door was partially open, offering a tantalising peek at her private corner of the tower. The red-and-gold banker he had nearly destroyed now covered a chest at the end of her bed. On the hearth, a pan of bubbling water and lavender scented the air. It seemed too personal, this view, a glimpse of hopes and dreams more intimate than a kiss.

He pushed the door, quietly. She sat up in the bed, still awake, stitching a falcon's hood.

The vision shocked him, for all the times he had imagined bedding her.

Her blonde hair, always pulled tight into a braid down her back, tumbled free across her shoulders and her breasts. It was fair, but not the sun-kissed gold of the Plantagenet kings. Instead, the strands glittered like icicles in moonlight.

The old man's laugh, and that of his lady, echoed from behind the door at the end of the hall. She looked up at the sound, frowning.

Then her eyes met his.

Her lips parted in surprise. There was an inheld breath. Hers? His?

'What a vision you are there, Mistress Clare,' he said, surprised the words came so calmly when his heart was galloping.

She pulled up the covers, though her breasts were twice covered already, by a gown and her hair.

'Go away.'

'Oh, I sleep here now, didn't you know? Your father asked me to move in, right up here next to you.'

She sighed. 'He told me.'

'But don't worry. I won't burn you in your bed.'

She stiffened and he regretted his words. But her eyes searched his for a long minute and her lips softened before she spoke.

'No,' she said, finally. 'You won't.'

The words shook him. For all the names she had called him, all the distrust, had she ultimately more faith in his goodness than he did?

Or was she merely rejecting him with new words?

He pushed away the desire for more of that softness. If she was to marry him, and he was not at all certain that she would, he must not remind her how far short he fell of the knights of her chivalric dreams, nor speak of what they really did in war. He must talk of harmless, cultured pleasures.

He leaned in the doorway, but came no further. 'You look pretty sitting there.' His voice was rough with emotion he did not want to feel. 'Like a wee lassie ready to say her prayers and drift off to sleep without a care in the world. Do you have a care in the world?'

Her moment of softness was gone. 'None I would share with you.'

Yet she had cares. He knew. Chasing after perfection according to rules made by others. A quest without end. 'You should be as happy and carefree as you were when you were a little girl with nothing to worry about but looking for robin's eggs.'

Was his wish for her? Or for himself?

'I was never that little girl, even as a bairn. My mother died when I was eight.'

He blinked. So they carried a common burden. He a fatherless son, she a motherless daughter.

'Well, then, maybe you should just put down your cares and act like that wee lassie should have.'

She closed her eyes and pursed her lips, as if struggling against the idea. Then, she looked at him and set it aside, as deliberately as the tiny leather hood. 'You have such a limited supply of charm, Fitzjohn. Don't waste it on me.'

He didn't let the smile waver. 'Oh? Didn't your father tell you? We're to be married.'

'Despite my father's misbegotten ideas, you are not looking at your future. I am more than a body to convey his land and his blood and his grandbabies. And I don't want you.'

Whatever the old man had told her, he wasn't making the wooing easy. 'Well, want me or not, I'm what you're going to have.'

'Not as long as I draw breath.'

'Do you have a better offer?' Cruel, yet he said it.

She lifted her chin to salvage her pride. 'You know the answer to that.'

He raised his brows in mock distress. 'Then how can you refuse my hand and heart?'

She shook her head. 'You have no heart, Fitzjohn.'

He wished that it were true. 'Now you malign me, Mistress Clare.' His smile stayed fixed.

'I don't think so. I want a man who's interested in me, not just my body and my property.'

Foolish dreams, for someone who longed for courtly ways.

'If you want to be a lady, that's all a husband *will* find of interest. But if you marry me, they'll say there goes Clare, married by her heartless father to that bastard fire-starter and it won't matter what they say.' He grinned, thinking of the nights. 'You'll wake every morning with a smile.'

An expression flashed across her face, then disappeared.

He might have called it hunger.

'You flatter yourself with that fantasy, Fitzjohn. I'm not just a demure maiden who needs a strong arm and a stronger pillicock.'

His smile sagged in shock.

'You didn't think I knew that word, did you?' She was the one who smiled now.

'Well, you are a woman of surprises.' He liked this Clare, the one who wasn't afraid to speak her mind.

'I am capable, clever and of passing appearance.' Yet the words seemed said to convince herself and not him.

'You are all that, Mistress Clare.' And much more. Beautiful and fierce, with eyes sharp and bright as her falcon's.

And just as trapped.

She lifted her chin and he saw high colour on her cheekbones. 'Wipe off that smile, Fitzjohn. It will never be you.'

'Never is a dangerous word.'

'I do not choose it lightly. You've been hoodwinked, Fitzjohn, blinded just like one of my birds who sits in contented ignorance as long as she sees nothing of what's around her. Whatever my father promised you, you'll never collect because I'm no party to that bargain.'

Still smiling, he tried to look offended. 'Is the Frenchman so much better?'

Her look said that was a question not worth answering. 'I have chosen the man I can share my life—' she stumbled over the words '—myself with.'

No woman and very few men could choose their lives. Yet she wanted to select the fist she would return to.

He would have to be sure it was his. 'Then tell me about this paragon you seek to wed.'

'He's nothing like you.'

'I'm deeply hurt that you would say that when you know so little of me.'

'I know enough.'

Like all of them, she knew all she needed to know. And she would think worse of him if she knew it all.

'Then tell me more of the marvelous Comte de Garencieres. Tell me why he's your ideal man.'

Her face softened. 'He is admired for his manners and gentility and his prowess in the field. A chivalrous knight who appreciates art and literature and is at ease with the courtly graces.'

He clenched his jaw, fighting a wave of bitter yearning. Birth and blood had denied him some of those. The rest, war had stripped away. Yet the Frenchman remained untouched by the horrors he had seen. For that alone, he would be worthy of envy.

At his silence, she continued. 'And he understands partnership and shared laughter.'

'Many men do.' The *comte,* she would discover to her sorrow, was not one of them. It seems she was as blinded as he, but he could not tell her so.

She threw back the covers, swung her legs over the side of the bed and slid to the floor, continuing her recitation as she walked towards him. 'The man I marry will appreciate that I brew the best brogat this side of Jedburgh.'

His heart beat faster and he searched for her curves under the shapeless gown. Who slept in clothes like that? What was she afraid of?

Him, of course. And she should be.

Or was it herself?

She still smiled, her chin lifted and her head cocked to one side. 'And he will dance with me, in the dark of the moon, seen only by the stars.'

Then her smile turned wistful, as if she spoke, finally, only to herself. 'And he will chase the falcons beside me, riding as fast as the bird can fly.'

I was the one who urged you to ride free.

But she had tied his tongue, as firmly as her falconer's knot held her bird.

In the darkening light, she shimmered like a ghostly angel. Pale gown, pale skin, pale hair. Moon to his sun—surely she would still glow beneath a dark sky.

Then, her eyes met his, as if she had come to herself again. 'For this man, for the right man, I will be the best wife a man could ever hope for. That is not, and will never be, you.'

She had reached the door now, smiling as if she had

bested him. All he wanted was to press her against her barren bed until she gave up the rest of her secrets.

And accepted his.

'When next the moon is new, Beltane will be upon us. Dance with me then.' He thought he saw an answer in her eyes. A whiff of desire. It gave him hope.

He put his hands on her arms, gently, so she would not run away. 'We'll sway under the stars together and pray that summer returns and light fires to make sure it does.'

In the dusk, her pale face turned whiter. And he realised the talk of fire had made him a villain again. 'Oh, don't worry,' he said, the smile that shielded him returning to his face. 'I never burn folks in their beds who've been nice to me. You will be nice to me, won't you, Mistress Clare?'

She pulled back, leaving him with empty hands. 'I will be as nice to you as you deserve, Fitzjohn. At the moment, that's very damn little.'

She shut the door in his face.

And his shout of laughter no doubt disturbed the old man and his woman.

The tercel returned to the mews a few days later and dropped a piece of food at Wee One's feet. Then Clare watched him swoop and bob above the falcon's perch.

'He's feeding her,' she said.

'He's trying to coax her into mating,' he said.

She looked at him, sharply, but he spoke only of the bird. Here, they had a truce.

Reluctantly, she let Fitzjohn help her exercise the birds. The falconer needed help and Alain had no interest in his own birds unless they were riding out to hunt. In truth, Fitzjohn knew as much, perhaps more, of the birds than either she or Neil.

She let the idea play in her mind again, without fear this time. 'Is that possible? Here?'

He shook his head. 'How would the young learn to fly? To hunt?'

A haggard bird, taken in the wild, already knew those things.

'The same way as does the fledgling you take from the nest or the branch. Wee One was a brancher.'

'But those at least have been taught to fly. How would they learn that here?'

She looked around the mews, which suddenly seemed small and dark. 'Surely a bird is born knowing how to fly.'

He shook his head. 'I've seen fledglings that have fallen from the nest unable to fly back.'

The world was a dangerous place. 'Maybe it would be better to raise it here, then, where her parents could teach her.'

Gavin studied her face. 'You really think to breed falcons in a mews?' His tone was puzzled. Curious.

At least he would discuss it with her. Alain and the falconer both thought the very idea akin to heresy. 'I just wondered whether you could.'

'Why would you want to? It's unnatural.'

'Is it any more unnatural than asking them to hunt with us?'

'They hunt naturally.'

She smiled. 'Well, from what you've told me, they breed naturally, too.'

He laughed, the rolling sound a comfort.

She furrowed her brow. 'But it's never done. Why not?'

He shrugged, looking sceptical. 'Try and you're sure to discover.'

It *wasn't* done, she knew. And there must be a reason. Surely disaster would strike if she tried it.

But still, there was something comforting about the thought of Wee One with a family. Birds always came back to the same place to nest, so if she did mate, this would be her home, the place she would never leave.

He interrupted her thoughts. 'But you're worrying about something that won't happen. I've never heard of falcons mating in a mews.'

But the idea took stubborn root in her head. The next time she saw the tercel, she'd shut the door with the bird inside.

It seemed as if it would take the same kind of force to bring Alain to a declaration before time ran out and her father again threatened her with Fitzjohn.

The day before Beltane Eve, she discovered the egg.

During the intervening weeks, Wee One had taken over a high, flat shelf in the mews. Together, she and the tercel filled it with bits of twig and grass, but this morning, instead of standing on her talons, she huddled down on the ledge, as if hiding something.

'What is that, Wee One?' Clare asked, as if the bird would understand her. 'What do you have there, sweetheart?'

The bird flared her wings, threatening, refusing to

let Clare closer, but beneath the feathers, she glimpsed a mottled brown egg.

Tears gathered in Clare's throat. This wild thing, her dear companion, had found a way to start a family. Even in captivity, the bird could do it.

Not she.

She tried to remember what Gavin had said of breeding falcons. It took weeks after mating before the bird could lay. So all this time she had been trying to encourage them, the two had already joined, perhaps that day she thought she had lost Wee One.

'Ah, there you are, *demoiselle*. I weary of the Scottish ale and have a taste for the claret tonight. Serve some with the meal.'

At the sound of Alain's voice, Wee One flapped violently and squealed in an angry, unstoppable rhythm.

'Look,' she whispered, as if somehow the falcon would hear and understand her. 'She's laid an egg.'

He barely glanced at it. 'Destroy it. The birds, they cannot be bred. Even if taken from the wild too early they are poor flyers.'

She could not make her hand reach for the egg to crush it. 'But this one would not be taken from the nest. Her own mother would train her to be a fine hunter.'

'You will not think the same when the eyas screeches all night and then refuses to fly because she knows you will feed her. The falconer was careless to let a tercel so close to her.' He shrugged, dismissing the whole affair. '*Ce n'est rien.* The mother is too small to be a good hunter.'

Anger straightened her spine and strengthened her

will. 'The egg is here and it is hers. I will not deprive her of it.'

He smiled. '*Bien sur.* Do as you like. How else will you learn? But prepare for the disappointment.'

They left the mews and Alain strode away after a kiss on her hand and a reminder about the claret.

She tasted the last of the tun of French wine in the cellar and stuck out her tongue. Alain would be displeased. It was on the edge of vinegar.

He was right about the bird, of course. Gavin had told her the same.

The afternoon of Beltane Eve, Clare felt restless and idle.

She left the preparations to Murine. Clare's mother, transplanted from France, had never understood the festival rituals and could not teach them to her daughter. Her mother, like Alain, had been a stranger to this land.

She was not.

Could she feel at home here if she could not persuade her father to change his mind?

If Alain—

She put the thought away. France would be her home. It was only the threat of darkness that caused her gloomy thoughts. Even as a child, Clare had huddled in her mother's skirts at the end of the day when all the fires were extinguished. What if the fire could not be rekindled? What if she were left alone in the long, dark night?

Now, she was too old to be afraid of the dark, but she was also old enough to know, better than she understood then, that starting a fire without a flame was very, very difficult.

What if, this time, the wood didn't spark?

What if Alain didn't speak?

Then she would speak to him, even if it violated everything she had been taught. He knew nothing of her father's demands. He would understand when she explained why she could not wait.

Relieved at the thought, she walked through the tower and the cottages, making sure every fire was extinguished. The blossoming rowan branches made her smile. As a child, she had loved the white flowers scattered beside cold hearths and cottage thresholds for good fortune. Loved them still. Pure. Clean. Unsullied.

The gloaming stretched across the sky and she left castle and cottage behind to join the rest as they walked up to the fire pits on the hill. Her heart lifted as she looked over the rippling hills. Soon, the sheep would move up to the high pasture and summer would come.

But she would not be here to see it. She would be on her way to France.

Yesterday, the men had prepared the pits for the two Beltane fires. They were re-used each year, and over the winter became clogged with grass and earth. Now, crisply dug anew, they were filled with dry wood, not even left out overnight for fear the dew would dampen the spark and prevent it from catching.

In her childhood, she remembered, there had been a large wheel built. Many men ran together, pushing it until enough friction was created to light the need-fire.

Now, lighting the fire had become an individual competition, not a community task. Men lined up to compete in a race to show which of them could start the fire most quickly. Her father used to be the first, and always the winner, but he had finally accepted that his hands were too tired.

Alain, offered the first seat, shook his head. 'Better a tournament to sharpen fighting skills than such a sacrilege during the month devoted to the Virgin Mother.'

She frowned. 'But the winner will be able to select the woman of his choice as partner for the evening. I thought—' She bit her lip. She had thought to have time alone with him.

He patted her hand. 'I will be your companion, of course, regardless of these men. No one else is worthy of you.'

Just as soon as the fire had kindled, then, she would draw him away from the others.

One by one, nine were chosen. Four men-at-arms. Four cottage lads.

The final place was empty.

Until Fitzjohn took the seat.

A flutter in her belly. Was it fear for him?

'Well,' Alain said, loudly enough for all to hear, 'I think we will see fire *très vite*.'

Whispers rustled through the crowd. Superstition had it that if a man could not spark a fire, it was because of a sin that stained his soul. They knew who he was now. And though his Robson raid had convinced some to accept him, others, despite the baron's support, were unconvinced.

Fitzjohn would lose either way. If he sparked a flame,

it would prove him a fire-starter. If he did not, it would prove the same: the sin of the fire in him.

Fitzjohn's eyes slid over hers and paused.

Dance with me.

His smile, that everlasting smile, showed no hesitation.

Her father laid out the rules. As soon as the sun slipped below the horizon, he would shout 'start.' The man who sparked the first fire would get his choice of partner for the evening.

Another part of the ritual she dreaded. They were good Christians, most of them, but some looked on the day as a chance to take licence. More than once, as a child, Clare had felt her mother's cool hands cover her eyes to shield her from the most lecherous acts.

Her father had first taken the widow Murine at Beltane, she had heard it whispered.

Murine, she was glad to see, had an arm firmly on Euphemia's shoulder, keeping the girl close.

With the rest, Clare turned her eyes to the west, waiting for the last edge of the sun to slip below the red-rimmed clouds and disappear behind the furthest, darkest ridge.

'Now!' her father roared.

There was no yelling, no cheering on of favourites. Instead, there was the hush of dozens of inheld breaths. It was always thus. This was serious business, for if no spark could be kindled, there would be no fire, no light, no warmth.

Fitzjohn was the only one she watched.

Each of them had a thin, round stick that fitted into a board with a hole carved into it. Crouched over it, he put his boot on the end of the board to hold it steady, then placed the stick in the hole and, palm on either side of the stick, rubbed it back and forth. A nest of dry tinder, nearby, was ready to catch the spark.

She held her breath. A few wisps of smoke drifted up from the point where stick met board. Drifted, then disappeared.

Concentration creased Gavin's brow, but unlike the others, his face held not worry, but a smile.

Wisps of smoke drifted from his board.

While the rest still frantically rolled their sticks, he picked up the little scoop that had caught the embers and blew on it, softly.

Another man, at about the same place, was so excited he blew his embers across the grass where the precious heat was lost and he was forced to begin again.

But Gavin kept the now-glowing spark steady in his left hand, picked up the mouse nest of dry grass, and dumped the burning brands into it. Then, he blew on the grass, breath gentle as a feather.

Everyone else stopped to watch, knowing he would be first or they could all start over again. The dry grass glowed.

A flame erupted.

A cheer, some handclaps, fluttered through the crowd.

Gavin walked to the waiting bonfire pit and touched the flame to the wood shavings on the edge. They were slow to light.

Angus ran to him and held out a torch soaked in pine pitch that would catch more easily than the wood.

Gavin, immobile, stared at it, silent.

Then, carefully, he held out the flaming nest. The torch lit and the last of the dry grass was burned away.

He dropped it into the fire pit as Angus lit the other fire.

But he stared into the flames a long time before he turned away.

'Well, my boy,' her father said, loudly, as the crowd dispersed. 'Who would you like as a companion for the evening?'

He blinked, as if just awakened, and lifted his head. 'Why, Mistress Clare, of course. If she would do me the honour.'

Chapter Ten

Alain's hand tightened on her arm.

Gavin strolled over and took her other hand in his, pressing a kiss on her fingers. *'Demoiselle.'*

His accent was perfect.

Rage masked Alain's face. 'You do not deserve her.'

Gavin's courtly manners did not falter. *'Au contraire, mon ami.* If you refuse to join the combat, you cannot claim the prize.'

'I will speak with you later,' she whispered to Alain, before he stomped away.

Fitzjohn's hand cupped her waist. Her father's knowing smile as they walked by was fuelled by more than ale.

She stepped away from Fitzjohn's hand. 'You and Alain, you both speak as if I were a prize instead of a person.'

'You wanted to be a knight's lady. And for a knight, winning the lady is the symbol of his prowess. He plays the game of love against his fellows, as well as the game of war.'

'I thought you did not believe that war was a chivalric game.'

'I don't.' He looked at her. 'And neither is love.'

The bonfire's flames cast light and shadow across his face. She saw a war in his eyes, war between a desire to believe in goodness and the knowledge of the darkness in his own soul.

And hers.

She tried to back away from his too-knowing look, but the gentle hand on her waist turned hard.

'If you want to play at love,' she said, 'I don't know why you would select me.'

'Don't you?' There was a world in those two words. They spoke of more than her father's wishes. They spoke of his own.

And just for a moment, she was wanted to learn his heart. Not just what people said of him, but the secrets no one knew.

No. There would be no sharing of those. For then he would demand hers in return.

'I'm a lady, Fitzjohn. And you're a rogue.'

'I can't help my birth.'

'I do not speak only of your parents. You're a schemer who expects to have your way in everything.'

'Well, that just proves you don't know me very well. Yet.'

'I know you well enough. You're too much like my father.'

'Why, thank you for the compliment, Mistress Clare. He's a wonderful man.'

'To you.'

'You don't like him much, do you?'

'Not since I was eight.' That was when she had given up on him.

Or he had given up on her. When her mother died, he didn't hold or comfort a frightened, lonely child. He sent her across the sea to strangers and took another woman into his bed and another daughter on to his knee.

'That's a large decision to make so quickly.'

'Now that I'm grown, it takes me less time. I judged you as soon as I saw your cold, blue eyes.'

She had glimpsed a perilous mixture there. Incredible lightness hiding shadows as dark as her own.

'You've judged the colour right, at least.'

'You said I was a good judge of character.' She pulled away from him, fighting temptation. 'Well, I judge you to be ruthless and dangerous, and I want nothing to do with you.'

She lied and he knew it. Too close and she would crave his kiss all over again.

'You want a marriage of money and a bedmate, Fitzjohn. I want more.' Her voice shook as she remembered, belatedly, that chivalric romance was to be saved for illicit relationships, not to be expected from a husband. 'I want a life away from this wilderness.' Away from the wildness in her soul. 'Neither you nor my father appreciate that world.'

'You talk a lot about what kind of man and what kind of life you want to get. What are you willing to *give* to this marriage of fantasies?'

'Why, everything, of course.' Or everything a man

should want. There would always be a part held back. The part she had buried, or tried to. The desires that took over her body late at night. Those, even a husband must not know. 'I would give all that I am.'

'Mistress Clare, you don't even *know* all that you are.' His lips hovered too close to hers, stirring those dark urges, the feelings she must never confess, even to herself.

Alain never raised those feelings. With Alain, she was safe.

But she was not with Alain, she was with Gavin, with Gavin on Beltane, a night to pray for fertility, and her body wanted to give the ancient, sinful answer.

If she closed her eyes, could she be like the blinded birds, unable to fear what could not be seen?

She lowered her gaze and leaned closer.

'Demoiselle Clare?'

She pulled away, stumbling, at the sound of Alain's voice. What had he seen? She smoothed her skirt as if Fitzjohn had rumpled her clothes. As if something had happened.

It hadn't, of course, but worse, she had wanted it to.

'Demoiselle Clare, I think you have wasted enough of your evening on this man. I have come to take you back.'

'Yes. Yes, thank you.' And she took her first deep breath, as Alain led her away, refusing to look at Gavin for fear he would call her back.

How much would you give? She was so ready to give herself to Alain. A lady would never push a man, never raise the question herself, yet she must.

Now. Or her father would force her to be the bastard's bride.

'Alain, it is time…' She paused, leaning against a boulder. Higher on the hill, twin bonfires still roared. The cattle were being driven between them as protection for the coming year. 'There are…I am…' She could scarce get words to form.

'*Chérie,* what is wrong? Did he bother you?'

'No. No!' A lie, but Alain must have no doubts of her. 'Not that.'

'Then what is it? Can I help?' He touched her cheek, gently, and met her eyes.

But in the dim light, she saw no hunger there.

She tried to smile. 'I must say some things and I don't even know how to begin.'

'How can it be difficult when we have spoken of so many things?'

So many things. Him. His home. His exploits. His preferences in food. His opinions on falconry. Had they ever talked of her? She couldn't remember. 'We've talked of many things, Alain, but never of the future.'

His face looked blank. And a bit uncomfortable. 'Future?'

'*L'avenir,*' she said, with a smile. 'Plans. Hopes. Dreams.' She dropped her head. 'This is too difficult. I can't.'

He put a finger on her chin and lifted her head. 'Speak of *l'avenir, chérie.*'

She searched his eyes. Calm. Comforting. Without rough edges. Without pain.

Without passion.

'Alain, I'd like *you* to speak of it. You've been here for

more than a year. We've spoken, ridden, talked, walked, spent time and company together. And I have come to expect, that is, I thought that you had feelings for me. Do you have feelings for me?'

He dropped his hand and leaned away. '*Bien sur.* Of course.'

This was wrong. All wrong. It was the knight who should be on his knees, professing his lovesick devotion. 'What kind of feelings?'

He looked at her as if she were a dog who had leaked against his leg. Loved, perhaps, but one who had committed an awkward, inconvenient, embarrassing act. 'Respect. Admiration.' He shrugged. The silver tongue tarnished.

Such words. Full of pity. Did he recognise what she was doing? 'Is that all?'

'All?'

'Is that the extent of your feelings?'

'Feelings. A difficult word to understand.'

'*Tendresse.*'

'My feelings for you are all that is appropriate.'

'Feelings enough to ask me to be your wife?'

He blinked, like a deer, seeing the hunter's arrow but unable to move.

She knew, then, what his answer would be. She should have known when his eyes met hers. Kind, but distant. Never really seeing beyond the surface.

And until Gavin Fitzjohn plundered her with a glance, she had not known the difference.

He coughed and cleared his throat. '*Ma femme?*'

Such a question. As if he had never considered it before. As if she were feeble-minded for misunderstanding. Well, she was beyond humiliation now. She had no more to lose. She would make it his turn to suffer and squirm.

'Yes. Your wife. Did you know my husband will have the tower and these lands, as long as he can hold them?'

'But you knew, of course, that I must return to France.'

Yes, she was enjoying it now. She would press him, press both of them, to the embarrassing and bitter end. 'Oh, yes. France is a second home to me, as you well know.'

'But there is more, an alliance there, my family...' He stumbled over what used to be smooth phrases. 'Surely you understood...'

'Une alliance.' Her words were a whisper. 'Of course, I knew.' She straightened her shoulders, unable to face her shame any longer. 'I wanted to be sure there was no misunderstanding that you, that you and I...' She looked away, into the sky, wishing she could fly as far away as her falcon could soar.

And then, she would turn, dive down from the sky, and rip out his eyes with her talons.

The thought gave her strength. 'No misunderstanding about our...future, because my father, you see...'

'Ah, *votre père.*' He sighed, relieved. *'Oui, je comprends.* Awkward. *Gauche, n'est pas?'*

Her dear, well-meaning father. Brimming with bluster, if missing some manners.

And Alain dismissed him with one word.

'I know it has been difficult, night after night.' Her dear, determined father, who wanted grandsons so badly that he would sacrifice his feelings, put aside his doubts about the man his daughter wanted in order to force him into her bedchamber to produce them.

It was love, in a strange way.

'I did not intend to mislead,' Alain said. 'You are sweet, graceful, intelligent. And your behaviour so perfect, never suggesting...'

Oh, how she had wanted to. How she had wanted to grab him and shake him, so many times, and say *kiss me, love me, marry me*. Instead, she had behaved perfectly because she was afraid of losing him.

And had lost him anyway.

'I'm so glad we talked, Alain, and that you agree we have no future. It would indeed have been awkward, for you to ask me to be your wife.' No reason to hide her feelings. No need to watch each word. 'I am like the finest of peregrines, you see, and I need a worthy falconer. And you, I think, are no better than a cadger.'

She left him there, walking away with her head high and her eyes wide, hoping the wind would dry her tears before they fell.

Days, months had slipped away, wasted. And the fault was hers, not his. She had had no mother to whisper in her ear and warn her of the man's true feelings. All the time that she had been pining after Alain, she was so stupid that she couldn't even tell he had no interest in her.

How could she trust herself to judge any man?

Full darkness had fallen. Dancers around the flickering bonfires cast strange shadows. Clare could face none of them.

Her father tapped his toes as he watched them, Murine snuggled against his side.

Clare averted her eyes.

'Daughter!' he called out.

She kept walking, to no avail. He caught up with her. 'I saw you with Alain. Is it settled?'

She gazed up at the moonless sky, knowing she would cry if she faced his hopeful eyes. 'Yes, it's settled.'

'Really?' Astonishment and disappointment mingled in the word. 'You've surprised me, daughter. I never thought. In fact, I had hoped…' He let the words fall away.

She turned, feeling her fury rise. Her moment of understanding and sympathy had gone. If he had not pressured her, she would never have asked, never have been so humiliated.

'You had hoped what? That I would prefer a fire-starting bastard to one of the most chivalrous knights of the realm? I do not. But I discovered the knight did not prefer me.' Anger clogged her throat and she wasn't sure whether it was directed at Alain or her father or herself. 'I'm just a foolish lass who's been pining over a man who has done nothing but dally with me to while away the boredom. And I, like an idiot, did not see it.'

'What are you sayin', lass?'

She took a breath. 'I am saying that Alain will not, and never intended to, marry me.'

Wrath cracked the crags of his face. 'I'll kill him. I'll—'

She grabbed his rough sleeves. 'No, you won't. I won't let you make it any worse than it already is.'

His arms went around her then, and she felt the quick rub of rough wool against her cheek. 'I'm sorry, lass.'

She bit her lip against the tears. He had never been so kind to her before. 'Don't. Please. I canna bear it.'

He pulled away, straightening his shoulders. 'Then it will be the other.'

'You can't mean it.' She had prayed that Fitzjohn had been only a threat, a way to force Alain to action. She waved her hands towards the men and women, raucous around the fire. 'They will never accept him as their lord.'

'They'll come around.'

'*I* won't.'

'You will if I say so. Have you no consideration for your father?'

'I've all the consideration that you have for me.' How could she trust anything at all? Alain, her father, Fitz-john—for each of them, she was no more than a means to an end. 'What about what I want?'

'Enough. It will be the other. Prepare for it. I'll go tell him.'

'No,' she said, surprised by how quiet and firm the word was. 'Wait.'

Reeling from the blow, she had not fully faced what Alain's rejection would mean. She was trapped in this hilly wasteland. She could refuse her father, but what would it gain? He would choose again. Another try, another man, a stranger, perhaps not even a knight. Someone with a strong arm and weak manners who had never even seen life beyond these hills.

Fitzjohn, at least, understood hawking.

'I am the one who will be his wife,' she said, drawing

her first clear breath since Alain's betrayal. 'I will tell him.'

She wanted to see Gavin's eyes when he learned his fate. She hoped she could trust what she saw.

'Do it quickly, girl.'

Now that the fires were safely lit and blazing, they let the younger lads practise with the sticks and boards so they might some day be starters. She found Gavin with Angus huddled over a board. Intent on the speed of his stick, the boy let Gavin guide his hands, showing him how to rub the stick more smoothly.

He looked up and met her eyes. Was there hope in his when he turned to see her? She couldn't be sure.

'I must speak with you,' she said, and turned away, certain he would follow.

Chapter Eleven

Clare dipped a small torch to the fire and, silent, led him halfway down the hill, stopping when they reached the barmkin surrounding the Tower. Behind them, the twin bonfires licked the sky, but they were beyond the sight of the revellers.

'You wanted to see me, Mistress Clare?'

She held her torch at an angle so it would not drip hot pitch on her fingers. 'You can call me Clare from now on, Gavin.' Gavin. She had never used his name.

He lifted an eyebrow. 'Oh? And why would you allow me such a privilege?'

'As a husband, it will be your prerogative. In fact, I think a husband can call his wife anything he wants.'

'A husband?' His smile disappeared, replaced by a look as intense as that of the falcon fixed on her prey.

'That's right. You have won the prize. Received the day's laurel from the lady's hand. In fact—' she laughed, because if she didn't, she would cry '—you have received the lady's hand itself. And everything that goes with it.'

Emotions chased each other across his eyes behind the flames, so fast she couldn't catch them. Was that one disbelief? Wonder? Lust?

Joy?

He took her free hand, bowed deeply and pressed his lips to her fingers. 'The *comte*'s loss is my gain.'

She snatched her hand away, hating the reminder of Alain's refusal. 'Of course, you've won something much more important than my hand. This tower and land, if you can hold it.'

She chattered to keep him, the thought of him, at bay. Otherwise, there would be only a man and a woman in the dark with the thought of what a husband and wife can do together.

'You chose your side of the border,' she began. 'Now, you must keep the border where it is. Because make no mistake, the Inglis on the other side of that ridge will nudge and shove and push, trying to make that line give way. And whether David or Edward or Robert or William or James or Matilda of Norway rules Scotland, they'll keep pushing. So you had better be ready, because in the end, holding that line will be a lot more important than holding me.'

The languid, bowing courtier rose, transformed into the dark warrior she had met that first day in the hills. 'I will hold it.' Certainty rang in his words.

And when he raised his eyes, she saw an emotion she recognised. Elation.

So now she knew. His joy was for Scotland, not for her.

She turned away, letting the torchlight play on the rugged stones of the wall. 'Good. Because that is the reason for this marriage. You have my hand, but that's the only part of me you *will* have.'

Gavin swallowed, unable to speak, thinking of her, a home, and everything he'd ever dared to want lying within reach. 'I hope our marriage will be about more than that.'

'Our marriage will be about *only* that. My father and Lord Douglas have the right to dispose of my life as they choose. They have chosen to give it to you. And now I will be tied to this wretched place for the rest of my life.'

She hunched her shoulders and gazed towards the hilltop, crowned with flame, looking like a falcon with clipped wings.

The truth of it hit him. It had not been Alain she wanted. It was France. 'You want to leave here as much as I want to come home.'

'You think this is your home?'

'It can be. I want it to be.'

'Well, now you will have what you want.'

'Not without you.'

She shook her head. 'You mean you can't have it without me, not that you don't want it without me.'

He started to protest, but she held up her hand. 'No flattering lies, Fitzjohn. You do not do them well. You encouraged my father's glorious little plan. But I won't play. If he wants to hold this castle so much, let him give it to you. Take it. Hold it. Make it yours.'

'That's not all he wants.'

'I know. He wants grandchildren, blood of his loins, manning the ramparts until the Second Coming. He wants to be remembered. So how does that make you feel? Like a breeding ram?'

Her vehemence left him speechless. What had become of the lady afraid of breaking the bounds of propriety? Alain's refusal had unleashed a new Clare: even more sharp-spoken than the one who had shut her chamber door in his face.

An ironic smile tilted his lips. 'I feel honoured that he'd trust my blood to mingle with his. Many would spit on it instead.'

Guilt flashed on her face, then the meek lady returned. 'I'm sorry. I should not have spoken so.'

'You do not believe you should have spoken, yet you believe what you said.' She coloured. 'You are no better at flattering lies than I.'

'I tried.' Her words were for herself. Not for him. 'I tried to be a lady worthy of a knight.'

'And I,' he whispered to himself, 'a knight worthy of a lady. So we both have failed.'

Yet knowing what would be his, he felt like the victor instead. He took the torch from her hand and pulled her to him with his other arm. 'Dance with me, Clare,' he said, giddy with the scent of her. 'No one can see us but the stars.'

She hid her face against his shoulder and he held her close. 'You see?' he said, as they swayed in silence. 'I can be that man, the one who dances with you under the new moon and rides with you across the hills.'

He had hoped to make her lift her head, laugh and smile. Instead, in the silence, he felt the dampness of her tears stain his tunic.

'Then a kiss,' he said, tightening his hold as he felt

her slip away. 'To seal the betrothal. To celebrate Beltane and pray for fertility.'

She stiffened, as if she would do no more than stand and endure, tolerating his embrace without yielding to it. But he wanted more than that. He wanted her spirit unleashed, as well as her tongue.

He bent to whisper in her ear, 'Think of it, Clare. Of you and me alone in the dark with no one to say us nae.'

Her breath quickened. 'A husband has rights. You will take them.'

'I want more than rights.' He wanted the core of this woman. He wanted that loving, laughing partnership she had spoken of. He wanted something he had never seen, and barely imagined. Maybe it didn't exist for someone like him. But just maybe…

'Come now, Clare. We know you can respond to a kiss.'

He took her lips.

She had refused seduction. This was claiming.

He could not take her here, now, but tonight, he would do more than dance. He would mark her as his.

His tongue plundered the sweetness of her mouth. Something deep within her responded, despite her resistance. He could feel her ease against him, her breasts pressing against his chest, her lips softening with eagerness.

Dance forgotten, he threw the torch to the ground, needing both hands. One held her close, while with the other he explored the land that would be his. He cupped her soft cheek against his palm, sweeping the tears away. Then he let his fingers trail down her neck and come to rest on her shoulder where his thumb could explore the hollows of her delicate collarbone.

Not lifting his lips from hers, he let his hand move lower, searching for her breast through the rough wool of her dress.

She stiffened when he found it, resistance returning, but he no longer made any pretence of chivalry. He curved his fingers around her breast, then pulled his hand away until he could tweak its tip, relishing her involuntary gasp.

Her fingers fisted on his shoulders, but she did not push him away.

Frustrated with the woollen armour that protected her, he let his hand leave her breast and move lower. At first, she sighed with relief, not knowing his intent. Then he rubbed the heel of his hand against her skirt, searching through the layers for the mound between her thighs, pushing the fabric between her legs with his finger.

She gasped.

Her legs parted, her knees gave way, and she sagged, crying out, as he would hear her, soon, in his bed. He reached for her hand, pressing it between his legs where she could feel his desire—

'Clare? Are you there?'

At the sound of Euphemia's voice, she pushed him so hard that he stumbled. 'Yes.' The word unrecognisable.

The girl's steps came closer. 'Is something wrong?'

'No. Nothing.'

He leaned down to pick up the low-burning torch,

grateful they had been outside the circle of light. Neither he, nor Clare, had an extra breath.

Euphemia joined them. 'It's time to pass the bannocks.'

Clare nodded. 'I'm coming.'

'We are not yet finished, Clare,' he muttered.

But unless he could persuade her heart as well as her body, he feared their marriage, indeed, might be finished before it started.

Chapter Twelve

Clare, still shaking, took one sack from Euphemia and let her keep the other.

The girl smiled. 'So you like him better now, do you?'

'Mind the affairs that are your own, Euphemia.'

You and me alone in the dark.

If she gave him all he asked for, would he want it still? Or perhaps they were a match, his darkness visible, hers hidden.

They started back up the hill.

She needed her mother tonight. Needed to know whether a woman might feel so desirous of a man she was to wed. Wanted to know what her mother would have thought of Fitzjohn, whether she would approve.

She scolded herself for even wondering. Her mother would have been appalled to know how close her daughter had come to succumbing to him tonight, outside, where anyone might have passed, like the most wanton harlot.

Your mother came out to play. Was that possible? Her vision of her mother, a child's, was turning inside out as she looked with a woman's eyes.

At the top of the hill, men, women and children jostled them, each grabbing for a cake of eggs, butter, milk and oatmeal, baked before the fires had gone dark and then brought out for feasting.

And one of them was crossed with charcoal.

Her mother had hated this part of the celebration. And so did she. It represented everything that was wrong with this pagan, superstitious place.

Good fellowship had become quarrelsome. This year, they celebrated not only the arrival of summer, but the departure of the Inglis and the war. Relief released demons. Fights broke out on the edge of the crowd.

Euphemia, flushed, happy, humming, trailed smiles in her wake, not just from the sweetness of the cakes. Could it be, after all, only her sunny disposition men liked? Like Murine, she seemed at peace, even happy, with the world, herself and her lot.

Envy stained Clare's heart. All her life, it seemed, she had wanted to be someone or somewhere else.

She felt Fitzjohn beside her and refused to look at him, uncertain what to do. How was it possible to be wild in a man's arms one moment and speak calmly before people the next?

She held out the sack, trying to calm her breath. 'Do you know what this is? Everyone takes a cake. Whoever gets the marked one is made Green Man.'

It sounded like an honour. It was not.

In the hills, long ago, perhaps the marked man had been an offering to the gods, given up to be devoured by the flames with a prayer for a fruitful summer. Now, the victim was pelted with eggshells, swung towards the fire as a mock sacrifice, then shunned for the night.

He put his hand into the sack and drew out a bannock. 'My mother's people did it a little differently, but yes, I remember.'

She lowered her gaze. And gasped.

He had the marked oat cake.

She reached for it, meaning to throw it back in the bag, but the man next to him had noticed. 'It's him!'

As the men and women around him saw what was in his hand, they fell silent and stared.

He dropped his gaze from her face, and when he saw what was in his hand, he sighed.

'So today, as on so many other days, I shall be treated as the man dead.'

He stared at the bannock, wishing he could drop it or crush it or throw it into the fire. Too late. God's confirmation of what so many of them already thought seemed branded on his hand.

Hope's whisper, drowned by the crowd's rising murmurs. No home here, either. Even his bride-to-be shunned him. Well, he'd been condemned for fire. Now he would be its symbolic sacrifice.

Would this, at last, burn all his sins away?

The first eggshell hit his face.

He squeezed the marked cake in his fist, refusing to flinch. It would do no good to run. His sins and his father's, true or false, would follow him. Inevitable.

Yet he would not, could not, deny who he was, nor seek redemption for things he had never done.

* * *

Clare flinched as an eggshell hit his cheek.

Then another. Then more. Hesitant at first. Then faster.

The custom was to be a jest, but snarls, not smiles, touched these faces. Ale fuelled suppressed fears. The mixed feelings so many held for him boiled over. He was, after all, a stranger still and easy to hate.

'Inglis bastard!'

'Whoreson!'

Mothers covered their children's ears and pulled them away.

Eggshells turned into rocks.

'Stop it! Now!' Strange, to hear herself scream. 'He's not what you think.'

And she wondered how she knew, she who had scorned him even more than the rest. But she had not intended this. Never this.

A few who heard her tried to hold back the others, but two of the peasants, emboldened by drink and the licence of the day, jumped on Gavin, knocking him to the ground.

'What if he *is* guilty?' one of them yelled. 'He started the fire too easily.'

'And you would have condemned his soul as unclean if he hadn't been able to spark it,' she said, barely able to hear herself over the pounding in her ears.

'Maybe this time,' he said, eyes meeting hers as he was dragged away, 'I will be reborn.'

What had she seen there? Resignation. Hope. Love. Farewell.

Angus ran up and clung to Gavin's leg, as if one small

boy could save him. But he was no match for two men, even if they were wobbly with drink.

'Angus! Find the baron!' Only he could stop this now.

Wide-eyed, he ran.

Two men-at-arms joined in. Men who had eaten beside him. Each took a leg and, with the two holding his arms, they swung him towards the leaping flames. It was the usual ritual, done in jest.

She heard no laughter now.

Alain appeared beside her, but made no move to intervene.

She grabbed his arm. 'Stop them!'

He crossed his arms, unmoving. 'Who cares about an English bastard's soul?'

His chivalry. All for show. 'You have no honour if you will not lift a finger for a fellow knight.'

She looked back at Gavin. What if they slipped and flung him into the flames?

And then someone's hand did slip. And the world stopped as he flew into the air.

But the men's throw was as loose as their grip. Instead of landing in the flames, he fell to earth, rolled on his side, then jumped to his feet to stand between the twin fires.

He faced a mob, ready to surge.

She ran, no thought now but prayer, circled behind the fire, and reached him first.

Ashes smeared his cheek and his clothes. The flickering flames glinted on the golden streaks in his hair.

He looked like an angel unfairly cast out of Heaven.

But which one? Michael or Lucifer?

She stepped in front of him, facing the mass of snarling faces. She was the mistress of Carr's Tower. Surely they would listen. 'Please—'

A rock sailed out of the crowd. Gavin blocked her body with his. She flinched as the rock hit his chest. 'It's too late,' he said. 'Get behind me.'

Funnelled into the narrow path between the fires, two men, one of them a man-at-arms, ran towards him, fists raised.

'Stop this!' her father bellowed from the mob's edge. 'Stop it right now!'

A few, still sober enough to recognise their lord's voice, paused, but most were too far gone to know anything except that they were spoiling for a fight.

The first man took a swing at Gavin, who countered with a punch to the stomach.

She crouched down to search for discarded wood she could use as a club, reluctant to pull her dagger against her own men.

Gavin felled the first man, but the next one stepped over him, fists ready. Two of the men-at-arms fought their way to the front to stand beside Gavin.

She found an unburned branch, grabbed it with both hands, and rose.

'Clare! Get out of here!' Gavin yelled.

The mêlée began.

Chapter Thirteen

Gavin and the two others fought side by side, protecting her from flailing fists and feet. Alain had disappeared, but Angus, determined to prove himself a man, ran back to stand with them.

She cringed as fist met flesh and strained to distinguish Gavin's shouts from Angus's cries and the howls of their foes. Her father had disappeared, but she thought she glimpsed Murine, tugging some of the stragglers away by their ears and slapping them sober.

Even in the flickering, uncertain light, she could see bruises near Gavin's eye, cuts on his knuckles and blood smeared across his torn tunic.

They seemed to gain the upper hand, slowly, as the opponents spent their energy and their intoxication.

Then, her father pushed past her, having worked his way around the crowd. Standing shoulder to shoulder with Gavin, he stretched out his arms.

'Stop it, the whole bungfued lot of you! This is the

man my daughter will marry! This is the man who will hold Carr's Tower!'

Stunned, they stopped.

The crackle of fading flames filled the uncertain silence.

One man, head down, wiped his hand on his tunic, then held it out. Gavin, gracious, shook it.

More, but not all, followed. Some, muttering, turned their backs.

It would not be easy, as she had warned her father, for Fitzjohn to be master here.

Celebration spent, mothers lit a stick from the bonfire and led sleepy children down the hill, crumbs clinging to their cheeks. The rest trailed behind, each taking a burning faggot to rekindle the home fire.

Her father's knees, suddenly weak, gave way. Gavin caught him. Murine came to his other side. He waved them away, but needed their support, one on either side, as he staggered back down the hill.

Clare grabbed a brand from the fire and followed, Angus at her side.

Inside the wall, Murine motioned Gavin to the left. 'We can take him to my cottage,' Murine said.

'No.' Clare put out a hand to stop them. 'He should be in his own room.'

Murine had little patience in her glance. 'Would you force him to mount the stairs to sooth your pride?'

The woman's question shrivelled her tongue. The world was upside down. Knights without honour. Men against master. What difference would it make, if a lord slept in a limmer's bed?

They carried him inside, weaker now. Angus ran for

water. Clare touched her brand to the neatly laid kindling on the hearth.

The white rowan blossoms had shrivelled.

The cottage was clean, but barren. Why would her father choose to stay here night after night?

'You may leave now, Murine. I'll take care of him.'

The woman drew herself up to her full height. 'No, Mistress Clare, I will nae. I am not his wife nor his daughter, but I have been by his side these ten years. I will not leave now.'

Clare was too tired to argue. Or she knew it would be useless.

Or, maybe, she knew the woman had earned her place.

So they worked together, wiping off the blood, soothing the bruises. Murine brewed a sleeping draught and applied the yarrow-leaf ointment to stop the bleeding and the pain.

And finally, Clare knew she must leave him there.

She rose, back aching, and looked around, wondering where Gavin had gone. Then she lit a brand to take to her room.

'Murine,' she said, pausing at the door.

The woman looked up, barely noticing her in her concentration on her father.

'Thank you.'

And she recognised the smile. It was the same as Euphemia's.

The flickering brand was a small circle of comfort as she crossed to the tower and climbed the stairs to the third level. All the time he had been at war, she had blocked the thought of her father's death. Now that he was home, it seemed impossible he could survive the battles and be bested in a drunken brawl.

To lose her father, too, was more than she could face. But the years ran swiftly. She could see frailty that she had wilfully ignored before. He must see it, too, knowing the road before was shorter than the one behind. And that his daughter must be protected before he reached the end.

Even if that meant marrying her to Gavin Fitzjohn.

In her chamber, she touched the flame to the wood on the hearth, rekindling the fire that had been smothered for the Beltane relighting.

The blaze illuminated the room, her small sanctuary of beauty and order, exactly as she had left it. Her ivory triptych. Her precious copy of *Miroir des preudes femmes*. The red-and-gold banker.

How could it look the same when all had changed?

When all was lost.

Her shoulders drooped. There would be no marriage to Alain. No home in France. No escape from the land of horror she had faced tonight. Nothing left of the hopes she had clung to in order to survive each day.

Numb, she changed into her night robe. She had thought she knew Alain. Had trusted her feelings and been so, so wrong. Alain had rejected her. She had even less reason to trust Gavin.

Unless she was wrong about him, too.

She heard his step in the hall. At the door.

Gavin walked in without asking leave, still covered with dirt and ash and sweat, his chest heaving as though he had run a long distance.

She had defended him against the mob, but the man

before her embodied everything she had feared in him from the first.

He stepped towards her, a dare, like dark fire in his eyes.

She reached for her dirk and pointed it at him, trying to keep the blade steady. She could see his wounds. A black eye. A bloody cheek. Swollen knuckles. Chest, bared by a shredded tunic, covered with cuts.

Yet his eyes were fierce as ever.

She swallowed, trying to choke down the fear. He had said he did not burn that church, but if he had, he would certainly not hesitate to lie about it.

Yet still, her chest rose and fell in time with his.

'No closer.' The dirk, at the end of her arm, quivered.

'Everywhere I've been tonight, someone has threatened me. Now, I'm going anywhere I please. So don't hold that blade on me unless you mean to use it.'

He leaned closer, making sure the knifepoint touched his bare chest, moved as if, with one more step, he might impale himself on the knife.

She watched it waver, knowing that she hadn't the strength, or the will, to push it in.

'Look at me.'

She did.

He grabbed her shaking hand and raised the blade to the hollow at the base of his throat. There, even she could inflict a fatal wound. 'Now,' he said, still holding her fingers captive. 'Run me through.'

He said it as if he would welcome death.

He let go of her hand, but his eyes did not release

hers. She tried to read them in the flickering light. What could she see? Despair? Surrender?

No. His eyes asked her to save him.

And she didn't know how.

She didn't move the blade, but he knew, now, that she wouldn't. He pushed her hand away and the dirk clattered to the floor.

Heat washed through her, and not just from the fire. She backed away. She should run, out of reach of his dirty, sweaty, bloody hands so they wouldn't stain her gown.

Or touch her lips.

Or expose the secret of her desire for him.

'You believe them, don't you?' Rage scorched his words. 'You believe them all. Despite everything I've told you, you believe every laidly thing they've said about me.'

Denial stuck in her throat.

'It's more than that, isn't it?' He turned his head, studying her as if he could strip away not only her clothes, but the façade that covered everything she tried to hide. 'Not only do you believe it. It excites you.'

'No.' But he was right. The game of love, he had called it. Whatever she would have with this man, it would be no game, but a wild flight of life and death.

And if she dared it, there would be no one to catch her when she fell.

Smiling. Always smiling as if he knew a jest she did not understand. 'And now that we're to be married, you know there will be more than kisses.'

'Stop! Go find someone who wants your kisses.'

'I have. *You* want them.' He gripped her arms and

pressed his body against her, his lips so close that she could feel his breath and almost taste the sweat on his skin.

Wanted to taste the blood on his lips.

'Now, Mistress Clare, I believe this is where we were when we were rudely interrupted.'

She held her breath, waiting, expecting, and closed her eyes.

He plundered her mouth, tasting, taking all that he had before and more. But this time, the limits, if there had ever been any, were gone.

Swept to places she wanted, and feared, to go, she kissed him back. His sweat stained her gown and his hand cupped her breast, not with a rough grab, but with an insistent rhythm that pulled her along, made her sway against him.

Where she could feel his hardness.

He broke from her mouth and his lips moved on to her throat, kissing the moan that rattled there. And at the vulnerable hollow, the place her dagger had hesitated on him, his tongue circled, gently, pausing before it trailed down.

Her gown slipped off one shoulder. The night air cooled her breast just before he covered it with his mouth. The soft tip became a craving void, the world no bigger than her breast and his mouth and desire.

She stumbled backwards and fell on to the bed.

He leaned on his arms over her, far enough away that she could see his eyes again. 'Not so afraid, after all.'

Dirt and blood smeared her sleeve. A stain that would never come out.

'Get out.' She tried to hit him with the words, but her breaths were coming fast as her heartbeat.

He stood, moving as comfortably as if the room were already his. 'It's not me you're fighting, Clare. It's yourself. So sleep well and dream of our wedding night.'

He had not taken her, but she knew he could.

And now, so did he.

Chapter Fourteen

Gavin relived the entire night in his dreams: the fire, the fight, her desire.

He woke to regrets.

The last shred of chivalry he clung to had been stripped from him last night. He had wanted to claim her, to mark her as his. Instead, he had proved again why she would never want to be his.

He had known there could be no home, no wife for him. Known that the escape he longed for would be brief. But he had allowed a waking dream, daring to want more. These hills, this tower.

Her.

He'd had women a-plenty, but he had let none of them get close enough to see whether he was as bad as they feared. Or hoped.

He had wanted someone who could accept, even share the darkness of his soul, to open a window and let in the light, so that he would not be so alone there.

But no one could. Least of all this wounded bird of a woman, tied to another man and her past.

Last night had proved why it was impossible. To most of them, he would for ever be the son of a hated enemy. Shunned, not trusted.

To her, he would be worse. He would be the man who could release everything within her she tried to hide.

He saw beneath her veil, glimpsed what bound them. Behind her cool eyes and her stone-hard stare was a woman who feared her own desires.

And hated him for unleashing them.

Married, alone together, would there be any boundaries they wouldn't cross?

Neither of them, he thought, was ready to find out.

No, there was no future for him here. It was time to move on.

He rose. He would tell the baron. Now.

He ducked to enter Murine's small cottage with the smoke-blackened walls. Humbler even than the rough stone tower, yet the old man preferred it. Maybe this was *his* escape, from demons or memories, Gavin couldn't guess.

The baron sat on the edge of the bed this morning, bandaged, but smiling. If he hadn't known better, Gavin would have wondered whether the old man had exaggerated last night's injuries.

Old man. He thought of him that way, for he was ten years older than his own father would have been.

'Ah, there ye are, Fitzjohn.'

Murine, stirring soup over the fire, nodded.

'How are you feeling this morning?' Gavin asked.

'Always better after a good brawl.' He rotated his shoulder, as if shaking off a final twinge. 'You?'

'Well enough.' He wished for someone to soothe and clean his cuts and put a compress on his bruises. Instead, he had washed in cold water, left in the basin. 'Last night, in the heat of the moment, you said some things.'

'Yes, I did. Told you I would.'

What could he say now? He'd sound ungrateful to refuse. 'I wanted to tell you I would understand. You can renege.'

Murine handed the man a cup and he slurped it, then licked his lips. 'Break my word? Why would I do that?'

Because Clare will never have me. And I can scarcely blame her.

'Your daughter would thank you.'

He snorted. 'She'll thank me when she's wed you, though she doesn't know it now.'

No wonder the woman struggled so. Had any man—her father, the *comte*, Douglas—ever considered her feelings? It was a woman's lot, of course, but she was treated with no more consideration than her birds, expected to fly and hunt on command.

'But you saw those men last night, even a few of the men-at-arms. They wanted to kill me.' And he had fought back.

It seemed, at least, that he was not yet ready to die.

'You held your own. They'll come around.'

The old man had more faith in him than he had in himself. Suddenly, he wanted to deserve it. 'Sir.'

The baron looked up from buckling his belt.

'Sir, I didn't burn that church.'

Clare's father sighed and shook his head. 'I know that.'

'How?'

'You said so before.'

That had not been enough for Clare. 'But everyone says—'

'What they want to hear. But I'm glad to know the truth.' The man clapped a hand on his shoulder. 'Come. I'll send a message to Lord Douglas. As soon as he and a priest arrive, we'll have a wedding!'

A wedding. To a woman who surely thought Gavin was Lucifer himself.

Well, a woman, even this one, could be lured. Like the falcon, trained to follow her natural instincts.

Even if she didn't yet know what they were.

If Clare had hopes her father would reconsider in the light of day, they were dashed. He made a formal announcement of their betrothal at the midday meal, right after he had told the men their ale portions would be cut for a week as punishment for the brawl.

A few of the men had grumbled under their breath, but some had grown to trust Fitzjohn, so the rest, ashamed of last night's clash, muted their complaints. She had even heard a few apologies, though not from Thom, the man-at-arms who had thrown the first blow.

Fitzjohn, at least, stood humbly quiet. She could not have borne it if he had celebrated his new power over her.

After the meal, she escaped to the mews, to cry unobserved. Through the blur of her tears, she watched

Wee One, hovering close to her nest, taking food from her mate.

'Ye'll lose them all,' Neil had grumbled, shaking his head. 'A rogue tercel. Breeding birds. Ye're courting calamity.'

She had blocked her ears. Wee One, at least, would raise a happy family. It was more than Clare could hope for now.

She came closer and saw one—no, two new eggs in the nest, each a rich, mottled reddish brown, so beautiful she wanted to cradle them in her hand.

The door to the mews opened and closed, softly. She heard Gavin's step, but refused to turn her head.

'You're determined to do this, aren't you?' His voice, gentle.

'As determined as you are for this wedding.' She looked over her shoulder. 'At least she chose her own mate. Now, she's building a family. How could I take that from her?'

Wee One turned to her nest, pushing one of the eggs towards the edge of the ledge with her beak until it fell off.

Heart pounding, Clare stuck out her hand in time and caught it. 'What's she doing?' She tried to put the egg back, but the bird screeched at her and she pulled her hand away, barely avoiding being pecked.

The egg, still warm, rested in her cupped palm. Poor babe, not even born, but already rejected. 'Why would a mother do that?'

'Look,' he said, pointing. A crack, barely visible, scarred the shell. 'It would never have hatched.'

She nodded, sadly, and put it aside. Another of life's

brutalities. 'I just thought of that poor chick, rejected before it was even born.' Clare swallowed foolish tears, railing against something inextricably part of God's plan.

'She has no soul. She's a wild animal.'

'She's a mother.' Something inside her wanted to scream 'How could she?'

Gavin's eyes searched hers, but he didn't answer. Silent, they turned and left the mews together. She had already let him see too much.

All over again, she felt angry at her mother, dead all these years, gone when Clare needed her. How was she to marry this savage stranger without a mother's guidance?

And beyond that, how was she to *be* a mother without a mother to teach her, without a mother to ask?

Facing her future, she felt as abandoned and unworthy as the damaged egg.

She must hide whatever it was that had made her so unlovable to her mother, to Alain. There could be no more sharing with this man by her side.

Bad as he was, she must not let him leave her, too.

Joyless and uncertain, Clare began wedding preparations.

What food should be served? What dress should she wear? Each step was solitary drudgery without her mother, or at least a woman of her own station, to share it with.

A few days later, Murine knocked on her chamber door. Clare, trying to choose among three dresses draped across the bed, refused to acknowledge her at first, but the short, plump woman with a few strands of grey in her chestnut hair waited, patient, but immovable.

'What is it, Murine?' Clare said, finally.

'Ye'll be worrying about the marriage.'

She flushed. The last thing she wanted was to discuss her impending marriage with her father's bedmate. 'I have nothing to say to you about it.'

'Well, I've a few things to say to ye and it's time ye listened.'

Clare blinked, taken aback. Common as she was, the woman had always known her place before.

'I know ye don't like me,' Murine began, as if these were words she had practiced, 'and why, but the truth is, I love yer fader and because I do, I love ye like me own.'

'I most certainly am not—'

'Hush and let me finish. Yer fader worries about ye.'

'He waited too long for that.' Tears stung her eyes. When she was a sad, frightened little girl who needed a father's comfort, he had sent her away so he could dally with this woman.

'Ye blame him for not mourning yer mither still. She was a fine woman, and he loved her dearly. But a man's not meant to live alone. And I've made him glad.'

It was true, and Clare begrudged it. 'Go on.'

'Can't ye accept him as he is instead of wishing he could be what ye want him to be?'

No. She could no more do that than she could accept Gavin that way.

Or herself.

'If he truly cared for me, he would never have

arranged this marriage. He did it to satisfy himself, not me.'

And even as she said it, she knew the folly of the words. What woman expected a marriage to be arranged for her pleasure?

'I tried to make ye happy, too, but...' Murine shrugged. 'No one can do that if ye insist on being unhappy.'

'You have no right to talk that way. Happiness comes to those who attain perfection with God in Heaven,' she said, knowing how far she was from that.

'Well, ye seem determined to avoid the bits some of us cling to here below.'

She opened her mouth to recite her woes. A motherless childhood. A distant father. A lover's rejection. A forced marriage with a man she feared and tied to a life she hated.

But right now, the dresses seemed more important than all that. She looked at the bed and the colours blurred before her eyes. Blue, red, cream. Which was a bride's? 'My mother should be here to help me.'

'Well, yer mither's been dead these ten years. That's a long time to carry grief.'

'My father certainly did not carry it so long.'

Murine's eyes met hers. 'I carried the pain of me husband's passing, too.'

Flushed with embarrassment, Clare gasped. 'I'm sorry,' she stammered. So good at seeing her own pain, she had been blind to others'. She thought she was the only one ever left alone, but all around her, people bore losses beyond speaking.

'Ye drag the past with you like the bells on those

birds of yers. Any time ye might forget, the bell rings so ye can remember and resent it all over again.'

Sinking to sit on the wooden chest, she let the tears go, and let Murine pat her shoulder. How could this woman know her so well? 'But I thought Alain…and then he…and I don't even know what I did wrong.' All her fault, in truth, and not her father's at all.

Murine held her at arm's length and looked her squarely in the eye. 'Ye? Me thinks it's the Frenchman who's a fool if he couldn't see how lucky he'd be to have ye.'

The blunt speech startled a laugh. She had not expected such words from a woman who had just criticised her roundly. She smiled, wiping her eyes on her sleeve, trying to remember whether her mother had ever lavished her with such praise.

'Well, this is the marriage Da wanted, so this is the one he'll get.' She sighed. 'Though I don't know why.'

Murine's smile was knowing. 'Ye will.' She patted Clare's cheek. 'Ye got the best part of the bargain.'

She put little store in the words. Murine had no concept of the courtly life. She spoke only out of her loyalty to Clare's father.

Still, a small corner of Clare's heart smiled. 'Well, at least I got the man who knows the falcons. The *comte* hunted no better than an ill-trained kyte.'

Their laughter mingled. Clare waved her hand at the dresses. 'So which one, Murine?'

The woman looked carefully at each, smoothing the fabric, picking away a stray thread. Then, she pointed. 'The blue. It will set off your eyes.' She grinned. 'And his.'

Clare found herself still smiling after Murine left.

Chapter Fifteen

Marry in May, rue for aye. That was how the saying went.

Yet it was June before they could gather Lord Douglas and a priest educated enough to perform a nuptial mass and Clare feared she would rue the day just as heartily.

At table the day before the wedding, her father, Douglas and his men celebrated more heartily than she or Gavin. Her husband-to-be, surrounded by an increasingly rowdy group, sat wearing his best half-smile, silent.

Clare, with Murine and Euphemia, worked tirelessly to keep the platters full. It was Clare's task to be sure that Lord Douglas had the best cut of meat and that his cup was never empty.

An easy task. The man drank little.

After the meal, he waved her over, refusing the brogat. 'Come. I would speak with you alone.'

He rose, and Clare glanced at Murine, who nodded that she would keep food and drink flowing.

'Lord Douglas.' Clare stepped quickly to match his strides as he left the Hall behind. 'We are honoured to have you here.'

'Of course,' was his only answer. After ten years as *de facto* ruler of the Borders, he was a man comfortable with his power.

He led her up the stairs to the gallery and fresh air. One lonely man had drawn the lot and been left to scan the countryside for danger. He straightened to see Lord Douglas, then moved out of earshot when the man motioned him away.

'Now,' Douglas said, turning his eyes on her, 'tell me of this man you are to marry.'

She cleared her throat, trying to think. Douglas had made his promise years ago. Faced with the real man to whom he would entrust these lands, he might rethink his pledge.

She chose her words carefully. 'What has my father told you?' If her father had kept Gavin's parentage a secret, everything could change once Lord Douglas discovered the truth.

And what would happen to her, to all of them, then?

His grim expression darkened. 'That he's Eltham's son.'

So he knew. She should have expected as much. Gavin had said that his name was reviled throughout Scotland.

'Why should I give these lands to an Inglis enemy? Has your father's brain gone feeble?'

She refused to admit she had wondered the same. She must give Douglas no reason to doubt her father.

'I'm sure he does not expect your blessing until you, too, can be satisfied that the man supports Scotland.'

He looked at her sharply. 'You're the woman he's to wed. Does he?'

What could she say? That he was not an enemy? Did she even believe that? Yet the consequences now, should everything crumble around them, were as frightening as the marriage.

'He has as much Scottis blood as Inglis.' The words he had said so often warmed her mouth.

'And as many ties to Edward as to David. And none to me.'

Douglas wanted a man as loyal to himself as to the Bruce. 'He has chosen his side.' She touched the stone wall, thinking of the hunger in Gavin's eyes when he looked at the land. 'He will die to hold this land for you.'

That, at least, she did believe.

He looked at her, assessing. 'So he will be loyal to me.'

Douglas. David. Scotland. She had never thought there to be a difference. 'Yes.' Even she could hear the wobble in the word.

The man was quiet for a time, looking north towards all of Scotland. Finally, he turned back to her. 'Be sure the man gets you with babe. That way, if something happens, I will name a guardian until the child is of age.'

Silent, she followed him back down the stairs. That's all you'll have of me, she had said. But it had not been true then and it was less so now. Scottis or Inglis, she would have to take him to her bed.

And the thought was not near as distasteful as it should have been.

* * *

The fire burned low as Gavin listened to Lord Douglas. The man, in a triumphant mood, regaled them with boastful tales as the evening tired. How he had hounded Edward back across the border. How he had then kept riding and rousted the English loyalists from Galloway and Kyle and even the mighty castle of Caerlaverock.

'There's the last of him,' he concluded, with a grim smile, directed at Gavin. 'Edward *and* his de Baliol puppet.'

He said it as if expecting Gavin to speak.

Standing on the other side of the border had not brought the peace he had hoped. Scottis as he was, Gavin could not rejoice in the English defeat, so he remained silent. He was Clare's intended, but promises to the baron notwithstanding, Douglas could undo everything with a word.

His eyes sought Clare, as they usually did when he was not aware of his thoughts.

Then, Douglas's hand fell on his shoulder, hearty as a blow. Brown eyes burrowed into Gavin's, as if reading his doubts.

'You're to keep this tower, Fitzjohn.'

He nodded. 'So I vow.'

Douglas did not relax his gaze. 'I've given you an easy task. I've made a truce with Northhampton until Michaelmas.'

Northhampton was English Warden of the March, as powerful on his side of the border as Douglas on his. 'You no longer need King David and King Edward to make war and peace?'

Douglas drew back his hand. 'I never did.'

The words chilled him. How many sides were there to this war? 'So you will press for King David's release now.'

Douglas sipped his brew. 'Perhaps.'

Gavin had not thought he asked a question. He wondered, not for the first time, whether Douglas really wanted David back. With the English gone and David captive, Lord Douglas, along with the Stewart, was as powerful as a king himself.

'What would stop us from bringing him home?' Gavin said, cautiously.

Lord Douglas grunted. 'The ransom they want would bleed us dry. I won't pay it.'

I. As if the decision, the money and the country were his.

'Besides,' Douglas continued, 'David thinks to give the throne to a son of England.' He spat.

'Instead of to Robert Stewart or to you?' he asked the question calmly, wondering whether the man would pull his dirk.

'Instead of to someone who has spent his life defending this land against the laidly Inglis while "David Drip-on-altar" warmed his toes by Edward's fire.'

He had not heard such a slur against King David in all his years in England. 'I shared that fire with him,' Gavin said, jaw tight. A life in exile was no life at all. 'He's spent ten years in England because his countrymen are too cheap and too stubborn to bring him home.'

'Which side are you on, Fitzjohn?'

When he chose Scotland, he chose King David. Were

his loyalties to be divided again? 'I've chosen my side, Douglas. Would you have me choose between you and my King?'

'You must choose Scotland, no matter who is King.' The man met his eyes, searching.

'I thought that as long as a Douglas had a say, a Bruce would be King.'

Lord Douglas blinked. He could not dispute that as long as the heart of a Bruce decorated Lord Douglas's shield. 'Tell me, Gavin Fitzjohn, why did you come back?'

'Scotland is my home.' Despite the years away, his feet had recognised the ground. 'And now, so is Carr's Tower.'

Douglas's glance was sceptical. 'Only by my grace and that of your strong right arm.'

'I've no doubts about the arm.'

Douglas frowned into his brew. 'I made a truce, not a peace. If you think holding the border will be easy, you are the wrong man.'

Must a man seek war instead of facing it to satisfy Douglas?

'Not easy, but I will hold it—for you and for Scotland, and for David the Bruce,' Gavin said. 'I'm sure you'd agree its time he sat on his throne again, instead of on Edward's chairs.'

Douglas's scowl was tinged with grudging admiration. 'Edward has appointed ten commissioners to sue for peace. I meet with them before I go to France.'

'I thought you were going on pilgrimage.'

'To Amiens.' He crossed himself. 'Thanks be to God for our defeat of the Inglis.'

The *comte* joined them. 'And if any Inglis dare to challenge us on French soil, we shall defeat them there, as well.' He raised his eyebrows, a challenge to Gavin, who had been an Englishman on French soil once.

'I've had my fill of war on French soil,' he answered. He let his eyes rest on Clare again. 'And I have a bride to enjoy.'

Beneath his moustache, the Frenchman's smile soured. 'It was not you that she wanted.'

Douglas's glance flickered from the *comte* to Gavin.

'It is now,' Gavin answered.

'Be sure of it,' Douglas said. 'I expect to see a babe in nine months.'

'Oh?' Gavin's unconcerned smile emerged to protect him again. 'Are there any other conditions of this union I need to know before I take the tower?'

Douglas's expression spoke of war, not of wedding. 'Only that you hold it. If you lose it to those men across the hill, you won't be the one to win it back.'

Gavin lifted his mug. 'I'll hold it.'

Douglas watched Clare approach with another round of brogat. Gavin saw their eyes meet, a glance exchanged, and wondered what they had talked about when they left the hall together.

The marriage had been the baron's idea. Douglas, like Clare, had been coerced into agreement.

Had his bride begged for release? To prevent the marriage?

Or something more sinister?

She had feared, even hated him. Enough for murder?

* * *

'Now leave the rest of this, Clare. Ye'll marry on the morrow and it's too late to be doing kitchen work.'

Clare untied her napron and smiled as Murine and Euphemia tried to shoo her away. Nothing could have been further from the castle of the de Garencieres family than the kitchen of Carr's Tower. Yet sharing with these women had given her a few bits of that happiness Murine had spoken of.

Maybe she could find a few to cling to with Gavin.

'Clare. A word.'

Startled, she looked up to see him at the door. Her body had begun to anticipate the wedding night. Each time she saw him now, it was harder to breathe.

'Now see?' Murine said. 'It's time for ye to go.'

But no smile touched Gavin's lips tonight, and her moment of anticipation wilted. He gripped her arm as if she were a captive as he pulled her towards the stairs.

On the dark level below, the empty dungeon and the cellar shared a floor that smelled of old wine, dried meat and mixed spices.

'You talked to Douglas,' he said, when they were alone.

'Yes.'

'Tell me what you said.'

'He wanted to know whether you would be loyal to him.'

'And if I wasn't?'

The doubts she had held at bay returned. 'I told him you were. I told him what you keep saying—that you have as much Scots blood as Inglis. Are you telling me I lied?'

'I am telling you nothing. I am asking whether you and Douglas are plotting a way to end this marriage.'

Jolted, she stared at him.

If something happens.

Douglas had promised a wedding. No one could promise long life. And he would not hesitate to slay Gavin if he felt his reasons were right. He had killed his own uncle to become leader of the family.

Being Douglas's enemy could be no more dangerous than being his friend.

'Well?' Gavin, impatient.

'I am not privy to his plans.' His eyes, so blue. As if he had stolen a piece of sky. She still feared him, but not for reasons she could share with Douglas. 'But mine include a wedding, not a burial.'

'A wedding and a birth.'

She shivered. Hot and cold, her blood rushed in anticipation. Close to him, in near darkness, he stirred her body without a touch.

After tomorrow, there would be no escape. She would be forced to accept this man into her body. Night after night, she would be caged with his darkness and her own. No rescue. No peace. And no idea where the path that joined them would lead.

She resented him, and her flesh, for making the idea so tempting.

'Yes, a birth. I know my duty.'

Was that shift in his gaze disappointment? 'And does your duty also include warning your husband if his life is threatened?'

'Yes.' She feared his touch, but she would not see him dead, and for reasons that went beyond wifely duty.

He touched her chin and turned her face towards the torchlight, searching her eyes in suspicious silence.

'Clare…' he said finally.

The word was a question.

She did not know how to answer.

He dropped his hand. 'Be sure of it.'

Turning his back, he mounted the stairs, leaving her alone and straddling a strange border between love and hate.

Chapter Sixteen

The wedding was over. The guests gone.

Alone in her room, Clare gazed out of her window as Alain, Douglas and their men rode away, the priest, on a slower horse, lagging behind. Douglas had no time to stay for a feast. They had left just after midday, heading for the ship that would take them to England and then to France.

Without her.

The hoofbeats faded, until only the wind's whine remained.

'Did you say your fond farewells?'

Gavin's voice startled her. She did not turn to meet his eyes.

'I bade our guests goodbye, of course.' She was glad Alain had gone. She could not have borne it, the next morning. The pounding at the door. The search for the bloody sheet. Alain's eyes looking at the evidence that she belonged to Gavin.

Behind her, she felt her husband move closer and waited for him to touch her as was now his right.

He didn't.

'He did not seem to mourn your marriage.'

She squeezed her eyes against the pain, more angry at Alain and herself than at Gavin because it was the truth.

'No. Only I do that.'

What a fool she had been. He had left with no more than a polite farewell, as if she had meant nothing to him.

No more than he, she realised now, had meant to her. A symbol, not a person. Someone who would have decorated her life like the banker graced her chest.

'Would you have me woo you now?'

She turned and he filled her eyes, too rough, too raw, too large, invading the space that had been her last haven.

'It's too late for that. We are wed. I have no escape.'

'Nor I.'

Fire and pain mixed in his eyes. She blinked against them. She didn't want to see his pain and feared the fire even more.

'If you wanted one,' she said, 'you should have spoken long ago.'

He did not want her. Not as she longed to be wanted. But at least he wanted the tower and the cattle and the sheep and the land that came with her. Alain had disdained even that.

'Come,' she said briskly, pushing him towards the bench beside the fire. The unfamiliar ring weighed heavy on her finger. 'I will tend to you.'

Eyes never leaving her, he sat. She knelt before him to unbutton his cote hardie. It was too tight, a gift from Lord Douglas since the man had carried nothing with him and there had been no time to send for fine cloth and make another.

Gifted. Just like his bride.

She fumbled with the buttons. He grabbed her hand. 'Since this duty displeases you so, I'll do it myself.'

She stood and backed away as he rose from the bench, pulled off the garment, and tossed it aside. He kicked off his soft boots and held out a hand.

She turned her back, refusing to yield to the desire to curl against his chest and lift her lips to his. But breaking the gaze changed nothing. Blood still pounded through her veins and pooled in her core.

She battled for a breath, resentment washed away by desire. She owed him the duty of a wife and would show him only that or she would drive him, too, away.

She fumbled with the ties at the back of her dress, trying to disrobe and get into bed quickly, as if hiding her body would hide her desire from him.

'Let me.' His fingers, deft, loosened the laces. His fingers, warm, brushed her back.

'No!' She ripped herself away from him, tugging awkwardly, until dress and chemise fell in a heap on the floor. She kicked them out of the way.

She had no more love for her wedding garb than he.

Keeping her back to him, she scrambled into her high, narrow bed and drew the covers to her chin. 'I am ready.'

He loomed over the bed, eyebrows raised. 'For what?'

Her heartbeat drowned his words. She swallowed. What words could she use for such intimacy? 'For... the act.'

Settling on the bed barely big enough for more than one, his knee nudged her legs. Yet when he leaned forwards, arm on his bent knee, he looked more comfortable than she.

'You appear ready for an execution.'

'Oh?' She sat up, but then slouched beneath the covers again as they fell away. 'Is my body not enough? Must you have heated glances and breathless moans? Then you must seek a different woman.'

She waited for him to simply take her, as he nearly had the night of Beltane. Or perhaps he would try to tempt her with the seductive smile that always coaxed the worst of her nature into the light of day.

But this time, no lazy smile lifted his lips or lit his eyes. This time, his furrowed brow reminded her of a golden eagle, about to destroy its prey.

He grabbed her shoulders, not gently, and the covers fell away, leaving her breasts cold and bare. And the moan she had disparaged threatened of its own.

'Hear me well.' Anger shimmered in every word. 'There will be no other woman. I may not be the chivalrous knight you dreamed of, but you forget that the token of such a knight's affections is a woman married to another man. I will not be so "chivalrous" as to court another man's wife, nor so generous as to forgive one who wants mine. Let there be no confusion. You married *me*.'

He released her shoulders, grabbed her left hand and held it up, rubbing the wedding ring circling her shaking finger. '*Vous et nul autre.*' The French words sounded like a death sentence. 'You and no other.' He leaned closer. 'Falcons mate for life.'

He dropped her hand and sat back.

She swallowed and nodded, unable to answer such intensity. His teasing smile had deceived her. She had assumed he cared no more for her than for any woman who tempted his eye. But the man meant to possess her entirely, whether because he owned her or because he cared for her was less certain.

He assessed her silent nod, and returned it. 'I would prefer that we both enjoy the marriage bed, but we are, and we will be, man and wife, in every sense.'

She held the blanket against her chest and straightened her bare shoulders, struggling to regain her composure, hoping he could not sense the rapid rise and fall in her breath. 'Yes, we are wed. And I will do all that is required of a wife. But do not ask me to enjoy it.'

The sensual shade returned to his gaze. 'I will not ask. I will simply make certain that you do.'

A soft flutter rippled between her legs. She wanted to call it fear, but it was not. 'What do you mean?'

'Before the falcon and the falconer can work as one, the bird must become accustomed to the new master.'

Now, her shiver *was* fear. The process of 'manning' a falcon, or making the bird comfortable around people, took weeks. During that time, bird and man were never apart. 'Do you mean to deprive me of sleep and food until you break me to your will?'

'Do you break a falcon when you train her?'

Reluctantly, she shook her head.

His finger trailed the side of her cheek, down her throat. 'And when the training is done, don't bird and master hunt better together than either could alone?'

She nodded, unable to speak.

His lazy smile reappeared. 'And doesn't the falconer tend to the bird's every need, finding her prey to hunt, food to eat and water to drink?'

'Of course.' His finger, feather light on her throat, still seemed to block the words.

'So the man also serves the bird, does he not?'

'Yes!' She threw the word at him, resentful. Even his slight touch made her tremble.

'Then who owns whom? And who trains whom?' His finger drifted over her left shoulder and lightly down her arm, pausing on the delicate skin inside her elbow. 'The falcon and the falconer are wedded to each other.'

She summoned the spite that would free her speech. 'The bird follows the gloved hand because it carries the food. Not the hand itself.'

But her eyes followed his hand, as his finger, whisper soft, hesitated on the blue veins of her wrist.

'Make no mistake, *mine* is the glove with the food. And you will learn to love it.'

And that threat was more frightening than anything that had come before, because he promised what she most feared.

She forced her eyes to his. 'You'll find I am not so gullible as the hawk. I can find my own food.'

The liquid smile touched his lips and he leaned close

to whisper, his breath tickling her ear, 'There are many kinds of food, my falcon.'

She could near taste the banquet he offered. All that she had resisted in herself seemed to find a mate in him. If she surrendered to her desires instead of her judgements, could she escape the bounds of earth?

No. That was just a dream. If she surrendered, he would learn her weakness and leave her, embarrassed and alone. 'You shall not trap me so easily.'

'You have trapped yourself,' he said. 'You've put on jesses and a hood without even choosing a worthy falconer. Now you have one who can teach you to fly higher. Faster. Further.'

Shaking at his words, she pulled away from his touch. Had she not thought the very same? But she could not submit without a struggle.

Her eyes clashed with his. A dare. 'Do you think to make me captive with your training?'

'I think, dear Clare, you have made yourself the captive. Shed your training. Then you'll be free,' he whispered in her ear now, so close he must have been able to sense her heart pounding at her temples, in her throat, in her breast. 'Let me teach you to soar as you were meant to.' He held her hands and squeezed, his fingers gentle enough to make her tremble. 'Now lie back, my dear. I shall keep you with me, day and night, until you learn to ride my fist and trust my touch.'

He pressed her back into the bedclothes. Her breath, her heart, fought with her blood. She knew he would touch her, could already feel his fingers.

And thought she would go mad with the wanting.

And with the fear.

Not of him. It was herself she feared, that she would break into pieces beneath his fingers.

He kneeled, legs on either side of her, leaving her unable to move.

The covers slipped down, leaving her breasts almost, almost exposed to his gaze. He towered above her, golden head, broad shoulders, strong arms. Then he pulled the covers the rest of the way down, sliding them across her breasts.

She bit back a scream.

Looking down, she tried to pull away from his hands. What would he do now? Worse, what would he cause *her* to do?

'Ah, I see, as with the bird, I shall need to keep you from seeing what goes on around you until you are accustomed to your new surroundings.'

Fresh foreboding beat in her throat. 'Do you mean to cover me in a leather hood?'

There was that smile again. The sensual one, full of promises and secrets. 'You are much more delicate than a haggard bird. You need something softer.'

He reached into his sack and pulled out a blue silk scarf, wrapped it across her eyes, and knotted it firmly behind her head before she could protest.

The smooth fabric, soft and not too tight, caressed her face. Without sight, each sound, acute, vibrated against her skin as well as in her ears. The whine of the wind at the tower's corner. The rustle of straw as he shifted his weight. The soft plop of feet hitting the floor.

Arms straight, she waved her hands, but caught only empty air. 'Darkness may comfort the birds. It does not comfort me.'

His palm cupped her shoulder, then slid down her back. 'If I do something you do not want, just say "stop,"' he said. 'Will you do that?'

She mouthed the word, silently. It gave her a strange sense of power. 'Yes.'

'Promise. Tell me you promise.'

And with those few words, she felt something tug at her heart more dangerous that lust. 'I promise.'

'Now turn over on your stomach.'

With relief, she turned her back to him, and pressed into the mattress, feeling safer with breasts and belly hidden.

She felt a tug on her braid, hanging down her back, as he unlaced the intertwined ropes of hair, then combed through it with his fingers. It rippled across her back, soft as the silk against her face.

'Now, I will touch your back, as you might stroke the falcon's feathers.'

The cloak of her hair was swept aside. His hand, at once sensual and comforting, stroked her skin from shoulder to spine to the small of her back. Again. And more. Relentless rhythm, until she thought she might go mad with it.

Until she wanted to scream *stop*.

Yet she did not speak and he did not stop.

Finally lulled, she fell under his spell, halfway between waking and sleep, day and dream, arousal and relaxation, barely knowing who or where she was floating in a world of sensation and darkness.

Hooded by scarf and pillow, she could not tell whether hours or minutes passed. Her fear ebbed.

She breathed in the scent of dried lavender stuffed

in her pillow, revelled in the smell of juniper, oak and pine crackling into flame on the hearth.

And always, the pressure of his hands.

Finally, she let go.

And slept.

She woke to darkness, opened her eyes and saw no light. Frightened, she sat up, then realised the cloth still covered her eyes. She started to pull it off.

'No.' His voice. Calm, firm.

Reaching out, she tried to see with her hands. Her fingers grazed bare skin. His. Warm.

She had seen his chest before, but never truly touched it. Now she pressed her palms against him, learning him by touch, reading him with her fingers, first exploring a soft tangle of hair on his chest, then letting her fingers follow the trail of warm skin down to his hip, naked now.

And then, discovering something straight, strong and alive between his legs.

She snatched back her hands, but he captured them in his and cupped them around his staff.

She felt him swell, heat against her palms. Strong, yet strangely fragile, too, jerking wobbly against her as would a staggering young lamb.

'Now let me touch you.'

She stiffened as his hands swept over the skin of her shoulders and arms. She faced him now, naked and exposed, no longer protected by the armour of her back. But a sliver of trust had grown within her and she stilled, allowing his touch.

Was this how the falcons became fearless of men?

His fingers found the tips of her breasts. She gasped, breath chasing the sensation. He moved, slipping away from her hands, and laid her gently against the bed.

He was not touching her now.

She turned her head, trying to see with her ears, sense him by smell. The bed shifted beneath her, releasing a whiff of lavender. Hot wax, melting from a candle.

Him. Him, ever him.

She gripped her breath, knowing he must be looking his fill.

Did he like what he saw?

His hand touched hers. She jumped, pulling away. Then, slowly, she laid her hand on the sheet again and his covered it, warm, strong and gentler than she expected.

'There is no hurry.'

Patient. She had not expected him to be so patient. Persistent as he had been when he stroked her back, he sat, touching only her hand, and moved no more.

A feeling of safety settled over her. An illusion. Temporary. Deprived of his touch, her skin craved it, ached for it. The very air kindled the feeling his hands had raised.

How long would he make her wait?

'What do you intend to do?' Her voice, unused for hours, rough in her throat.

'Teach you to trust me. And yourself.'

Herself. The word ripped away her blindness. She was naked with a man who called to the wickedest longings that lurked beneath her skin. A man she should not trust or want.

But did.

She pulled her hand from his and folded hers in her lap. 'That will be hard.'

'Not as hard as you think.'

Be sure the man gets you with babe. And she must. 'You are my husband. Do as you like. I'll submit.'

'I don't want you to submit!' She felt the air move. Was he waving his arms in frustration? 'I want you to *choose*. To come to me with desire.'

'I never will.' But she lied. 'Do it. Now.'

'Not until *you* want this union. Not your father or Lord Douglas. You.'

She raised her head, still blindfolded, wishing she could see his eyes. 'I have no choice here.'

'I give it to you now.'

'The falcon does not choose.'

'Every flight is a choice. Each time, the bird can choose freedom instead of returning to you.'

Did he fear to lose her, too? Did he want more from this marriage than land and a home?

No. She could not believe that. Because if she did and were disappointed, it would be worse than if she had expected nothing at all.

His hands, his lips, touched her again, covering her skin, whispering in her ear, stealing her doubts.

Stealing her choice.

She ripped off the scarf, needing to see his eyes, read his intentions.

But the first thing that assaulted her was his body. Naked.

And hers.

Wavering candlelight cast moving shadows across their skin, hers pale, his more golden.

She wanted to cover her eyes again. This was too coarse, bodies no longer disguised by colour and cloth.

But then, her eyes feasted on him as her hands had done. Muscles of his arms softly rounded as the hills. Golden hair a soft contrast to the strength of his chest. A wandering warrior, as much a stranger in her bed as the tercel in the mews.

He let her look, unmoving beneath her eyes, as if he knew what she was looking for.

You'll wake with a smile on your face.

And that was just what she feared.

Words. She wanted words. She wanted reassurance that if she howled like the lowest limmer he had ever bedded, she would not regret it.

But to ask for words would guarantee nothing. Alain had given her such pretty words. All lies.

So she searched his eyes by the wavering firelight. 'I cannot choose. I do not trust you.'

His gaze, dark and intense, did not reassure her. 'It's not me you distrust. It's yourself.'

This man, reviled, had made his own choices, refusing to explain or defend himself against the vilest accusations. And he challenged her to do the same.

No. That was a risk beyond taking.

He wanted her to choose. Very well. She could submit and still hold herself away from him. She did not have to give him all to give him a child. He would not know the difference.

She stretched out her arm in the dark, palm up, fingers spread. He met it. Their fingers entwined. 'If I say yes, it is only for tonight.'

'Only for one flight.'

'Yes.'

He blew out the candle, leaving her in the safety of darkness again, and his lips took hers.

His hands, firm, but not forcing, flickered over her skin, teasing the tips of her breasts, lower, caressing her waist, hips, then the secrets hidden between her legs.

As she had lost herself and time in his touch before, she did so again. Her legs parted, her body seemed to open of itself, eager for more of his lips, his fingers, of things she couldn't yet express or understand.

He mounted her, finally, filling her slowly and fully, as the hand of the falconer fits the glove. She moaned. Or did he?

Then he started moving.

Something within her surged to meet him, desire spiralling like the falcon towards the sun. And if he took her too high, she would lose herself in the golden glare and never find her way back to earth.

She felt herself start to break into pieces and wanted to shriek, to yell, to scream like a wild thing.

She had said yes, but to something she didn't know. Now, faced with it, she pulled back. The creature in this bed was a succubus, with no connection to what a lady must be, think and do.

Panting, she pushed against him. 'Stop!'

He paused, leaning on his arms over her, breathing hard, as if reining in a galloping horse. 'Are you sure?'

'I can't do this. I can't be this.' If she let go, if she went where he was leading her, everything she knew of who she was would be lost.

'Have you the courage to choose what *you* want?'

Eyes open, she could see him fighting his desires, waiting for her answer. She didn't want to choose, didn't want to reveal her hidden demons, demanding to join his.

It will kill me, she thought. If I reach for this and seize it, I will die.

But if I don't, I will die, too.

'Yes.'

And there were no more questions, no more doubts, no more words. He took her higher, faster, until there was nothing but flight, joined to him. Until he and she and now were the whole world.

And then the world exploded.

Light. Blind feeling wiped everything else away. A scream? A moment so close to the sun she must be aflame.

Another person. New. Free.

And she waited for him to recoil.

He didn't. He held her as she drifted down from the sky and found herself in bed, her arms clinging to his neck, not wanting to let go. Here was a moment of happiness she must savour, fleeting as a breath. Calm. At peace. In the arms of her husband.

A half-English fire-starter.

She curled against him, her face buried in the curve of his shoulder, wanting the darkness, the blindness again so she would not have to face what she had done with him.

For as the madness faded, the fear returned.

That he would leave her, too.

Chapter Seventeen

Afterwards, Gavin lay beside her, holding her gently, letting her shake, thinking what a beautiful creature she was.

Her outer calm, her certainty, yes, he admired that. But to discover the passion underneath—she astonished him. He had thought, he had hoped, but she was so much more than he could have imagined.

He closed his eyes against the morning sun, seeing her again as she was last night. Her half-parted lips. Her pale hair, like moonlight spilling across his body.

Her hand, raised to meet his.

Only now, as he held her fully within his embrace, did he realise how delicate she was. Wrists, fingers, collarbone, toes, dwarfed in his arms. No match for a warrior's strength.

Had he forced her? He asked the question, fearful of the answer. That had not been his intent. He had wanted to bind her loyalty with his body, but he had wanted her to come to him freely, although they had been caged together in this marriage like trapped birds.

At first, as his entire body screamed at him to take her, she lay, clothed in emotional armour strong as any warrior's.

Slowly, gradually, he had stripped that away.

What had he given her in return?

How would she feel when she wakened? Would she sense the deep joining that he did?

One night. One flight. That had been his promise.

And so it would be. She must choose to come to him next time, although he did not know how he would keep his hands, his lips, away from her. He had dreams of what they might do together next. He would be ready when she was.

But unless she had chosen freely, he could never risk revealing what lay beneath the armour that shielded his soul.

Because it mattered, finally, what someone else thought.

Clare slipped from the bed as he slept, afraid to face him so soon. Now she knew the feel of the skin below his waist, the strength of his arms braced beside her, the unbelievable moment when he, too, had shuddered.

Did he feel as vulnerable as she? When he gave himself to her, had he given more than his seed?

She had revealed herself, fully, without saying a word. He held her heart in his hand, now.

And could crush it at any time.

She pulled her hair back and tied it with a ribbon, not taking the time for a braid. Her father must have kept the men away, for no one had come to pound on the door. She glanced out of the window at the sun. Was it midday already? Had they stayed in bed for a day?

Hand on the door, she paused, afraid to go out and face the knowing eyes. Even if they had not heard her moans, everyone knew how a bride and groom spent a wedding night.

The noise from the Hall reassured her. Murine must have prepared the midday meal. Quietly, she tiptoed down the stairs and past the Hall, unseen.

Smiling, she marvelled at a world still right side up. It seemed impossible that the sky still stretched blue above, dotted with drifting clouds. She should be walking on stars, looking up at trees grounded in heaven, their leaves stretching down to reach earth.

Her steps, of their own, took her to the mews. In the days before the wedding, she had had no time to visit Wee One.

As her eyes adjusted to the dimmer light, she heard something new.

A tiny chirp. More than one.

Wee One's eggs had hatched.

She held her breath and crept closer. Two fluffy chicks cheeped in the nest. Wee One stood beside them, wings hunched, as fierce as when she stooped to take a duck in flight. Her head followed Clare's every step. She and Wee One exchanged a long look. Then, carefully, Clare leaned closer, holding her breath.

Eyes closed, pink beaks open, the chicks looked like chubby balls covered with fur. So young. So fragile. They could be no more than days old.

She had opened the high window in the mews and kept all the birds on the creance so the tercel could come and go. His bits of food and fluff littered the gravel nest.

But the chicks cheeped as if they were hungry. Perhaps the bird had not brought enough for them to eat. She reached for the falconer's food sack, wondering whether the babies ate what grown birds did.

She retrieved a morsel and held it between her thumb and finger, keeping an eye on Wee One. She had fed her falcon this way. Perhaps she could feed the chicks, as well. If she stretched her arm gently—

'Stop.'

She turned. Gavin, voice harsh, smile gentle, stood at the door. Freshly washed, hair still damp, he wore a young squire's smile instead of a warrior's frown.

Her breasts burned with the memory of his lips. She swallowed, unable to speak, thinking of all they had done.

And wanting it all over again.

He put his hand on her arm and she realised she had not moved. Her arm was still outstretched to feed the chick.

'If you feed them, they will scream for food every time you come near.'

Heartless man. 'They're too young to hunt. How are they to eat?'

'The tercel will bring food. Unless you want to release Wee One to help.'

She pulled back her hand, but made no move to untie Wee One. 'How do you know so much about falcons?'

'They were good companions for a child in exile. The King's falconer was patient with me.'

'Which King?'

They shared a smile.

'Both. David keeps a falcon with him. Edward allows him to hunt.'

'That is kind of Edward.'

'They send their armies to war, yet they are related by marriage. Some days, in private, they are as cordial as family.'

What hopes there had been, when King David married King Edward's sister, both of them children. Joan Makepeace, they had dubbed her. And yet, she had not.

But she did not want to speak of borders and wars when her relationship with her husband was as fragile as the chicks.

'What else did he teach you about the falcons? Did he ever raise a bird in the mews?'

He shook his head. 'Once or twice he scooped a fledgling from the nest. Without training by their parents, they never became good hunters.'

Her heart cramped. Even the birds needed a mother to teach them. She looked back at the cheeping balls of fluff. 'Then I shall leave them to Wee One.'

'Come.' His arm sheltered her shoulder and he guided her towards the door. 'We must face the household.'

She sighed, knowing the comments would be ribald, and walked with him back to the tower.

What would you tell me, Mother? she wondered, as she accepted hugs from Murine and Euphemia. *What am I to do now?*

She watched him spar with the men over his prowess of the night. Most gathered around and raised a cup. Thom, who had led the fight at Beltane, and one or two others still hung back, muttering in their brew.

Their suspicious glances rekindled her doubts

Do I truly know him? Can I trust him? Can I trust the way I feel?

Well, if he truly wanted her, wanted a marriage she had glimpsed in the dark last night, he would come to her again.

She would not ask.

June melted into July, fast as clouds skittering across the sky. The sheep, shorn of their wool, were herded into the hills to fatten on summer grass.

Yet he did not come to her again.

She went to their bed alone, night after night, as he pleaded the need to inspect the armoury or review the records of the wool sales.

Then, he would wait long enough to be sure that she slept.

She did not, always. Many nights, she lay on her side, eyes closed, listening to the soft clunk of his boots, the whoosh of his tunic, the rustle of the straw as the bed shifted beneath him.

Each night, she lay, hoping, her skin aching for his fingers. Once, twice, she almost turned to touch him, but she clenched her fingers to stop her hands. A lady would never reach out first.

So night after night they lay beside each other, backs touching, and he never reached out.

Some nights, he did not come to bed at all.

Gradually, her hopes faded. He had not left her as Alain had done, but he had left her in spirit. There would be no more secret sharing. Her moans and her screams must have driven him away.

She tried not to care.

They lived in front of others, every word and gesture for all to see. Each had daily duties. Meals were taken with the entire household. And if she watched him sometimes, wistfully, as he shed his tunic and lifted strong arms to show Angus how to hold a sword, only Murine noticed.

Her silent, sympathetic smile was small comfort.

The only time they spoke alone was in the mews.

The chicks grew rapidly. Within six weeks, long, dark feathers replaced the white fluff. Eager to grow, the birds pecked at what remained of their baby down, pulling out the final feathers.

Strutting to the edge of the ledge, they flapped their wings, as if preparing to jump.

Clare closed the shutters, afraid they would fly away and not be able to find their way home. But though they seemed to know what was expected, neither had been willing to take the final leap off the ledge.

Her monthly time came. And she knew she must confront him.

If they were to produce an heir, they must share more than a bed again.

That night, she lay quietly, pretending to sleep, until he settled in. Then she turned and placed her palm on his shoulder.

He bolted upright, as if her touch was a signal the enemy had come. 'What?'

'My monthly time came.'

It was hard to get the words out. Surely she would not have to say more.

But he said nothing. And he did not touch her. 'Is that not a usual occurrence?' His choked question sounded as awkward as her admission.

She felt her cheeks burning. 'It is.'

He looked at her blankly, as if he had no idea what she meant.

'So I am not with child.'

A smile flickered over his face. 'That I do know.'

She swallowed, unsure she would be able to say the words. How could a lady ask for such things? 'And that means we must—' her eyes went from him to her to the sheets '—again.'

He crossed his legs, mercifully under the covers, and leaned towards her. 'We *must?*'

'Without a babe, you will lose the tower.'

'It will not be the first thing I have lost in my life.' His voice, husky, echoed with empty years.

Did he hate her so much that he would relinquish everything to avoid her? Well, she knew the price of allegiance if he did not. 'It is our duty to have a child.'

He dropped his head to his hands, sighing. 'Is that all this is to you? Duty?'

'What do you mean?'

He started to reach for her, then pulled back, knotting one arm over the other. But still, he touched her with his eyes. 'I told you every flight was a choice. Do you choose solely for duty?'

'I thought…' What could she say? Yet here was this man, her husband, looking at her with eyes full of hunger. No, more than that. 'I thought you did not want me.'

Shock first. Eyes blank. Mouth open. A sword's blow could not have stunned him so completely.

Then, a smile, large now, blessed his face and he pulled her into his arms.

Safely surrounded, his chin on top of her head, she felt a chuckle rumble in his chest. 'And I thought you did not want me.'

Fear, coiled in her every muscle, ebbed, released by giddy anticipation. 'You waited for me?' What man would ever do so?

He nodded against her head. 'I promised you could choose.'

Now her laughter bubbled up, belly deep. 'Then it seems, my husband, that we have kept our babe-to-be waiting unduly.'

Bold, eyes open, she raised her lips to his. This time, she would see his every move.

Yet without the freedom of darkness, she saw too much. Their noses bumped. Her hands, first clasped around his neck, then gripping his forearms, rested gracefully nowhere. She dropped them to dangle, uselessly, at her sides.

His tongue teased hers, and she dutifully replied in kind, trying to please him. But instead of a sensual gesture, it felt like a child's tantrum.

The first night, she had feared the wantonness he released in her. Now, instead, she was a woman so awkward and unsure that she knew she could never please a husband.

Tired of doing everything wrong, she turned limp, returning to simple submission. Let him do as he liked.

The kisses that had cascaded over her ears, her cheek, her throat and her shoulders slowed, then stopped. He pulled away, studying her.

'I thought you wanted this.'

'I did. I do. Truly.'

'Then what's wrong?'

She turned her head away. 'I am still a nestling, I fear.' She thought of the baby birds, hopping on the edge of the nest, flapping their wings, unwilling to jump. 'When I see everything...' Her voice faded. How could she explain? 'I am like the falcon who needs to be blinded to her fears.'

His smile, impossibly, was at once tender and lewd. 'Ah, I see we went too quickly. We must return to your training.'

The silk kissed her cheek again. Returned to the safety of darkness, all her senses re-awakened, ready again for his touch. She lay back with a sigh of relief.

'Before a falcon is made,' he said, his voice coaxing, 'she must be trained to the lure.'

Beneath her, the straw shifted as he rose. She tried to picture him moving around the room. 'What are you doing?' Impatient now. Ready for his touch.

'Preparing to train my beautiful nestling.' The lid of a chest opened and closed. 'I will not risk losing her. And for that...'

He stretched her arm to the edge of the bed and as quickly as she hooded Wee One, she felt a thin leather strap around one wrist.

'...she must wear a creance.'

Her other wrist, now, secured the same way.

'Now, my wife, we are ready to resume your training.'

Immediately, something tingled in her breasts, pulsed between her legs. Now, totally at his mercy, desire and fear mingled, difficult to distinguish.

'Are you comfortable?'

She swallowed, and nodded.

'Remember. Just say "stop."'

'I remember.' But she remembered more. How difficult it had been for him to stop. And how she knew, now, that it would be impossible for her, as well.

Something soft, a feather's edge, tickled her ankle, then started a lazy trail up the inside of her bare leg. She sensed where it would end. And already she was slick with wanting.

She swallowed against the throbbing of her heart, unsure she would be able to speak. 'Will you be patient with me?' Had she misjudged him? 'You won't hurt me?'

The feather's trail stopped. 'No falconer would harm a bird. But it must be your choice. Do you want to take this flight?'

His hand, large, gentle, rested over hers, waiting.

Have you the courage to choose what you want?

Last time, frightened by longing so intense, she thought she would go mad with it. Instead, she had discovered a vast sky, a new world, and the freedom to explore it.

She laced her fingers with his. 'Yes.'

He sighed, with more relief that she expected, and pressed his lips to her brow. 'Then fly as far and as fast and as high as you dare. I will be here for you. I will catch you.'

The feather resumed its wanderings, exploring the inside of her knee, then stroking, ever so softly, up her thigh. 'And like the bird when he is fed, you will learn by this sign to expect the food of love.'

He gave a whistle, soft and low.

Then, she felt his lips on the delicate skin of her inner thigh, and she knew there would be no stopping either of them.

Chapter Eighteen

After her release, Gavin held her, still trembling, in his arms.

Or was he the one who shook?

He had not realised, when he urged her on, how much he asked. No woman had ever given herself so completely. She had nothing left, nothing hidden, nothing of herself that she had not exposed to him.

If she were a falcon, there would be none better. And he would never, never allow her to be lost.

To know that she, that part of her, belonged to him alone, made him feel for the first time, as if he was more than a bastard without a country.

He held her closer and kissed the sensitive spot he had found on her neck, just behind her ear, hidden by her hair. Not intending to excite her now, but to comfort her. To tell her without words that he would keep her safe. Always.

In this bed, alone, they were sheltered within the borders of their own kingdom. But that, he knew, was temporary. Douglas, David, Edward, the quarrels of the world would come to them again.

It was only a question of when.

She lay in his arms, shaking, ashamed to raise her eyes to his. What must he think of her now? At the end, something had moved through her. Powerless to stop it, she felt as if she had been cracked open and the spirit, the core, the essence she had been fighting all her life had finally broken free.

The spasming of her body. How total. As if there were nothing more in that moment than a howling banshee. She had moaned, she was sure, wild as an animal, unable to stop. With no more control and no way to hold on to her mask.

Surely, now that he had seen this wild, screaming woman he would recoil in horror.

Alain would have.

Yet her husband still lay beside her, his arms protectively around her. And she felt, for the first time, that she could drop her defences. They had been replaced by his arms.

It would be their secret, these terrible things they did together, the wild feelings that surged between a man and a woman. Had anyone else ever felt them before? Surely not. No one could have survived this—vulnerability. She was weak, exposed, defenceless, and yet he made her feel safe. As if everything she had done and felt was as perfect as the falcon following her nature.

He nuzzled her neck behind her ear, his breath was soft, his kiss gentle.

His whisper, not in her ear, but close, was barely loud enough to hear.

'A perfect flight, my fearless falcon. You soar above the rest.'

She snuggled against his shoulder. The freedom she had sought, chased across the hills, lay instead in the dark of a shared bed.

So their days became light and the evenings shade. With every joining, she was satiated, only to crave his touch again, hours, minutes after.

She resented the long, endless summer days that kept them from bed. But they used the time to work with the two fledglings, Wee Twa and Wee Thre. First in the weathering yard, then in the wild, she and Gavin taught them to chase the lure. Each successful catch was rewarded with food, as it would be when they hunted live prey.

But they could not spend all day with the birds. As she worked in the kitchen, or picked herbs from the garden, her hands moved of their own accord while she remembered the night before. Her father and Murine exchanged sly smiles when they saw her.

She ignored them.

And sometimes, a low whistle, vibrating, would tickle her ear and she would catch him watching her, his smile a promise of the night to come in their secret world, unacknowledged in daylight.

After joining, they talked, as intimately as they loved. Of daily tasks, and whether they should imp the feathers of a short-winged hawk so that she could fly again. And of their days as children in exile. For Clare, lonely, motherless days in France, as she struggled to shed her Scots accent and memorise every new rule of conduct. For Gavin, days as a young page, serving King David on foreign soil, said to be his own.

Yet as much as she craved his touch, the silken scarf hung close at hand, for she needed the protection of the blindfold and darkness, before she could truly surrender.

'Not so much cannelle, Euphemia. The recipe calls for half that.'

Clare was trying to teach the girl how to help with the brogat. The task was trying her patience. 'You must weigh and measure carefully, not just fling handfuls into the brew.'

'But I like cannelle!'

'I like it, too, but that doesn't mean I can have as much as I want.' The brown, spicy quills were dear. She looked into the sack, trying to assess how much was left. 'I am trying to teach you how to do it properly.'

Euphemia shrugged and still kept smiling. 'And I thank you for that, mistress.' She stuck her nose over the malt mixture, inhaled, then released a happy sigh. 'It smells good, though.'

Clare wrinkled her nose over the brew and sniffed, savouring the whiff of cinnamon, trying to assess how much the girl had used. Maybe, if she liked the taste, she'd adjust the recipe. She had discovered, grudgingly, that Euphemia was able to cook without the benefit of instructions.

They worked in silence for a few minutes. 'I saw you with Walter last night and Thom the night before,' Clare began. Thom was one of the louts who had attacked Gavin at Beltane. Walter was apprenticed to the farrier. A good, steady lad. 'Have either of them mentioned marriage?'

She'll marry the first man who asks her, her father had said. If he didn't get her with child first.

She shook her head. 'Fitzjohn keeps Walter busy with the horses and Thom keeps busy complaining about Fitzjohn.'

'Complaining?' She asked the question with more calm than she felt. Men-at-arms grumbled, always. But this one seemed to have a special grudge. 'What does Thom say?'

'That Fitzjohn is more Inglis than Scots.'

Safe in bed with Gavin, she had allowed herself to forget that he was still Inglis to many of the men. 'Do others say the same?'

She shrugged. 'A few. I always tell them how kind he's been to me.'

Clare smiled, suddenly wishing to hug the girl. It was not an argument that would sway a fighting man, but it was a sweet sentiment, all the same. 'Do you think it is more than talk?'

Euphemia tilted her head and thought for a moment. 'I don't know.'

Gavin had worried about Douglas. Maybe he had been right. Maybe Douglas had left spies in their walls.

She put down her spoon and wiped her hands on her napron. 'Euphemia, I need you to find out. Can you do that for me?'

She nodded.

'And if you hear anything, anything that threatens him, come tell me.'

'And Fitzjohn?'

'No. Come to me first.' The girl was too young to distinguish a complaint from a conspiracy. No reason to disturb her husband unless the threat was real.

'You like being married to him, don't you?'

'Yes, I do.' What a miracle, to say it.

'I told you he was braw.'

Clare's laughter bubbled. 'And now I suppose you'll say that you were the one who invited him home with us.'

The girl grinned. 'Well, I did, didn't I?'

'And you deserve proper thanks for it. So thank you.' The words tasted as sweet as the brogat.

It was time to fly Wee Twa free.

She knew that. But if the fledgling was ready, Clare wasn't.

'Today,' Gavin said. 'We should fly her.'

She looked up at the sky as if assessing the weather. But the August rain had stopped. The sky was clear blue, the clouds puffy and benevolent. 'It's a little windy. Perhaps tomorrow.'

'You have said tomorrow these last seven days.'

'But Wee Thre is sick. We should wait until she is well and they can fly together.'

He cupped her cheeks in his hands and turned her face to his. 'Now. Or she'll never fly.'

She nodded, knowing he was right. Her fingers shook as they gathered the creance and the lure and rode into the hills. She tried to take comfort from the familiar routine.

She had trained Wee One well. Unfailingly, the bird would return to the fist at her whistle. But this younger bird was an untried thing. They had trained her, of course, letting her free and calling her from post to fist in the weathering yard, then outside the walls. But Clare had never yet risked a free flight. Daring to raise the chicks, she had flouted hundreds of years of falconers' experience.

Now, she would discover whether she had been right, or a fool.

They rode high enough that the trees gave way to brush. She looked out over the hills, hoping there would be less chance of losing her here than in the forested slopes.

'It's too soon, Gavin. She needs more training.'

He helped her off the horse. 'Clare, now is the time. She's trained and she wants us to know what she can do. It is her nature to fly.' He touched his wife's cheek and she blushed.

Just as it had been her nature to join with him.

She looked at the bird, hooded on her leather gauntlet. Had she done everything right? Would it keep her safe? Yet Wee Twa was a hunter and must fly as she was meant to.

She transferred the bird to Gavin's wrist and took the lure in her hand. The weight of it swung comfortably on the end of the rope. She tested it, swinging it in the familiar pattern, up and down, side to side like a great cross, then left, then right, then overhead.

She nodded at Gavin, ready.

He removed the creance and the hood. The bird looked around. They had worked with her here before, still tethered, so the place was familiar.

Gavin, a length away, let the bird go, lifting his fist, and Wee Twa flew up, up and higher.

Clare could hear the wings, flapping as hard as the pulse in her throat, the endless wind, the jingle of the bells.

She started to swing the lure.

At first, the bird didn't turn. She flew straight, as if ready to soar into the sky she was bred for and never return to earth.

Then, the lure caught her eye.

Once she saw it, the sky held no appeal.

It was an easy matter, at first, to keep the lure just ahead of her. Close enough so that she could see it, almost reach it. Close enough that she would not get discouraged, but far enough to keep her flying.

Clare did a complete round, twirling the lure, her skirts flaring in the wind, feeling as if she and the bird danced. Wee Twa, still new to the hunt, was easy to stay ahead of.

On the third pass, she slowed, ever so slightly, and the bird pounced, 'killing,' the lure. Clare rushed to her, calling the bird to her wrist.

She came, as she was trained, to eat her reward.

Gavin joined her, putting his arm around her shoulder. The wind had blown her hair free and she felt her whole body smiling. 'Again?'

The bird did as she had been taught, faster each time, until even Gavin could barely keep the lure ahead of her.

Clare, buoyed by the day's victory, finished the practice with laughter.

'As soon as he's well, we'll fly Wee Thre, then we can take them both after game,' she babbled happily, as they put away the gear and hooded the bird to head home. 'You see? It is possible to raise a bird from the nest. She'll come to the fist as well as her mother does, every time.'

Instead of sharing her joy, he frowned. 'There is no surety with the birds. Ever.'

Or with us, he seemed to say.

That night, he finally spoke of his birth.

'My mother lived on the land near Halidon Hill,' he began, softly, 'where my father helped lead the English troops to their victory.'

She wanted to know, yet she resented having the past thrust into their bed. The battle's very name was poison in a Scottis man's mouth. More than a battle lost, it was the death of a generation of leaders. Twenty years later, some said Scotland had not yet recovered from the loss.

'So was she one of the spoils of war?' She winced at a sudden vision of a prince, maddened with battle lust, a son, born of a rough taking.

'No!' His arms tensed about her. Then, in softer words, he continued. 'At least, that is not how she told me the story. They met before the battle.'

He rolled away from her and lay on his back, looking up at the ceiling.

'How,' she whispered, 'did her story go?'

'It seems,' he began, as if reciting a favourite tale, 'that the King's younger brother, John of Eltham, had spent so much time in Scotland that he developed a fondness for the land. There was talk of making him its King, if he could subdue the place.'

She heard the chuckle in his voice and answered it. 'A Scot is harder to tame than a falcon.'

'So he discovered.'

She placed her hand, small, pale, over his, encouragement.

He kept his gaze on the heavens, but finally spoke again.

'One day, he was leading his soldiers in the land above Berwick, in the East March. This was a few months before the great battle. They stopped at a nunnery, hungry, thirsty and wanting shelter. The nuns, of course, could not attend the soldiers, but some of the daughters of the local families had been sent there for safekeeping. One of them was my mother, Margaret MacGuffin.'

She had heard of the family, distant relations of a Highland clan.

'As she told me, they were taken with each other on sight. He was only seventeen then and she was the same. One night. And in the morning, he was gone.'

Clare held her breath, seeing the young lovers of memory. John of Eltham. No doubt a golden eagle, like his son. Margaret MacGuffin. Eager, rebellious, perhaps, and too young to know better.

Or perhaps too swept away to care. She could understand that feeling now.

Even forgive it.

She curled her fingers tight between his as Gavin continued.

'She told me he promised to marry her.'

Impossible. A romantic fabrication by a woman attempting to salvage her pride.

'But he was the brother of the Inglis King,' she said.

His eyes met hers and she saw his wistful desire to believe. 'But plausible if he were to rule Scotland, to have chosen a Scottish bride.'

She could not destroy his illusion. She, too, clung to a childhood memory of a mother's perfection. 'What happened to her then?'

'The nuns protected her. And me. But when she took me home, her family was furious, ready to disown her and her English bastard. This was after the battle, and my father had become one of the most hated enemies of Scotland.' Bitterness touched his face. 'And with good reason.'

'So she never saw him again.'

He frowned, seeing the doubt in her eyes. 'The tale's not so simple. She *did* see him. He was on his way to Perth, where he died. I was only a child, but I saw him embrace and kiss my mother.' He paused. 'And after he left, she cried. For a long, long time.'

'Because he abandoned her?'

'No. Because she knew by then that he was a monster willing to torch a church full of supplicants who had sought sanctuary. And I carried his blood.'

His words, bleak and sharp as January's wind.

'A few weeks later, he was dead.'

Dead. Killed by his brother's hand. All of Scotland knew the story of Edward's fury. Even the King of the Inglis could not tolerate such sacrilege, at least, he couldn't then.

Cruel, though, to remind Gavin of that.

He squeezed her hand. 'Dead, leaving me to fight his poisoned blood.' He sat up and looked at her. 'And I have fought it.' His hands, gripping hers hard enough to hurt. 'Every day of my life. And I swear to you, of all the deeds I did in war, I did *not* kill those people.'

'I believe you,' she whispered. And for the first time, she truly did.

'But I wanted to. Don't you understand? For one dreadful moment I wanted to.'

She took him in her arms, rocked him against her, thinking tears might come, but she felt only a long, painful shudder, and she was not sure whether it was his or hers.

She had put herself at his mercy and now, she wondered whether she really knew this man at all.

Was she blindfolded in more than one way?

Chapter Nineteen

No surety with the birds, he had said. Early in October, she found out he was right.

Wee One and Wee Twa were ready to hunt, eager for the start of the season. But when Wee Thre had been sick, Clare had cared for her like a child and the bird lost all fear of humans and all interest in hunting. Finally, they moved her out of the mews and into the hall, where everyone petted her and she screamed for leftovers from the midday meal.

Today, they left Wee One in the mews and took Wee Twa for her first real flight. The crisp, sunny air and the scent of heather mixed into a perfect day as the new hunter caught her first prey: a small pigeon. She missed the second bird, but the third time, she plucked her second pigeon in the air.

One more flight, Clare thought, as the sun drifted down towards the mountains. One more and we'll turn home.

Perhaps she had become careless, too confident that

all would be well. Perhaps she was tired. Or the bird was. Or perhaps after her catch she was no longer hungry and the sky was more tempting than a meal.

Whatever the reason, this time, when they flushed out a black grouse, and looked skywards, Wee Twa did not turn.

Instead, she kept flying, fast and straight, into the gloaming settling over the mountains. Straight towards the border as if she knew where she was going.

'No!' The wind whipped Clare's scream out of her mouth and flung it behind her.

Wee Twa was barely visible now.

Clare whistled, shrieking over and over until her lips shook too much and she could not hold them firm.

The bird, if she heard, paid no heed.

Behind her, Gavin enfolded her, pulling her to him. No words. He did not need to say words.

But she needed to hear them. 'I flew her too long. I fed her too much.' She tried to remember all the steps of the training. Which one had she done wrong?

He rocked her against his chest. 'It is in their nature to fly.'

'Not this one.' She squeezed her eyes against the tears. 'She knows nothing but the mews. She cannot want what she does not know.'

'You did.'

Her hands flew to cover her mouth. Things she wanted. Things she had flown to him seeking, even though she did not know what they were until she found them.

All her training had not extinguished the fire of those wants.

'We'll look for her,' he said.

She pulled out of his arms. 'It will do no good.' Though she wanted to believe. 'A lost falcon is as good as dead.'

'I said we would look. I did not promise we would find her.'

But he was willing to try. For her. A comforting gesture, but it would not change the truth.

She had flouted convention deliberately, thinking that she knew better than generations of falconers just because she wanted so much.

No surety with the birds.

This was the price. Or was it only the first of many payments?

They rode out again the next day, passing the shepherds herding some of the flocks down from the hills. In the valley, mist hung in the air, like frost suspended. Towards the top, the wind started again, blowing the sky clear.

They dismounted, leaving the horses while they climbed higher. Where the ground became a soggy bog, the shepherds had moved a few stones into a rough path. Wind, relentless, whipped her cloak, whistled in her ears and scrubbed the tears from her cheeks.

How could a poor wee bird fly against such a gale?

She gazed towards the crest as the wind, suddenly, held its breath. In a moment, fog settled in, blinding her as effectively as a hood.

'It's here. Somewhere.' Gavin, barely visible, looked at the ground as if seeking something he'd dropped.

'What?'

'The line.'

The chill that gripped her did not come from the mist.

Had the bird noticed when she crossed it? Did the sky look bluer on Edward's side, offering something Clare could not?

Where is the border in my body? Gavin had asked her, that first night. Now, he stood, perhaps straddling that line carved by men.

With their joining, she had thought his split, and hers, would heal. That all divisions and wounds would disappear and they would be woven together, whole, a seamless cloth and he would be a Scottis man indeed.

Instead, like their fingers laced together, they could not be fully joined, only interwoven like the plaid, made of distinct hues, but combined in a new pattern.

But the pattern was not yet clear and she feared he still battled a darker self she had only glimpsed.

The fog thickened. There was no reason to keep searching. The bird was gone.

She hoped that Wee Twa would find those things she sought.

Clare held out a hand to Gavin, but while she had been searching the sky, he had looked at the ground. Now, he crouched to study the frozen grass. 'What is it?'

'Tracks.'

Now, she saw it too, imprinted in the frost.

Horses had been here. Coming from the English side.

Her eyes met his. 'Scouting.'

He nodded. 'They'll be wanting those cattle back. And more.'

They turned, together, to leave the mountain.

Douglas's truce was over.

Mindless loving no longer filled their nights.

On edge, Gavin barely slept, rising to check the guards and hear reports from the lookouts twice a night. Clare, no longer able to depend on his warmth beside her, took to wearing her night robe again.

The walls were strong. As long as the livestock were kept inside, the Inglis wouldn't bother with a direct assault.

But Gavin had ordered some of the flock and a few cattle to be left outside the barmkin wall.

She woke, one night, disturbed as he rose from bed yet again, tearing his heat from beneath the blanket. 'Where do you go now?'

'To the tower.'

'You've guards on the tower.'

He grabbed his cloak, not looking at her. 'I trust my own eyes and ears.'

'If you would only keep the animals inside the walls, you could sleep through the night.'

'Then I would have to lie awake all season, waiting for them to try again.' Metal rubbed on leather, signalling that he had tied on his belt and picked up his dagger.

'They only take what they can steal in the dark.'

'And I want them to think that's exactly what they are getting.'

'Are you sure your plan isn't to give them our sheep?'

He stilled. In the darkness, she could not see his face, but she knew it was touched with anger. 'What do you take me for? I'm trying to protect this tower and everything that belongs to it.'

'Is that worth losing the animals?'

'If the plan works, we won't lose them.'

'And if it doesn't?'

'I must take that chance.'

'You need take no chance at all! Keep them inside and there will be no risk.'

'No, there will be certainty that they'll return to plague us again and again. You want promises, guarantees?'

'I want you to follow the rules.'

'The enemy doesn't.'

And that was why she hated this place. There would be no brave battle on an open field. No knightly challenge made and accepted. No gallant win or loss. Only skulking in the dark to steal and kill. 'Which is why they are the enemy.'

He sighed and sat on the bed, cupping her head in his hands and bringing her forehead to his. 'Ah, Clare. You would have me ride to war in the sunshine, waving colours and wearing untarnished armour.'

She nodded, feeling foolish for thinking maxims would save them.

He kissed her, hard and fast, and rose. 'You must trust me. I'll do what is best.'

The door closed, leaving her alone to pound her pillow in frustration.

Following long-held wisdom was best. When custom was flouted, anything could happen. She had allowed Wee One to keep her eggs, thinking, in her arrogance, that she knew better, that she could train them to hunt as if they had been born wild.

Instead, one bird was useless, the other gone.

Gavin, too, had flouted the rules, but gradually, she had been lulled into forgetting that. Now the world's dangers intruded again. She pulled the blanket over her shoulder and shivered, alone in the dark, listening for sounds that might mean battle.

An owl hooted. Or was it the sentry's warning?

Or the Robsons, ready to strike?

Could she discern Gavin's loyalties any more clearly?

The thought of the lines she had crossed in this very bed made her shudder. In time, she would have to pay for that, and the price would be much higher than a lost falcon.

Gavin mounted the stairs to the tower, relieving Thom early. Instead of being grateful, the man snarled as he left, tired and surly.

Gavin would keep watch himself until dawn. He had pushed the men hard. All of them.

He had not slept well in weeks. And would not until the Robsons were bested. He spent days and nights going over the plans, discussing them with the baron, making changes, and then reviewing them again.

When the Robsons came, he intended for Carr's Tower to be ready.

Clare's father had argued for them to attack first.

'And break Douglas's truce?' That would do nothing to endear him to the man.

'Bah,' the baron said. 'When did the Inglis bother to keep the peace?'

But he persuaded him, finally, that if they broke the truce, the Robsons would have them tried before the Wardens of the March. The fine would be high and Douglas disgraced if his peace were broken in his absence.

And while Gavin was not averse to a fight, what he wanted now was peace. On the border and in his bed.

A tense truce now ruled in what had been their place of secret pleasure. Something had shifted. The looming fight, the loss of her bird, his confession—something had snatched away his uninhibited bedmate.

But he wondered now whether the pleasure had been too much his. He had wanted her to enjoy their lovemaking, thought that she had. But had he forced her instead of freed her? Gone beyond what she truly wanted?

He needed to know whether their lovemaking had truly been shared pleasure. That she would come to him without the tricks and games.

When the fighting was over, he must find out.

'Fire!'

Clare bolted from bed a few nights later, shaking, not even donning shoes before she dashed to the stairs. Running feet. Galloping hooves. Screams.

Where was Gavin?

As she ran down, cottagers, the women and children, fleeing into the tower for safety, forced their way past her. Buffeted by the crowd, pushed to the narrow end of the step, Clare's foot slipped and she fell.

'Stop!' She grabbed the sleeve of the falconer's wife. 'What's happened?'

'The Robsons.' She jerked her head. 'They're inside.'

Clare crept through the crowd to the base of the tower, then paused in the doorway, trying to absorb the confusion.

Flames leapt from the cottage next to the mews. Carr men and strangers on horseback faced each other in a space so small, the horses were stepping on squealing sheep. Battle cries mingled with shrieks from wounded men and bleating cattle.

Neil ran past her, carrying a bucket. 'The mews will be next,' he said, not pausing.

She looked over to see the first spark hit the roof.

'Here! You!' she yelled at the next cottager who passed her. 'Grab a bucket. Over there.'

Shaking, he was of little mind to listen.

'Angus!'

She grabbed his shoulder or he would not have stopped. Wild-eyed, dagger drawn, he was rushing towards the fray.

'Angus! Get these men to fight the fire.'

'But—'

'Now!'

He cast an eye on the battle before him and did as she asked. Murine and Euphemia appeared through the smoke with buckets.

Men, horses, the mêlée surrounded her, blocking her path. She searched for Gavin, finally seeing him near the gate where Robson men still galloped into the tower yard.

The gate was wide open.

She looked back at the mews. The smoke from the cottage roof drifted into the windows.

Wee One.

Angus had recruited a few men and a line now snaked from inside the tower, where the well was protected, out into the bailey and to the burning cottage. Several pails had doused the flaming room, but smoke still poured off the fire.

Wee One's screech pierced the chaos.

Running for the mews, she kept close to the tower walls to avoid the horses' hooves.

When she opened the door, smoke stung her eyes and she coughed. Neil appeared beside her. 'I'll get the goshawk,' he said, not pausing. 'Ye must set them free.'

Already, Wee One strained at the end of her leash. Clare pulled on it, bringing her within reach, but even close to Clare's touch and her murmured words, the bird still flapped her wings.

Clare could barely keep her still enough so that she could slip off the hood. Now able to see the drifting smoke, the bird strained harder to escape. Clare could not get enough slack on the leather to release the knot, which only tightened more, as it was meant to.

The falconer had already freed the goshawk, who headed for the open door. The man came to help, coughing now. 'Ye hold her. I'll loosen it.'

She put her hands on each side of the body, avoiding the wings for fear of hurting them. She cradled Wee

One, soft and delicate, able to feel the bird's frantic heartbeat against her palms. A creature born to kill, yet still so small, so vulnerable.

'There. It's done.' The falconer ran towards the door. 'The fire's on the roof now! Let her go.'

She didn't want to. She wanted to hold the bird safe, always.

But the corner of the ceiling nearest the cottage was in flames now, spewing smoke high into the room. If she let Wee One loose, she'd fly into the smoke and be lost.

Holding on to her, Clare ran for the door.

Chapter Twenty

Gavin sat on his horse, surveying the battlefield within the barmkin walls. The smoke's stench permeated his clothes, bringing back memories he had tried to escape.

Carr losses had been more than he hoped, but the Robsons had suffered worse.

His men had rallied quickly, the battle brief, but bloody. One Robson and one Carr man lay dead. One cottage destroyed and the mews damaged. Twenty sheep lost. Four horses gained.

And when the outcome was clear and the Robsons had retreated, they left three behind, now imprisoned in the windowless chamber behind the cellar storage.

They would not raid again soon.

The baron brought his horse alongside.

Gavin sighed. 'My planning did not take treachery into account,' he said.

'But I killed a Robson man.' No smile softened the words. 'I still wish we'd hit them first, but we got the best of them in the end.'

'Clare won't think so.' And she might be right.

'Well, you are right, there's a traitor in our midst, that's asure.'

Gavin nodded. 'And I'll find him.'

All his plans, all his preparations, nearly for naught. The ambush had gone awry, because someone had opened the gate.

And in all his careful plans, he had not prepared for the one threat he of all people should have thought of.

Fire.

He found Clare standing in the mews, staring at the burned-out hole in the roof. The room reeked of smoke.

'Are you all right?' he asked, holding his breath.

She turned and he gasped.

Soot smudged her cheeks. The gown she wore for sleep was grey with ash, pitted with cinder marks. Cuts and burns marred her hands and bare feet.

'We'll have to tear it down,' she said, voice numb with fatigue and sorrow. 'I can't bear the smell of it.'

Neither could he. 'What about the birds? Wee One?'

'She…I…' Tears and smoke seemed caught in her throat. 'Gone. Released. All of them. I carried her…' She crossed her empty arms as if still cradling the bird, then looked towards the door.

He took a step towards her, uncertain whether she would welcome his arms. My fault, he thought, wishing he could do it all again. He would keep the sheep, the birds, his wife and his people, all of them, locked safely behind the gates.

But how could he protect them safe from betrayal from within?

'We'll build another mews. A better one.'

She dropped her empty arms to her side. 'Why? There are no birds.'

He put his arms around her. 'There will be. I promise you, there will be.'

He felt her shudder with tears, not sure whether she wept for the birds or herself or the death of her illusions.

'The risk you took,' she said, finally, her words muffled against his chest, 'was it worth this?'

You need take no risk at all, she had told him. He wished it were true, for in all his calculations, he had never expected her beloved birds would be part of the cost.

'Clare, the ambush failed because we were betrayed.'

She lifted her head, the despair in her eyes giving way to confusion. 'What do you mean?'

'We had them surrounded. And then someone opened the gate and let them in.'

'Who?'

'I don't know yet, but I *will* find him, and when I do, the traitor will die.'

She wiped her eyes and he glimpsed something he did not understand. 'There are wounded to tend. Food to prepare.' She began to list all that she must do in the aftermath, walking towards the door.

He kept his arm around her and drew her out of the mews into the daylight. The sun was high in the sky, although it seemed impossible that this was the same day that had begun too late for night, too early for dawn, with the Robson battle cry beneath his window.

A screech split the air.

She raised her head, face lit with hope.

Wee One perched on the wall, screaming for attention.

Clare whistled. The bird flew to her wrist.

And not even the grip of the talons digging into the reddened skin of her wrist could erase the joy on her face.

Clare washed and changed into a wool gown, but the smell of smoke clung. Downstairs, work waited. Bandaging the wounded. Feeding the hungry.

Digging the graves.

But before all of that, she must talk to Euphemia.

She caught a glimpse of Thom and searched for guilt on his face. Anger, she saw, and disgust. Both familiar expressions.

Nothing else. Nothing new.

Gavin and her father had begun supervising the work. Walter had ridden to Jedburgh to beg a priest for burial rites. Some of the men were digging graves in the consecrated ground next to the chapel that had been without a priest since the Great Death. One for their fellow, who would be mourned. One for the Robson man, who would not.

Another group cleared the debris from the cottage that was lost and knocked down the mews.

Tomorrow, they would rebuild. Tonight, the homeless family would sleep in the Hall.

Clare found Euphemia in the kitchen, helping the

cook with soup for the hungry men. She motioned her to follow her up the stairs to the tower.

Only one guard was left. What they had been watching for had already come.

The wind cut through her gown as she looked out on the hills the enemy had crossed to reach them. The heather had faded. Frost would fall tonight.

Euphemia's eyes, normally merry, drooped, weary with tears.

I should have told him, Clare thought. I should have told Gavin what she had said about Thom.

'Euphemia, someone opened our doors to the enemy.'

She waited for some sign the girl had known. Instead, her mouth sagged in surprise. 'Are you sure?'

Clare nodded. 'What did Thom say? Did he say anything, anything at all about this?'

'No! Nothing.'

'I need you to find out.' She would make the girl a spy if she must.

'But it can't be true. He was unhappy with Fitzjohn, but give us to the Inglis? Never.'

She studied the teary eyes, wondering whether the girl was right or just blinded by young love.

Suddenly, the same question shook her. She could not envision even the most disgruntled soldier opening the gates to the Inglis.

The only man in the tower who had ties across the border was Gavin.

'I know you think so,' she said, fighting the tremble in her voice. 'But sometimes we do not know even those closest to us. Please. Try to find out.'

And she would have to do the same.

* * *

Her bones ached and she could barely lift her feet by the time she and Gavin mounted the stairs to the family floor that night. The smell of smoke followed them into their chamber.

She dropped her gown on the floor beside the ruined nightdress, vowing never to don either of them again.

'Do you know who might have done it?' She held tight to her voice, hoping to mask her suspicions. 'Opened the gates?'

Shaking his head, he sank on to the stool by the hearth and pulled off his boots. 'I questioned the Robson men. They swore not to know and I think they are telling the truth.'

She stirred dried lavender into the small pot of water bubbling over the fire, hoping it would rid the air of the stench. Standing next to him in her chemise, she felt that vulnerability of their first days. Could he see her doubts on her skin?

He put a hand on her arm, forcing her to face him. 'Who do you think might have done it?'

She swallowed. She could not accuse Thom without proof.

His grip tightened. 'You know something. What?'

'I don't know. I'm not sure.' Poisoned blood, he had said. Something like fear flickered through her.

'Then tell me what you think. Certain or not.'

I wanted to.

He didn't burn the church, but he had wanted to. What if there were other transgressions, like the sins committed in their bed, ones he could not resist?

She tugged against his grip, but his fingers chained her. 'Tell me!'

'You! It might have been you!'

Stunned, he dropped her arm. 'Me?'

She tried to read his eyes, no longer the peaceful blue of a summer sky. Fear? Anger? What did she see? 'Who else would want the Inglis to win?'

He stood and backed away from her, as if he could not bear to be so close. 'You? My wife? How can you—?' His throat tried to force words that would not come. When he spoke again, she could barely hear him. 'Do you really believe that? After—' he looked at the bed, then back at her '—everything...how can you believe that?'

Pain. That was what was in his eyes.

She dropped her glance to the bed. They had been naked together there. Souls as well as bodies. Guilt swamped her now. She should have told him long ago.

'Thom.'

'What?'

'It might be Thom. Euphemia said...it was so little. Just a sentence.'

'What did she say? Tell me!'

'She said Thom was...unhappy with you.'

'He has been since before Beltane.'

'He said you were more Inglis than Scots.'

The sentence lingered, floating in the air. She watched him suppress his pain and anger, so he could examine the idea. 'But if he's such a Scot, why would he let a Robson in? What if they had won? Why risk that? It makes no sense. Unless...'

His eyes met hers. 'Unless he wanted people to think as you did. That I was the one.'

'Could he hate you so much?' Her faith so weak that she would even think Gavin could betray them. Yet she had. For a while, even she had.

Gavin's expression darkened. 'I will find out.'

As he left, she prayed she had named the right man.

He went down to the hall, pulled Thom awake, and forced him outside. Damp, chill fog smudged the waning moon.

'Why?' he said. 'Why did you do it?'

'Do what?' he sneered the question.

Gavin's fist caught the man without warning, knocking him into the dirt. 'Because of you, one of our men is dead, there's a family homeless, and we lost twenty sheep, a mews and a trained goshawk.'

Slow down, he thought, grabbing hold of his fury. A falcon circles until the right time to strike.

Realising he was caught, then looked up, defiant eyes blazing with hatred. 'And because of *you,* good Scots men have to bow to an Inglis bastard who has already killed too many of our own.'

'Are there more?' How many? Did all the men think the same?

Thom laughed. 'What if I said all? What if I told you that none of them think you have any right to be master here? They would rather see the Robsons rule than you.'

Gavin fought the hum of rage in his head. To slay the man at his feet would only raise more suspicion.

He could not be the only one to hear his confession of guilt.

'But I *am* master here. And I am going to let you get well acquainted with the Robsons.'

The man turned pale. Gavin pulled him to his feet. 'Yes, spend some time in the cell with them and see if you think the same.'

But as he locked the man in the cell, his feeling of triumph ebbed. He had done everything he knew to make this his home, to protect it, yet he had not found peace. How many thought as Thom did?

Even his own wife doubted him.

Chapter Twenty-One

In the end, it seemed, Thom had acted alone.

Neither the baron's interrogation nor Euphemia's casual questions uncovered any allies in the man's plot. Instead, one by one, the men came to Gavin to pledge their loyalty anew.

A few even offered to wield the sword to execute the culprit, but Gavin persuaded them to wait for Douglas's return. He wanted justice, not vengeance.

They did not have to wait long. November's crisp frost sprinkled the Cheviot, when Lord Douglas and his men rode up to Carr's Tower.

Gavin smiled at his wife as she stepped forwards to greet their guests. She had begged his forgiveness for doubting him. He had given it. And yet as he saw her with Douglas again, he felt his own doubts rise anew.

'Lord Douglas,' Clare began, in her most ladylike voice, 'your presence honours us, and we—'

Douglas spat in the dirt.

Clare crossed her hands over her ribs, recoiling. Gavin stepped in to shield her. 'Lord Douglas—'

'We're finished. Hundreds dead. French, Scots. Edward now holds two kings prisoner, the French Jean beside David.'

Even Gavin, who knew the strengths and weaknesses of both opponents, was stunned.

The local war forgotten, they brought the men into the hall, offered food and drink, and listened to the tale of the battle at Poitiers. The English, outnumbered but still victorious. Arrows raining down on the charging chevaliers. Horses and men left dying in the dirt. Thousands dead or captured.

'And the *comte?*'

Clare's quick glance told him she was surprised that he asked.

'Captured,' Douglas said. 'Held for more than a thousand pounds. As are some of our best men.'

Gavin refrained from asking by what miracle of chivalry Lord Douglas had escaped the same fate.

Gloom settled over the hall as Douglas's words died away in defeat. Gavin exchanged a silent glance with the baron.

England had not simply won the battle. The war was over.

'Edward will turn his attention to Scotland again,' Gavin said, 'now that he does not have to fight on French soil. And this time, we'll be alone.'

'The French were little help to us,' the baron said, with feigned bravado. 'We don't need them.'

Gavin shrugged, not disagreeing. *Edward now holds both Kings prisoner.* But Douglas was to have met with

Edward's commissioners before he left for France. Why was David still in exile?

'Perhaps,' Gavin began, 'Edward would negotiate for David's release now. This war has been expensive. The ransom would be welcome.'

Lord Douglas stared into the fire, nodding.

Edward had not been the obstacle to bringing David home. In the last ten years, Stewart and Lord Douglas had divided the country and ruled it as they chose, in no hurry for the return of the rightful King.

The Lord finished his ale and wiped his lips. 'Aye. I guess it's time to bring the poor man home.'

Relief released a smile. Home. David, too, could come home.

'I've already applied for a safe conduct to send some men to England.' Douglas raised his gaze from the flames and smiled at Gavin. 'Join them.'

'I am honoured, Lord Douglas—' Douglas, no doubt, could hear the edge in Gavin's acceptance '—to represent Scotland.'

Peace between Scotland and England. David restored to the throne. It would be all he had ever hoped.

And his return to England? Well, it was time to make peace with his uncle. And to get the answers to questions he should have asked long ago.

'I'll call a council meeting. We will set the parameters, pick the rest of the delegation.' Douglas looked at him. 'But this isn't the first time we've tangled with the Inglis over these terms.'

Douglas's power, it was clear, was not based solely on his prowess in war. If Gavin came back with terms he did not like, he would blame Gavin and reject them.

No matter what happened with King David, Gavin thought, Douglas would have to be reckoned with.

'I promise you,' he replied, his gaze never faltering, 'it *will* be the last.'

With the plan settled, he and the baron spoke of their battle, the betrayal, and the prisoners held beneath them.

'When did they attack?' Douglas asked.

'October,' the baron answered. 'Early.'

Douglas shook his head. 'They waited until the truce expired. Clever bastards.' He looked into the fire, silent for a time, and then raised his head. 'Kill them.'

One more night, Clare thought, tucking a sprig of lavender into Gavin's bag to remind him of home. One more night and he would be gone.

Her weeks of doubts, their tug of war, all those things had defined the ebb and flow of days. Yet she had expected them to have time. Time to forgive. Time to reconcile fully. Time she had foolishly wasted.

Now there was no time.

She clung to him, not wanting to face the coming months she would spend alone until he returned.

She tugged him towards the bed for a last joining, a memory to last the empty months.

He did not move. 'It's time for your maiden flight.'

'What do you mean?'

'You must take off the hood, unleash the tether and test your wings.'

She covered her eyes with her hands, frightened of the very thought. She could never fly without the freedom of darkness; never dare look at him as she became this other being. In the dark, she could pretend she succumbed only because he insisted. Eyes opened, she would have to admit her own desires.

'I can't.'

His hands circled her wrists and he pulled them away from her eyes. 'Can't?' Quiet, he searched her eyes, and she glimpsed in his the doubts of the boy with no father and no home. 'Or haven't the courage?'

Did he, too, wonder whether his partner came from choice or from duty? How strange to think that a man could know the most intimate secrets of her body and still not know her heart. 'I fear my flight will disappoint you.'

'I am willing to take that risk. Are you?'

No, she wanted to scream. What if I fail? What if I disappoint you? What if I am awkward and it becomes a chore and not a pleasure?

Yet the question in his eyes was so strong, she had to answer it. She had to try for his sake, so that he would know how much he had brought her to herself.

'Yes. Yes, and because I want to.'

But this time, she would not expect to reach the soaring freedom she had come to love there in the dark. How ironic that she must be tethered to feel free.

'Begin,' he said, 'by disrobing.'

Since that first night, she had not undressed herself. He had always done it for her. Self-conscious, she reached for a lace, unable to look at him.

Yet something still tickled deep inside her as she felt his eyes on her, knowing what was to come. Knowing what had come before. He had trained her body to crave the mating. That desire, at least, had not disappeared with the blindfold.

The *frisson* of longing gave her confidence.

She lifted her eyes to his. There was a strange sense of strength, having her clothes, the power, in her own hands. As she removed the gown, she watched his eyes. Without the blindfold, she could see for the first time how just the sight of her sparked his desire.

It caught on the dry tinder of her body, giving her hope.

Finally, she stood naked before him. The heat in his eyes warmed her, but she did not know where to look with eyes now free to see, or where to touch with hands free to feel. 'What do I do now?'

'Whatever you want.'

When had she ever been allowed to do that?

What did the falcon want? To fly. To hunt. To eat. To mate. 'I want you to be naked.'

He opened his arms as if offering himself to her. 'Then make it so.'

She knelt at his feet as he sat on the bench, taking off his boots, using the excuse to explore with her fingers and her eyes. First, she touched his hair, golden like the eagle's, but with gentle waves hidden for her fingers to find. Then, she slipped her hands under the loose sleeves of his tunic, feeling the strength just beneath his skin. Arms as powerful as wings, able to propel death as well as love.

'Stand,' she commanded, wanting free access.

He did.

She pulled down the chausses.

She had left the tunic on, but he could not hide. He was aroused. More than aroused. Ready.

His eyes closed. She caught the whisper of a moan. 'Now,' he said, reaching for her.

She stood and held him at arm's length. He opened his eyes and she smiled, savouring her unaccustomed power. 'Not now. When I say.'

He rolled his eyes. 'I have unleashed a monster.' But when his eyes met hers, the hot desire was melded with something else. Trust. Love.

Had it been there all along, beyond the blindfold, out of her sight?

Could he indeed love someone so imperfect?

Could she?

She pointed to the bed. 'If I am free, it is time for you to taste darkness and feel leather's hold.'

How simple men are, she thought. For he was unable to hide his reaction, unlike a woman. She had hidden from him the excitement she felt at their joining, even hidden it from herself until his hands, fingers, tongue, staff swept her away and she could hide it no longer.

But he could not. 'I am not well trained enough to wait on your convenience, wife.'

'Then I must train you. The tercel is not allowed to hunt when he chooses, but must wait upon the falconer.'

She made him lie on the bed, draped the leather straps over his arms and legs. The bonds were only symbolic. She would not want to wait long before feeling him surround her.

Then she tied the scarf over his eyes.

Restless beneath her hands, he could not lie still. 'I must trust you with my life now, wife.'

'Have you the courage to take the risk, husband?'

His sigh, like a growl, rattled in his throat. 'I have trained you too well.'

She left his tunic on, remembering the rough feel of fabric against skin, the contrast between nakedness and covering that had heightened her pleasure in both.

His staff waved like a banner's stick, as if determined to get her attention.

She rubbed her palms along its length. Miraculously, it seemed to grow longer.

'For the love of God,' he said, barely able to grind out the words. 'Have mercy.'

She laughed. How strange to laugh in the middle of lovemaking. But it was their world here in the dark. No rules but those they created together.

'I don't recall,' she said, 'receiving any mercy from you when I begged.'

But she knew, now, what that meant. That he was on fire. That his desire was straining to break free.

She decided to give him release.

She opened her lips and took him fully inside her mouth.

Gavin, in shock, struggled for control, afraid he would let go immediately.

'Clare, you can't, are you sure…?' He couldn't finish the question, uncertain now how to speak.

All he heard was a murmur. All he felt was the track of her tongue swirling warm and wet around him. Then, her lips tightened at the tip of his staff.

After that, he knew nothing but the freedom of the falcon in flight.

* * *

This time, she held him as he fell back to earth, knowing, finally, she was truly mated.

He whispered, near her ear, as his breathing slowed, 'My falcon has become the falconer. You have trained me in truth. No, more, tamed me.'

Her arms tightened as he slipped into sleep.

She lay awake, unable to lose one moment of their last night. No longer blindfolded, she saw only her fears. More than vows bound them now, yet she still did not know this man. Tomorrow he would fly alone. And she could not be sure whether he would return or, like the falcon, escape to the victorious border.

And what will happen, her heart whispered, if you lose him now?

Chapter Twenty-Two

Spring had come to the south by the time Gavin confronted the King face to face.

He had spent the months since leaving home meeting with the council, where Stewart and Douglas had wrangled over whose men would travel to England to represent Scotland and what terms they could accept.

Then came the long, hard trip south. With each mile, he retraced the path that had brought him north, remembering how Edward had left France when he heard the Scots had taken Berwick. How they had galloped north, heedless of the winter cold, to wrest the town away from the enemy. And how he had crossed the border, riding by Edward's side, until he realised he could not make war on his own people.

Since arriving in London, he'd been in endless meetings and negotiations with Edward's representatives.

But never with Edward himself until now, when, finally, his uncle had granted his request to meet alone.

He stood before the man's chambers, uncertain how Edward would receive him. The last time they had seen each other, Fitzjohn had thrown his torch to the ground and ridden off without a word to join the enemy. No apology would salve Gavin's rejection of their shared blood.

But Gavin had not come to apologise.

The King dismissed the servants and they were alone. He bowed and waited as Edward examined him.

It was for the King to speak first.

'You've chosen a side, then,' he said, finally.

Gavin swallowed. Edward had been uncle as well as King, as much of a father as he had ever had. 'It is my hope, your Grace, that with this peace, I will have chosen a side of the border, not of a battlefield.'

Edward, flush with his victory in France, smiled, triumphant. He held both the King of Scotland and the King of France captive. He expected no more battles. 'So you've finally convinced those stubborn Scots to accept the terms.'

He nodded. 'We are very close, your Grace.'

'Scotland will be mine in the end, you know.'

'Or Lionel's.' David had been open to letting one of Edward's sons succeed him, something Douglas and Stewart were reluctant to accept.

'It is the same thing. My son. Myself.'

'Not always.' He knew that now.

Edward studied him in silence, and Gavin wondered whether he saw his brother in his brother's son.

'You wanted to see me,' he said, finally. 'Why?'

'I have questions.'

'*You* have questions?' The King's temper threatened.

'You were not the one left sitting in the cold looking at the charred remains of his dead brother's coat-of-arms heaped in the mud!'

Gavin paused. 'I could not set the church afire.'

He knew that now. Not only *did* not, but *could* not. He was not perfect, no man was, but he was not as evil as he had feared for so long.

With her, he had learned that.

Edward had the grace to glance away. 'War tests the resolve of even the most chivalrous. Sometimes, we fail.'

Had his father failed? Men with nerves pitched for battle could do things they would otherwise condemn. 'But they say I did it. That I burned the church. And that it was full of people.'

Had Edward heard the stories? Helped to spread them?

Edward waved his hand. 'People will say what they will. It's not true.'

'*I* know that. But what happened after I left?'

Edward's temper exploded. 'I burned it, yes! The church, the nunnery, the whole rebel-filled town! And Edinburgh and Whitekirk!'

'And the people?' Gavin heard himself yell, too. 'What about the people?'

The King rose from his chair. 'No!'

As the echo bounced off the wall, he slumped back in his seat, head back, eyes closed. 'Not the people.'

'And my father?'

Edward lifted his head and stared ahead, silent.

'They said,' Gavin began, the words rough in his throat, 'the same thing of my father. Was it true?'

His words seemed to take Edward back. He didn't speak and no longer seemed to see the man before him. 'He was not a bad man,' he said, finally. 'Just a young one.'

'Is that how you excuse him? He was of royal blood. He had led armies, ruled the country when you were in France. Was he not a man who knew right and wrong?'

'He knew.'

'And yet he did it anyway?'

'I don't know!' A shout.

Gavin wouldn't stop now. 'What about what they say of you? Is that true or as much a lie as their tales of me?'

'Is what true?'

'Did you kill my father?'

His question echoed in the silence. He had waited so long, waited since he had first come to court and wanted to challenge the King to combat to avenge his father's death.

Waited so long that it almost didn't matter any more.

Almost.

'Is that what they've told you?' He didn't deny it. 'He was so young in those days. We both were.'

'So that's your excuse, too? For murder?'

Edward's blue eyes met his, and he wondered at the mirror he saw. 'How can you even ask? He was my brother.'

As if that said it all.

But it didn't. Edward, after all, had had a hand in the death of his own father.

'I *have* asked. But you have not answered.' Relentless now. Nothing to lose. It was all gone except the need to know. Had his father been so evil, so terrible that his own brother had killed him?

Edward put a hand on his shoulder. 'No.'

His body sagged with relief, yet he still struggled to believe. 'But they said you had nightmares.'

'Wouldn't you if someone you loved had been taken from you?'

'I did. Your brother was taken, but so was my father.'

The King turned away, pacing. 'He loved your mother, that Scottish slut. Did she tell you? Maybe she didn't even know.' He shook his head. 'We suggested half-a-dozen wives for him and though he cleverly never said no, he never accepted any of them either. There was never a betrothal.'

Had his mother been right? He scoffed at his thoughts. Even Clare, raised on tales of chivalrous love, could not have sustained such a fantasy.

'And when I saw him that last time, he said he was going marry your mother. Can you imagine what would have happened then?'

He tried. If the King's brother had married a woman from a minor Scottish family, even become King of Scotland, the peace he had longed for might have come years before.

And Edward might have had an even stronger rival on Scotland's throne.

And a reason to want him dead.

'Then how did he die?'

'A fever? Spoiled food? Who knows why God takes

some men? And when you appeared, looking like John reborn, holding the testament to your birth, I thought he had come back to me. That it could end differently this time.

'It did.' He met Edward's eyes, calm from a lifetime of uncertainty settling over him.

'Yes. You chose her side.'

'So perhaps I am like my father in that way as well.'

Edward's smile was wistful. 'Perhaps even better.'

Strange, to have accomplished what his father had not: lived past twenty and married. His father had died too soon to learn the painful lessons of experience.

Or appreciate its joys.

'There will be peace,' he said, looking at his uncle, golden-haired, blue-eyed, and twice his age. Like the mirror of a future he hoped to see.

Edward sighed, thirty years of rule weighing on him, heavy. 'Some day.'

Gavin left the King and went to Westminster Abbey. He approached his father's tomb slowly. Edward had made sure his brother was buried with full honours. A canopy covered an alabaster sculpture of John, laid out in his armour, hands clasped in a final prayer.

Below were weeping figures. The Queen? His brother and sisters?

His mother had wept. But she was not pictured here.

He crept closer to look on his father's face. Straight, strong nose. Moustache. Full lower lip. A face younger than his own. Was there anything of this man in him?

He knelt on the stone floor and prayed.

And when he left, he had finally forgiven his father.

And himself.

Gavin entered King David's rooms in the Tower of London, noting the laxness of the guards. It was David's birthday and King Edward had graciously allowed him visitors.

'Whose man are you now, Fitzjohn?' David snapped, sharply. He looked older and more tired than Gavin had remembered. 'You left me to fight Edward's battles.'

At thirty-three, after ten years in captivity, David faced the fullness of age, a King who had lived more years away from his country than in it.

Yet, as Gavin knew, that didn't matter. The call of home would still be strong.

'And I left Edward,' he began, 'to come home again.'

'Home? To Scotland?'

He nodded, unable to stop the smile. Had it been only a year since he first rode on to Carr lands? He itched to be on his way back. 'Douglas has given me Carr's Tower and the woman to match it.'

'Douglas, eh? So you're Douglas's man now?' He said it with deep resignation, knowing that Douglas's man would not always be David's.

Gavin shook his head. 'I'm *your* man. We're near finished with negotiations. You'll be coming home.'

He outlined the terms. The ransom payment, the free movement of money and scholars, the list of hostages. Not a perfect treaty, but the best they could get.

David's smile, sad. 'Why couldn't they have done

that three years ago? The provisions are virtually the same.' His voice, after all this time, carried only a hint of his homeland inflection.

'I cannot say,' Gavin said, though he had his suspicions.

'You don't have to. Edward and I were too friendly for most. And Douglas and Stewart were more comfortable without me.' He let go a sigh, then squared his shoulders. 'In case of default of payment, who is on the list of hostages to be sent to Edward?'

Gavin gave him the names.

A sly smile touched David's lips. 'Let's be sure that Douglas and Stewart are added to that list.'

Gavin smiled. No wonder Douglas was hesitant to bring David home. He would have to answer to a king at last.

Neither Gavin, nor the tercel, returned in the spring.

Clare flew Wee One alone, riding into the hills, staring to the south without ever crossing the border. The bird seemed to share her feeling of abandonment.

She told herself Gavin only stayed in England because he must so that he could conclude a treaty that would include everything Scotland wanted. Without him, the sweetness of ordinary days deserted her, yet the memory of their lovemaking, instead of bringing consolation, made her toss and turn, desire mingling with discomfiture. How could she have done those things?

Months passed, until he had been away longer than they had been together. Memories dimmed. Doubts grew brighter. Did he mean to come home at all?

* * *

She went down to the cellar one June afternoon, trying to count the days. Had it been a year ago they wed?

The sounds of panting, gasping moans came to her ears like memories come alive. Then she realised it was not memory.

Euphemia and Walter, half-naked, were coupling in the corner.

Clare froze at the sight. His hips, thrusting into hers. Her eyes, closed in ecstasy. Neither of them aware of anything beyond each other. No better than animals.

Heat rushed through her, first unwelcome desire, then embarrassment, anger, fear, shame. In their joining, she saw everything that was wrong with her world, everything her own failings had created.

'Stop! Both of you!'

They did, jaws sagging in shock. Euphemia had the good grace to duck her head. Walter curved his body around hers, trying to hide her nakedness.

'Get up. Cover yourselves.' She turned her back and put her hands over her eyes, remembering her mother's cool fingers, shielding her sight. But that did not block the familiar sounds of cloth on skin. A kiss. 'Go upstairs. I will speak to you later.'

She wanted to screech curses at them, but all the words that formed were hurled at herself.

Once, she would have expected no better of Murine's daughter, but Clare had tried to teach her, had treated them both almost as kin. Euphemia's behaviour reflected on her.

And she had been a poor example.

Despite all her training, she had listened to her heart;

nae, worse, she had listened to her body, untrustworthy vessel, and lulled herself into thinking that an Inglis bastard could be a proper husband.

No one knew what she and Gavin had done alone together, but she did. She had violated every tenet she had been taught. And now she knew that she was no better than the women she despised, no more virtuous than Murine and Euphemia.

In the dark cellar, listening to their steps fade, she made a muddled vow. When, if, he came home, things would be different. They would share a bed, yes, but she would once again be the virtuous woman she had been taught.

And Gavin? He would have to prove that his heart was fully on this side of the border.

The Treaty was signed in Berwick in October. Gavin breathed easier as he and David rode across the border, filling his lungs with the scent of home.

The King was free.

And now, so was he.

They pulled up the horses at the crossroads where Gavin would turn for home. 'Here's where I leave you.'

'I must form a new government.' Sitting taller on his horse, wind whipping his hair, David seemed to have left ten years at the English line. 'I need men I can trust.'

Gavin knew that Lord Douglas and Stewart were not necessarily counted among them, though that would not be said aloud. 'Lord Douglas will be ready to serve, I'm sure.'

He nodded. 'He's to be made an Earl.'

'That'll please him.'

'You're sure you won't come to Edinburgh with me?'

Gavin shook his head. 'I have a falcon at home, ready to fly.'

'Some day we'll fly the hawks together again.'

They clasped arms and Gavin turned his horse to the west.

He was going home. And the falcon he wanted to fly was one he would share with no man.

Chapter Twenty-Three

As the hills of home appeared, his body grew more eager for her. First he would kiss her all over. Then, he would tease her until she was crazed with wanting. Then—

He stifled the rest as he rode into the tower's yard. Angus, trying to be a proper squire, took his horse to the stables. His father by marriage, Murine and Euphemia surrounded him with hugs and kisses.

His wife, finally, stepped forwards and gave him a decorous hug. 'Ye broke nae rules, did ye?' she whispered.

He smiled. Only in a homecoming welcome did she lapse into the accent of the borders. 'None I'll tell you about,' he answered.

And then, he gave a soft, low whistle, tickling her ear, hoping no one was looking below his waist as he leaped to return to his falconer's wrist.

He did not see the knowing, private smile he had hoped for.

And now, instead of a retreat to their aerie, he faced a painful hour of public display for the benefit of the rest, who insisted he outline the tale of the last ten months and the terms of the treaty.

Clare, running up and down stairs from Hall to kitchen to laundry, did not hear the story start to finish. Only as he neared the end, did she linger to listen.

But she did not sit beside him. And she would not meet his eyes.

Finally, pleading fatigue he did not feel, he excused himself, grabbed Clare's hand and headed for their bed-chamber, ignoring the knowing smiles from the baron and Murine.

But Clare's steps were slow and they climbed the stairs in silence.

Shy again, perhaps. That would not take long to mend. The last time they had made love, her eyes had been wide open, her mouth on him…

He quickened his steps.

Once inside their room, he kicked the door closed, lifted her in his arms, carried her to the bed, and lay down beside her.

'I'll have no more of your maiden's mattress,' he said, between kisses, as his feet hung off the side of the bed. 'We need one big enough for us both.'

She stretched against him, silent, and he sat up, stripping his boots and chausses, already hard for her. 'I must have you now, my lady. Our games will have to wait.'

He unlaced her gown, breath taken by the first sight of her breasts. Learning her again, he worshipped the curve of her hip and her belly with his lips. Both, still trim and firm as when he left.

'With all the times we've mated, I cannot believe you're not yet with babe,' he murmured, pressing his lips into her skin.

But he was glad of it. He had been away so long, she could have born a babe without him. He would have regretted that. 'I must make up for lost time.' Soon enough, there would be a son and a harvest of peace.

Yet beneath his eager lips, she lay quiescent, unmoving, eyes closed, not in ecstasy, but as if to shut him out.

His kisses slowed and he pulled himself up, leaning on his arms over her until she finally opened her eyes. 'What's wrong?'

'Wrong?' The arch of her eyebrow was as sharp as her voice. 'Whatever could be wrong, my lord?'

He rolled to one side, leaned on his elbow, and sighed. This was not a lady in the mood for lovemaking. 'Don't play with me, now.' Was it her time of month? Some domestic detail she must share with him first? Euphemia looked as if she might have a babe on the way. 'Tell me what troubles you.' He stroked the hair back from her forehead, impatient to hear her out, comfort her and move on.

'Tell me the terms of the Treaty.'

He groaned. 'Did you not hear enough of that already?'

Had he known it would delay their lovemaking he would have held her to his side as he explained, so she would miss no specifics.

'Some things, yes. But I need to be sure of what I heard.'

He laid back, arm covering his eyes, waiting for his

stiff staff to relinquish its hold so his brain could resume control.

'David is released, a ransom paid and hostages to be given to Edward in surety for the payment.'

'How much?' The bed shifted as she sat up.

He clasped his hands together on his ribs, ready to recite again. 'One hundred thousand marks.'

She looked at him open mouthed. 'What did you say?'

'One hundred thousand marks.'

'Is there so much in all Scotland?'

'It's a bargain for a king. For France's Jean, he'll get eight times as much.' David's stature with Edward had dropped once he had seized the real prize.

She slipped off the bed and out of his reach. 'You sound happy.'

He sighed and sat up, cross-legged, willing his staff to calmness. This would be no brief conversation. 'And you do not.'

'Why should I not be happy when I have a King again?' Her brittle lilt was forced.

'Aye. You do.' Patience. Patience. 'But can't these worldly affairs wait?' He reached for her, hoping to woo her back to a loving frame of mind.

She pulled herself away from his hands. 'And what about the succession? Who's to be king if David dies childless?'

This answer, he knew, would not improve her mood. 'The Treaty is silent.'

England and Scotland could both claim victory as long as the central issue remained unsettled.

'Did Edward give up his claims to the throne?'

'No.'

'No?' Her voice slid up the scale as she paced the floor. 'Then I've no country left! If we manage to pay the ransom, what will we buy? A few years? Then Edward will claim again what he wanted all along. Scotland.' She laughed bitterly. 'And we'll have paid him to take it!'

'There's no certainty of that. David is a young man. He could have children still.'

She scoffed, with the assurance of womanhood. 'He has been married since childhood and fathered no heir. There will be no children now.'

He sighed. David had confessed near the same.

'How could you allow this?'

She would not care about the other provisions he had fought for. That neither King could harbour rebels against the other. That the clergy from Scotland might study at Oxford. That England must accept Scotland's coin so trade could flourish. Provisions concerning Papal letters would mean nothing to her. 'These were not my terms alone. The other Douglas and Stewart men and King David approved them.'

'But Parliament refused the same three years ago.'

'Three years ago, we had French gold to fund our fight. Now, they must ransom their own King. There is no money to send to us.'

'Us? How can you use the word us?'

'Because it is us!' He drew himself to his feet, the bed a barrier between them. 'Do you only love the half of me that's Scots?'

Had she ever said she loved him at all?

'I should have known from the beginning.' She was

again the stern, judgemental woman he had met on the moor. 'You came here disguised to gain our trust. And now you've betrayed Lord Douglas.'

'Me?' Anger, deep, turned his desire to ash. 'It's Lord Douglas who betrayed the King. Ten years in captivity and why? Because Douglas wanted no rivals to his own rule. That's why these terms weren't accepted years ago. And despite that, David will make him an Earl and I've no doubt he'll take it. They'll both be satisfied. Why aren't you?'

'Because a Scot fights for freedom! We would have dethroned the Bruce himself if he had dared to subjugate us to England.'

'When the falcon flies, she doesn't see Scotland or England. She sees one island. One body. No more able to be cleaved than my own. Is it worth endless war to be sure no one steps across a line we cannot even see?'

'Yes.' The word. Cold. Immovable.

No way to convince her that these two countries must share an isle in peace. No compromise. Only what should be.

'I will never forgive them,' she said, 'for what they have done to Scotland. Churches, fields, everything burned.'

Them. The English.

Him.

Yet he tried to argue. Useless, when it was her heart that was unconvinced. 'You criticise Edward, yet against their enemies the Bruces did the same.'

She blinked. 'What do you mean?'

'Have you ever heard of the herschip of Buchan?'

The colour on her cheeks told him she had.

'Then you know what David's father did to his enemies. To men who were also Scots. Destroyed their
homes, burned their castles, crops, cattle, killed all who
were loyal to his enemies and left the rest without food
or shelter on lands where they had lived peaceably for
a hundred years. Terrorised the poor folk so thoroughly
that they have never raised their heads in fifty years.'

Fury shook him. Was it for her or himself?

But he could not stop now. 'So don't sit there and
wax righteously against the evils of the English. At war,
all men are devils, capable of things no man should see
and no woman should know of. In the midst of battle,
no man clings to chivalry. Not if he wants to live.'

His chest was heaving as if he'd been wielding a
sword against an enemy. 'And we all, Mistress Clare,
want to live. More than we want food or drink or air or
sex. We want to live and we will do anything, anything,
to be sure that we do.'

'So that is your excuse? You expect me to forgive the
English because they are no worse than anyone else?'

He shuddered at her words. 'I expected, at least, that
you had forgiven me.'

'How can I? You, Edward, you set fire to everything,
the church, even the people—'

'I didn't!'

'But you wanted to!'

His confession, hurled back at him. He had managed
to come to terms with the horror of war. To accept himself and the conquered darkness within.

She had not.

To her, he was still a monster who could burn a
church full of innocents. And without her trust, he was

still the same divided man who had faced the Lamp of
Lothian, holding a torch.

'This isn't about Scotland or England at all, is it? It's
my English blood you can't forgive.'

'The others…' She hesitated, searching for the words.
'Those men who did those things you speak of, they do
not sleep in my bed.'

The nights of loving acceptance. The dark desires
shared only with each other. That union that had united
his warring blood.

Surely all these things could not lie?

He reached for her, wanting their bodies to speak
again, beyond the hateful words. Her body would
remember his touch. He had simply been too long away.
Once they joined, all would be as it was.

She stood, stiff in his arms.

'You're afraid,' he said, truth finally sinking into his
thick skull. 'Afraid of what other people will think of
me.'

'No!'

'What, then?' He watched her eyes, no longer trusting.
Worse, ashamed, regretting what they had done together.
'This isn't even about trusting me.' Her silence con-
firmed his fears. Too long away from his body, she had
let her doubts intrude. 'It's about trusting yourself.'

She closed her eyes. Pursed her lips.

He knew he was right. And knew that with a kiss, a
touch, the gentlest of force, he could release her again
to fly with him.

But now, he could not do it.

She pushed him away, as if she knew his thoughts
and had to get away before his touch removed all her

resistance. 'I've had time to think. Time to realise those things we did…' Her shudder spoke more of longing than of revulsion. She opened her eyes and the ones that met his were hard, cold green-grey again. 'They went beyond all boundaries. You are not a man I could love.'

'Love is not perfection. It's messier than that. It's what happens in the dark corners between two souls. Good and bad mix in us all. Things we are proud of. Things we hope no one else ever sees. But when you love someone, you love even the parts that are not perfect.'

She did not speak. Did not move. Did not reach out to touch him.

With all the others, he had brushed off what was said of him, not expecting to live long enough for it to matter. Waiting only for an outer battle to bring the one within to a fatal, inevitable conclusion.

But with her, he had seen himself as something more than a knight whose task was to kill, known that the darkest impulses could be resisted, even channelled to create light.

And now, too late, he had brought them outer peace, and shattered the peace within.

Each flight was a choice. Each flight was a risk. And by her silence he knew he had lost her.

'Nae. Enough. I'll trouble you no more.' He grabbed the sack, still full of what he had taken on his travels.

'Where will you go?'

He heard no curiosity in her words.

Where *would* he go? What was a knight to do when the war had ended?

'Why, I'll do what the most chivalrous knight would do,' he said, forcing the edge of laughter back into his voice. 'I'll go to England as Edward's hostage so that one of those with real Scots blood can come home. That will spare one of Douglas's relatives a long, lonely stint in exile.'

As for him? Well, he would be again a man divided, as much of a wandering stranger as the falcon, without a country to call home.

Chapter Twenty-Four

She watched him, frozen with guilt. She had done nothing right, not from the very first. 'But you promised to protect…the land. To protect me.'

'Peace will protect you.'

'You think the Robsons care for the Kings' peace?'

She saw it then, a pang of pain, on his face. 'If they did attack again, you would only wonder whether I aided them.'

He stepped closer and she clenched her fists to keep herself from falling into his arms and reaching for his kiss.

He did not give it. Instead, he touched his fingers to her cheek, then smoothed them over her hair, tightly braided today, with no room for his fingers to roam.

He lifted her chin and she closed her eyes, waiting.

With a kiss, he could sweep her away. She could lose herself in his arms, surrender to his desires, and pretend that it was not her choice, but his that drew them together and made her do those things.

She waited, but his lips did not meet hers.

She opened her eyes.

His fingers fell to his side. 'Farewell, my falcon.'

Gavin protected her even as he left, giving her father a smooth, clever lie of explanation. Yes, he had known all along that he would have to return as a hostage. No, he had not told them because he had not wanted to spoil the homecoming.

No, he could not delay. Someone needed to carry the first ransom payment to England and he had volunteered. He had come all this way just to see home again.

He looked at her when he said it.

And, no, he did not know when he would be able to return. It might be years.

The men, disappointed and confused at losing the leader they had come to respect, gathered at the gate to wish him well.

She did not join them.

Alone again, Clare clung to her righteousness. It did not comfort her.

The bed they had shared was wide and cold now. Sleep, which had come so gently when he held her, no longer came at all.

Weeks later, she huddled beneath the covers long after sunrise, unwilling to face the damp autumn chill.

A knock jarred the door. She didn't answer.

Murine opened it anyway and stood, solid and stubborn, at the end of her bed.

Clare burrowed beneath the blanket. 'Leave me alone. I have nothing to say to you.'

The woman ripped back the covers and stepped up to perch her spreading hips on the edge of the bed. 'Well, I have some things to say to ye, so wake up and listen.'

Clare scrambled to sit, leaning against the headboard, and pulled her knees close to her chest beneath her nightdress. She had avoided the woman since coming upon Euphemia and Walter, but it was a waste of breath to argue with Murine. 'I'm listening.'

'Walter and Euphemia want to wed.'

Clare nodded. Not a moment too soon. A babe would arrive, no doubt, by March. 'I'll send for the priest, then.'

'And let Fitzjohn know.'

His name bludgeoned her heart. 'He's no longer master here.'

'That's not for ye to decide.'

'His loyalty lies with the Inglis, not with us, that's plain.'

Murine snorted. 'There's them I might accuse of that. He's not of them.'

'The Treaty he gave us will bring nothing but sorrow. That proves which side of the border owns his heart.'

The woman raised her brows and gave her a sideways look. 'Your Da worries. And not about the Treaty.'

'Did he send you here?'

Murine shook her head, but Clare knew, now, that more than bodies joined when a man and a woman shared a bed. He would not have had to ask. 'It's my father's fault I married the man. I rue the day I met him.'

'Do ye, now?'

Clare nodded. 'If he hadn't come here, I would be married to the *comte*.'

'And ye accuse Fitzjohn's heart of lying across the border? Ye sound more like a Frenchwoman that a Scottis one.' Murine shook her head and patted Clare's hand. 'Besides, ye're talking like a child. The lily livered man never asked ye and even if he had, ye would have been miserable.'

Resentful, she pulled her hand away and crossed her arms. There were no secrets in this house. 'Fitzjohn left us, Murine. That's the end of it.'

'Left? I'd say ye sent him back into exile.'

Something hot and hard seemed to burst in her chest. 'He left me, Murine! He left me.' The fire blurred through her tears and all the words tumbled out. 'I knew what I should do, what kind of woman I should be and I failed.' *You're perfect. Just the way you are.* He had said it, but he had lied. If she had been perfect, he would still be here. 'I failed.'

Murine hugged her, rocked her, and let her cry. 'All of us do, child. Ye've no special claim to perfection.' She shook her head. 'That's too great a burden for any earthly sinner.'

'But I tried so hard...' Not good enough for Alain, not good enough for Gavin.

You're perfect. He had not said it when she behaved like a virtuous lady, but when she had fallen apart in his arms, wanton desires laid bare.

'Seems to me ye have more rules for yerself and everyone else than Saint Peter. That's a hard way for a woman to live. And harder for a man.'

Suddenly, she wondered how many rules her mother had brought from France.

She sat up and wiped her tears on her sleeve, ashamed at having cried before this woman. 'Forgive me. You're right. I'm behaving like a child.' She lifted her head and straightened her shoulders, trying to be the lady of the household again. 'Walter and Euphemia will have my blessing and a cottage of their own before the child arrives. Is there anything else?'

Murine sighed. 'Are ye going to throw away happiness just because it doesn't come according to your rules?'

'Good day, Murine.'

The woman left, shaking her head.

She had tried to explain, but Murine couldn't understand. Rules were the only armour she had, the only way to ensure nothing bad would ever happen again, that she would lose no one else.

She'd broken those rules with the falcons. Warned not to raise birds in the mews, she had ignored the advice. Disaster had followed. One bird was useless for the hunt and the other had disappeared.

And with Gavin, she had done everything, been everything wrong from the moment she saw him emerge from the fog.

That's why he, too, had left her alone.

Unless Murine was right. What if she *had* pushed him back into exile because he did not behave according to some rules she had memorised, rules no one ever really followed?

She found herself staring at the red-and-gold banker and noticed, for the first time, that it was a poorly woven piece. She folded it, put it inside the chest, and dressed to meet the day.

A message went to the priest in Jedburgh before midday.

She sent no word to Fitzjohn.

Late in November, the rain and fog cleared one day so she rode out again. She found no game, though Angus, with one wary eye on her, kept looking.

They slowed the horses to a walk and she looked at the bird, suddenly feeling cruel. She was trained to hunt, as was her nature, but she was starved in order to be hungry enough to kill on command. Everything seemed turned around. As if everything were different.

But since Wee One's mate had come to the mews, everything had been different. Perhaps with him, the bird had remembered she was more than a trained hunter, only allowed to feed at a human's whim. Remembered what it had been like, to fly without a hood, jesses and bells.

Clare looked at the falcon, who had been her closest companion. Only a bird. Not a pet. Not a person. How could she put all her hopes, all her love, into a creature with wings when a man, a real man, had stood before her, trusting her with the darkest secrets of his soul?

And she hadn't even trusted him to be loyal to the blood that ran in his veins.

Falcons mate for life. He had told her that on her wedding night. Yet she had driven her mate away. Left herself alone as she'd been alone as a child. As she'd been all her life. And no matter what she had tried to do, how perfect she had tried to be, it wasn't enough.

She looked at Wee One. No, she had not done

everything right with this one. She had broken one important rule.

She had kept the bird too long.

'Angus, come. We're going to Hen Hole.'

He frowned, but didn't argue.

It was cold as she climbed higher, but she pressed on, hugging her cloak more tightly.

At the top of the ridge, the mountain dropped off steeply. Hen Hole was there below, in the deep cut created by the burn that wended its way towards a gentler valley. From here down would be an easy flight, but a long, dangerous ride.

She looked over the hills, thinking, foolishly, that she would see the tercel waiting for his mate, as if that would be a sign that she was doing the right thing.

The sky was stubbornly empty.

She fumbled with the falcon's hood, her fingers stiff in the cold.

'What are you doing, Mistress Clare? There's no game here.'

A gust of wind swayed the jesses and jangled the bells. Calm, deliberate now, she started to untie them.

'Give me the sack with the food, Angus.'

'But if you feed her, she might not come back!'

'I know that. I'm going to release her.'

'But she's your favourite!'

'Yes, she is. That's why I'm going to let her go.' To give her a choice. A warm, safe home in the mews or the life she had been born for. A chance to find her mate and their life together, here in the wild crags where the falcons nested and in the land across the sea where they would winter.

She reached into the bag and pulled out a piece of food. Unaccustomed to being fed if she had not hunted, Wee One didn't touch the titbit.

Clare poked it towards her beak again. This time, Wee One gobbled it down.

And the next.

And the next until the bird seemed heavier on her wrist.

Clare let out her breath. Wee One would be able to live for days now, while she remembered how to hunt and eat without help from people.

She handed the bird to Angus, then dismounted, taking back the falcon and leaving the horse, to walk carefully the last few steps of the winter-slick trail. Wind, ceaseless, whipped her hair free, tangling the strands as they flew behind her.

Wee One sat patiently as she'd been taught, even without her hood and jesses. Clare stroked her black-and-white striped breast, savouring her final touch of the soft downy feathers.

'Come home if you want, Wee One. The mews will always have a place for you.'

The bird turned her head, as if to hear better, but Clare knew she spoke only to herself.

She met the falcon's sharp glance, then lifted her gloved hand.

The bird rose and circled, confused. Never had she been fed before being released and she paused, expecting prey to be sent her way.

Maybe the bird would follow her home, Clare thought.

But she grasped at a vain hope. Wee One turned, and flew south.

'She's gone, Mistress.' The boy, stunned, stared at the empty sky.

'And so must you be, Angus.' Yet another dear one she had kept too long. The boy was past ready for squire-hood. 'My father has spoken to Lord Douglas. He's agreed that you can join his men.'

His grateful smile eased her emptiness.

He held her horse while she mounted and they turned for the tower, riding in silence. Only the whistle of the wind challenged her thoughts.

She, too, had learned to fly without hood, jesses and bells. Now, she needed the courage that Wee One had, courage to leave the safety of captivity and fly free.

Love is messier than that.

Could she love him as he was?

Could he possibly love her that way?

In order to be sure, she would have to break every rule she knew.

Chapter Twenty-Five

England—January 1358

'England is colder than Scotland.'

'No, it isn't. England is further south. It's always warmer in the south.'

Gavin put another log on the fire, letting his fellow hostages argue without taking a side. The dreary January dampness seeped through the stones of Odiham Castle, but cold or colder, England wasn't home.

If Gavin had feared Edward might ease his captivity for his father's sake, he was wrong. And glad of it. The other two hostages held here, a Stewart and a Ross, were confused enough when he appeared to replace the Douglas cousin whose name had been at the top of the list.

'Why you?' Stewart asked.

All the arguments he had given King David went through his head. Because it will ease Lord Douglas's anger. Because it will prove my loyalty to Scotland.

Because I am half-English. Because I can atone for my father's sins.

Because she no longer wants me.

'This I can do to give Scotland back her King. What more could I do, sitting on a border?'

'Sip good brogat and love your woman,' answered Ross.

There was no answer to that. His marriage and his hopes for it were done. Like King David and his wife Joan Makepeace, they would live apart, for she could no longer bear the sight of him.

Returning to Odiham Castle was like returning to the banishment of his youth. The life of a hostage was certainly better than that of a man in the dungeon, but the castle felt little more welcoming than the Tower of London. It was simply endless exile.

Had this country ever really been his home?

Where were the hills that brought the changeable weather, the light and shadow that shifted as the eye blinked, the scent of heather that softened the edge of autumn?

He longed for all that and more.

At first, he kept the lavender under his pillow, so his room would smell of home, but after the first week, he threw it away. It was too painful a reminder of what he had lost.

King David had left his falcon behind and they were graciously allowed one last hunt before the season came to a close and winter came on.

The bird, while worthy of a King, would have been no match for Wee One.

A page appeared at the door. 'There's a visitor for Sir Gavin Fitzjohn,' he began, nervously. 'A lady.'

The others stared at him, then Ross broke into a laugh. 'Well, I guess you've found a way to have the lady, if not the brogat.'

'Did she give her name?' He could think of no woman in England who would know, or care, that he was here.

The page shook his head. 'But she wanted to see you alone.'

Now both of his fellow prisoners whistled, though Stewart's expression held more than a touch of jealousy.

'In my solar, please,' he said, grateful that Edward had at least provided each man with his own room. If one of his former lady friends thought to rekindle their relationship, he would not subject her to an audience for his rejection. On the other hand, he thought, as he climbed the stairs, Joan Makepeace had returned to England. Perhaps his aunt brought a message from the King not intended for other ears. 'Just give me a moment.'

He looked around the barren room. There was little to neaten for a visitor. But the scent of lavender still hung faintly in the air, even though he had thrown it out months ago.

There was a knock on the door.

'Come.'

The door swung open and Clare stepped across the threshold.

Wordless, he watched her smile at his surprise. 'My lady,' he said, uncertain how he managed to make his tongue work. 'You seem to find yourself on the wrong side of the border.'

She raised her eyebrows. 'In faith, husband, I do not know when I crossed it.' Her glance was a mixture of shyness and confidence. 'I have lost a beloved tercel who respects no boundaries and have travelled miles to find the bird and bring it home.'

He thought to explain to her about kings and treaties, but all he could to do was look. 'But the bird now belongs to the King, who will not give him up.' His heart, pounding, his mouth, dry. 'Ye broke nae rules, did ye?'

'A few I'll have to tell ye about.' She smiled. 'I have spoken to the King. Both of them. And they now understand that this bird and his falconer are wedded. And since the bird has been gone, it is the falconer's heart that has broken.'

Could she have turned two courts upside down for him? 'Perhaps, then' he began, barely able to whisper, 'if you whistle, the bird will return to your fist.'

She pursed her lips. What escaped was not the shrill, high-pitched shriek that had called Wee One to her, but the low, coaxing warble of their private moments. The one that grabbed his body's memories.

He took a step towards her, wanting to hold her, but afraid, now, as he had never been in battle. He had not been afraid of death. But to lose her twice, that he could not bear. 'This bird you seek, I fear, will never be faultless.'

'I have learned that perfection does not exist in following the rules, but in being true to our nature. Yours has two sides. Scots. English. Dark. Light. And in that, you are perfect.'

'And so are you, my wee one.' He would tell her over and over again until she believed him. 'You soar above all others.'

Epilogue

❧❧❧

Carr's Tower—spring 1359

She must have screamed in ecstasy after she came back to earth, for when she opened her eyes, he was leaning on his elbow, smiling at her as if she were the moon and the sun and the stars.

She gave him a playful blow.

'What was that for?' he asked, eyes wide with fake innocence.

She kissed him and when their lips reluctantly parted, she snuggled under the covers. 'Inglisman.'

'Frenchwoman.' He swooped over and tickled her and she screamed with the glee of a child who is safely scared.

She had wintered with him in England, and when the next ransom payment had come from David, Edward had allowed them to leave for home. She had learned, during that sojourn, that all Englishmen were not devils.

And all Scots were not saints.

And that peace blessed the heart as well as the land.

She sighed, content. 'Well, I can't loll abed this morning. I've Beltane to bake for and Euphemia will be of little help this year.' Walter and Euphemia had wed and their second boy had been born a few days before.

'And we'll dance beneath the stars,' he said, a rough whisper in her ear, and they lolled abed some more.

Finally, he squeezed her in a hug and they started to rise. 'To think that it was only King David's long captivity that gave me to you.'

'What do you mean?'

'Douglas's promise that your father could choose your husband.'

She sat up in the bed. 'Because of my mother's dying wish that my father choose my husband.'

Now Gavin sat up slowly, questioning eyes locked on hers. 'Your mother? He told *me* it was because of the death of your brother and David's captivity.'

'What brother?'

Her realisation was reflected in his eyes.

They leapt from bed, each throwing on only enough clothes to get to down the hall to the baron's room. Gavin pounded, then pushed the door open, not caring what they might interrupt.

'You lied—'

'You conniving, sneaky—'

'You made up the whole story!'

'Both stories!'

'What really happened?' She was out of breath now, but out of anger, too.

Her father, still sitting before the fire with Murine,

laughed. 'Finally found out, did you? I was lucky that
you were fighting with each other so long or you might
have caught me earlier.'

She laughed then. Gavin joined in. And her father,
the most satisfied of all, roared.

'Well, here's the real story. The part I told you about
getting William Douglas good and bungfued was true.
But it was not to remind him of a promise he'd made
to my wife or even to me because of having no sons. I
gambled him for it.'

'You staked my future on the dice?'

'If I had lost, your future would have been the same
as it was before. He'd have picked some man for reasons
of his own. Some man whose favour he wanted. Who
might not care a fig about our land. I wanted a man who
belonged here.' His grin softened. 'And I found him.'

Arm around her, Gavin nodded.

She looked up at her husband, smiling. She had hesitated to give him her heart. The safety she had sought
would not be found in this man. Loving him would
always be a risk.

Yet each of them would choose, always, to return to
the other. Like the peregrines, mated for life.

Later that morning, she looked to the skies. A few
high clouds, a hint of warmth in the damp air. She
inhaled the spring.

In the barmkin, a new mews sat empty. Until now,
her heart had not been ready for another bird. Maybe
when summer came, she could search Hen Hole for a
new falcon.

Looking up, she saw a bird—no, two—flying closer.

She squinted and blinked, trying to bring the shapes into focus, afraid to believe what she saw. But they flew together, down to the tower, and settled on the edge of the roof of the mews.

'Returning to nest,' she whispered. Wee One had found her mate, just as Clare had hoped.

Yes, this season, Clare would look for a new brancher to train. Wee One's.

The birds flew away and Clare walked back to the house.

By August, if Murine was right, she and Gavin would have a wee one of their own.

* * * * *

Author's Note

The peace that Gavin and Clare longed for did not last
for ever, but King Edward never invaded Scotland again.
That was left to his successor, Richard II, nearly thirty
years later. The results—no engagement on the field of
battle and the disgust of Scotland's French allies—were
remarkably similar to Edward's experience in 1356. I
explored the subsequent Scottish invasion of England in
1388 from the other side of the border in my previous
book, *In the Master's Bed*.

King Edward, his brother John of Eltham, King David
and Lord Douglas, later the first Earl of Douglas, are all
real people and I have tried to be true to the facts we
know.

Gavin Fitzjohn, bastard son of John of Eltham, is my
creation. John did die in Scotland, suddenly and with
no clear explanation, at the age of twenty. Despite many
brides that had been proposed for him, he was never
formally betrothed. He did burn the abbey church at
Lesmahagow. The legend in Scotland was that Edward

killed his brother in anger for that act, but subsequent scholarship has refuted that claim.

Lord Douglas, like many Scottish lords, had an on-and-off relationship with King David. David did make Douglas an Earl when he returned from England and just a few years later, Douglas rebelled—briefly—when the cost of payment of the ransom became too burdensome.

The King's cordial relationship with his brother-in-law Edward did not endear him to his fellow Scots. He did promote the solution of putting one of Edward's sons on the Scottish throne should he die childless, a proposal universally rejected north of the border.

When he did die without issue, his nephew, the 'Stewart' in this story, assumed the throne as Robert II, after a protest from Lord Douglas. It was the descendants of this Stewart/Stuart line, after marrying an English royal along the way, who finally united Scotland and England under one king, a Scot, more than two hundred years later.

Gavin and Clare would both have been satisfied.

HISTORICAL

Regency

LADY DRUSILLA'S ROAD TO RUIN
by Christine Merrill

Considered a spinster, Lady Drusilla Rudney has only one role in life: to chaperon her sister. So when her flighty sibling elopes Dru knows she has to stop her! She employs the help of a fellow travelling companion, ex-army captain John Hendricks, who *looks* harmless enough...

Regency

GLORY AND THE RAKE
by Deborah Simmons

Miss Glory Sutton has two annoyances in her life. One: the precious spa she's determined to renovate keeps getting damaged by vandals. Two: the arrogant Duke of Westfield—the man assigned to help her find the perpetrators.

TO MARRY A MATCHMAKER
by Michelle Styles

Robert Montemorcy is both amused and exasperated by Lady Henrietta Thorndike's compulsive matchmaking! When his ward pays an unexpected visit, Robert bets Henri she won't be able to resist meddling...only to lose his own heart into the bargain!

On sale from 1st July 2011
Don't miss out!

HISTORICAL

THE MERCENARY'S BRIDE
by Terri Brisbin

Brice Fitzwilliam is finally paid his due: awarded the title and lands of Thaxted, the warrior waits to claim his promised virgin bride! Gillian of Thaxted will *not* submit to the conquering knight's powerful physique, or the bold way his arm drapes protectively over her at night...

Regency

FROM WAIF TO GENTLEMAN'S WIFE
by Julia Justiss

When a destitute governess faints on Sir Edward Greaves' threshold, chivalry demands that he offer her temporary shelter. However, the desire Ned feels when he catches her in his arms isn't at all gentlemanly...

WHIRLWIND BRIDE
by Debra Cowan

Can a hothouse flower bloom under burning Texas skies? Riley Holt doesn't think so. Susannah Phelps is fair, fragile... and wholly unsuited for frontier life. And being pregnant doesn't help matters. What she needs is a ticket back east— or at least someone to protect her. And damned if fate doesn't keep volunteering *him* for the job!

On sale from 1st July 2011
Don't miss out!

*Available at WHSmith, Tesco, ASDA, Eason
and all good bookshops*

www.millsandboon.co.uk

are proud to present

June 2011
Ordinary Girl in a Tiara
by Jessica Hart
from Mills & Boon® Riva™

Caro Cartwright's had enough of romance – she's after a quiet life. Until an old school friend begs her to stage a gossip-worthy royal diversion! Reluctantly, Caro prepares to masquerade as a European prince's latest squeeze...

Available 3rd June 2011

July 2011
Lady Drusilla's Road to Ruin
by Christine Merrill
from Mills & Boon® Historical

Considered a spinster, Lady Drusilla Rudney has only one role in life: to chaperon her sister. So when her flighty sibling elopes, Dru employs the help of a fellow travelling companion, ex-army captain John Hendricks, who looks harmless enough...

Available 1st July 2011

Tell us what you think!

millsandboon.co.uk/community
facebook.com/romancehq
twitter.com/millsandboonuk

REGENCY
Collection

*Let these sparklingly seductive delights whirl
you away to the ballrooms—and
bedrooms—of Polite Society!*

Volume 1 – 4th February 2011
Regency Pleasures by Louise Allen

Volume 2 – 4th March 2011
Regency Secrets by Julia Justiss

Volume 3 – 1st April 2011
Regency Rumours by Juliet Landon

Volume 4 – 6th May 2011
Regency Redemption by Christine Merrill

Volume 5 – 3rd June 2011
Regency Debutantes by Margaret McPhee

Volume 6 – 1st July 2011
Regency Improprieties by Diane Gaston

12 volumes in all to collect!

MILLS & BOON

www.millsandboon.co.uk

REGENCY
Collection

*Let these sparklingly seductive delights whirl
you away to the ballrooms—and
bedrooms—of Polite Society!*

Volume 7 – 5th August 2011
Regency Mistresses by Mary Brendan

Volume 8 – 2nd September 2011
Regency Rebels by Deb Marlowe

Volume 9 – 7th October 2011
Regency Scandals by Sophia James

Volume 10 – 4th November 2011
Regency Marriages by Elizabeth Rolls

Volume 11 – 2nd December 2011
Regency Innocents by Annie Burrows

Volume 12 – 6th January 2012
Regency Sins by Bronwyn Scott

12 volumes in all to collect!

MILLS
BOON

www.millsandboon.co.uk

2 FREE BOOKS
AND A SURPRISE GIFT

We would like to take this opportunity to thank you for reading this Mills & Boon® book by offering you the chance to take TWO more specially selected books from the Historical series absolutely FREE! We're also making this offer to introduce you to the benefits of the Mills & Boon® Book Club™—

- **FREE home delivery**
- **FREE gifts and competitions**
- **FREE monthly Newsletter**
- **Exclusive Mills & Boon Book Club offers**
- **Books available before they're in the shops**

Accepting these FREE books and gift places you under no obligation to buy, you may cancel at any time, even after receiving your free books. Simply complete your details below and return the entire page to the address below. You don't even need a stamp!

YES Please send me 2 free Historical books and a surprise gift. I understand that unless you hear from me, I will receive 4 superb new books every month for just £3.99 each, postage and packing free. I am under no obligation to purchase any books and may cancel my subscription at any time. The free books and gift will be mine to keep in any case.

Ms/Mrs/Miss/Mr ———————— Initials ————————

Surname ——————————————————————

Address ——————————————————————

———————————————————— Postcode ————————

E-mail ——————————————————————

Send this whole page to: Mills & Boon Book Club, Free Book Offer, FREEPOST NAT 10298, Richmond, TW9 1BR

Offer valid in UK only and is not available to current Mills & Boon Book Club subscribers to this series. Overseas and Eire please write for details. We reserve the right to refuse an application and applicants must be aged 18 years or over. Only one application per household. Terms and prices subject to change without notice. Offer expires 31st August 2011. As a result of this application, you may receive offers from Harlequin (UK) and other carefully selected companies. If you would prefer not to share in this opportunity please write to The Data Manager, PO Box 676, Richmond, TW9 1WU.

Mills & Boon® is a registered trademark owned by Harlequin (UK) Limited.
The Mills & Boon® Book Club™ is being used as a trademark.